THE MYSTERY OF THE
YELLOW ROOM

THE MYSTERY OF
THE YELLOW ROOM

Gaston Leroux

with an Introduction by
Mark Valentine

WORDSWORTH EDITIONS

For my husband
ANTHONY JOHN RANSON
with love from your wife, the publisher
Eternally grateful for your
unconditional love

Readers who are interested in other titles from
Wordsworth Editions are invited to visit our
website at www.wordsworth-editions.com

For our latest list and a full mail order service contact
Bibliophile Books, Unit 5 Datapoint,
South Crescent, London E16 4TL
Tel: +44 (0) 20 74 74 24 74
Fax: +44 (0) 20 74 74 85 89
orders@bibliophilebooks.com
www.bibliophilebooks.com

First published 2010 by Wordsworth Editions Limited
8B East Street, Ware, Hertfordshire SG12 9HJ

ISBN 978 1 84022 647 8

© Wordsworth Editions Limited 2010

Wordsworth® is a registered trademark of
Wordsworth Editions Limited

Wordsworth Editions is
the company founded in 1987 by
MICHAEL TRAYLER

Typeset in Great Britain by Antony Gray
Printed and bound by Clays Ltd, St Ives plc

CONTENTS

INTRODUCTION   vii

THE MYSTERY OF THE YELLOW ROOM   1

Chapter 1: *In which we begin not to understand*   3

Chapter 2: *In which Joseph Rouletabille appears for the first time*   11

Chapter 3: *'A man has passed like a shadow through the shutters'*   17

Chapter 4: *'Amidst wild nature'*   25

Chapter 5: *In which Joseph Rouletabille addresses to M. Robert Darzac a few words which produce a mysterious effect*   29

Chapter 6: *In the depths of the oak grove*   33

Chapter 7: *In which Rouletabille makes investigations under the bed*   43

Chapter 8: *The examining magistrate takes the evidence of Mlle Stangerson*   50

Chapter 9: *Reporter and detective*   56

Chapter 10: *'We shall have to eat red meat now'*   63

Chapter 11: *In which Frédéric Larsan explains how the assassin was able to get out of the yellow room*   69

Chapter 12: *Frédéric Larsan's stick*   86

Chapter 13: *'The vicarage has lost nothing of its charm, nor the garden of its brightness'*   91

Chapter 14: *'I expect the assassin this evening'*   101

Chapter 15: *The trap*   107

Chapter 16: *Phenomenon of the dissociation of matter*   116

Chapter 17: *The mysterious gallery*   119

Chapter 18: *Rouletabille has drawn a circle between the two bumps on his forehead*   125

Chapter 19: *Rouletabille invites me to lunch at the Castle Inn*   127

Chapter 20: *An act of Mlle Stangerson*   137

Chapter 21: *On the watch*   141

Chapter 22: *The incredible body*   149

Chapter 23: *The double trail*   153

Chapter 24: *Rouletabille knows the two halves of the assassin*   157

Chapter 25: *Rouletabille goes on a journey*   165

Chapter 26: *In which Joseph Rouletabille is impatiently expected*   167

Chapter 27: *In which Joseph Rouletabille appears in all his glory*   174

Chapter 28: *In which it is proved that one does not always think of everything*   202

Chapter 29: *The mystery of Mlle Stangerson*   207

INTRODUCTION

There has never been any doubt about who is the greatest detective in fiction, and not a great deal of debate about who was the first. And so Gaston Leroux turned to these two great examples when he decided, as he approached the age of forty, to create his own investigator of strange crimes. He was always quite clear that Arthur Conan Doyle's Sherlock Holmes and Edgar Allan Poe's M. Dupin were his models. But he was also determined to bring his own ideas to the form, and in particular he decided to create a much younger, more volatile, more mysterious sleuth, who would unravel cases of extraordinary complexity. Leroux's success was so great that he in turn left little room for dispute about the greatest French detective in fiction: his own Joseph Rouletabille, an eighteen-year-old journalist and prodigy with a formidable intellect matched by all the audacity and restlessness of youth.

Leroux certainly gave his character a fiendishly difficult first case to solve in *The Mystery of the Yellow Room*, which he wrote in 1907. It is one of the most remarkable examples of what has become a particular type of crime fiction, the 'locked room mystery'. There must now be hundreds of examples of this type of tale, all with varying degrees of ingenuity or improbability, but Leroux's was an early foray and remains one of the very best. The requirement is in essence simple: the crime must take place in a way which seems impossible; it must be inconceivable how the criminal could have got in, or got away, through locks, barriers, sealed doors or windows, or constantly watched places. 'I knew I must do better than Poe and Conan Doyle,' Leroux said, 'so I decided to have a murder committed in a room which was hermetically sealed.' Poe had been one of the first to try this sort of plot, with his 'The Mystery of the Rue Morgue', a remarkable, if not wholly convincing, pioneer of the field, and Conan Doyle's 'The Speckled Band' was a further strange and ingenious example . However, Leroux set himself the challenge of not using any of the more obvious solutions, such as a secret passage or trapdoor, duplicate keys, or the chimney. The reader was to be absolutely sure the crime could not have happened – yet it did.

Such was Leroux's confidence in his abilities that he achieves this not once, but twice, in this book, both in circumstances that are thoroughly baffling for the reader. Anyone who does not sneak a look at the explanation at the end – and I do urge you not to, however tempting it may be – will find themselves increasingly awed and impressed as Leroux builds up the tension and drama to an ever higher pitch, so that we are incredulous about how the plot can ever be resolved.

Yet the mystery element is not the only attraction of the book. The character of Rouletabille is also engaging, and we find ourselves enjoying his fervour, his occasional naiveties, his sly ways of insinuating himself into the investigation, his self-doubts and then, when he is on the right track again, his bombast. It seems to me likely that Leroux had in his mind something of the nature of the controversial young poet Arthur Rimbaud, who had taken the French literary world by storm at the age of seventeen, just as Rouletabille defies all the grand old men of detection. Of the young sleuth's characteristics, his habitual little pipe, his disreputable soft hat, his gaucherie, his arrogance, and his sheer genius, are all to be found in Rimbaud.

Nor are Rouletabille's rivals any less colourful. We enjoy the vanity of the examining magistrate who is also a playwright, and who leaps at the chance of investigating a crime that might give him another plot. And we are impressed that the man from the Sûreté, the Paris equivalent of Scotland Yard, is not a rather ponderous, workaday type like some of those who came to Sherlock Holmes for help, but is himself also a clever and resourceful thinker. The subsidiary characters – the local villagers, the servants of the estate, the distinguished owner and guests of the château – are also well-drawn and full of foibles and qualities which make them much more than pawns on the chessboard of the plot. And Rouletabille inevitably has his own Dr Watson, the loyal, if often bewildered, Sainclair, who is also, like Holmes's faithful chronicler, unmercifully tantalised by his friend, sent off on obscure errands, invited to share unknown dangers, reproached for not keeping up or observing things, and invariably expected to cope with the ever-changing moods of the great detective.

In brief, *The Mystery of the Yellow Room* was not only the first but one of the finest of Gaston Leroux's crime novels, rivalling even his rather better known *The Phantom of the Opera*. It was a remarkable achievement for an author fairly new to fiction. Yet in many ways its author had had the ideal preparation to create just this sort of book: a hectic, unsettled existence, gaining him plenty of experience of crime, strange characters, and with a good familiarity with brisk and efficient writing, and popular tastes.

Leroux was born in Paris in 1868, though he grew up in Normandy and went to school locally in Caen. He remembered his childhood among the fishing villages and busy ports with affection, and soon showed signs of being a writer when young, making up his own stories and dramatic sketches. This wasn't quite the career his parents had in mind for him, and he was at first sent to the capital to study law – a useful apprenticeship for a crime writer – but in his early twenties, he abandoned this and became a journalist, specialising in reports from the courts, often covering the most sensational cases. He was soon snapped up by *Le Matin*, the prestigious Paris daily paper, and it was here, just like the character he later created, that he demonstrated his unorthodoxy and restless energy. For example, he was one of the first journalists to have the idea of interviewing accused criminals in their cell, to get their version of events, a proceeding which, in its simple audacity, outraged his rivals on other papers and offended legal circles, who were not quite sure that it should be allowed.

It was a natural development from this for the youthful court reporter to do some investigating himself, rather than just report the official proceedings – again, an unheard-of thing. Leroux was also a prolific, vivid and energetic writer, never afraid of the flourish and the exclamation, and all of this must have seemed like a whirlwind to his more staid contemporaries. Some of the flavour of all that is certainly present in this novel, and we can see that, in Rouletabille, the author is in good measure remembering with affection and amusement his own youth.

He was soon in demand for wider journalistic assignments than just the courts, and went on expeditions to what were then remote or secret parts of the world – the Caucasus, on the very eastern edge of Europe, the Atlas Mountains of Morocco, on the tip of North Africa, and the frozen margins of Finland. During this period, he built up a reputation as the leading travel writer of his time, and continued to be adept at scenting out the real stories behind events and at securing interviews with unwilling or suspicious eminent people – royalty, statesmen, soldiers, explorers. He was shameless in using faked papers or made-up excuses to secure an entrée to them, but once in their presence his charm and sympathy usually prevailed.

But in the first years of the twentieth century, as if the change of era had given him even more impetus, he decided to turn to fiction. With his newspaper reputation, he was easily able to sell stories or instalments of novels to the daily press or periodicals, and his excited, headlong style was ideal for keeping readers in breathless suspense. *The Mystery of the Yellow Room* was one such commission, and it was a great success, with no-one able to guess the solution or follow the impeccable logic, or the labyrinthine twists in the plot. It was recognised as a real tour-de-force where at every turn the reader cannot quite believe how Leroux can hold everything together and still deliver a plausible resolution.

The serial came out in book form in France in 1908 and the first English translation appeared the same year, as a sixpenny paperback from the *Daily Mail* – evidence of how successful it was. A hardback edition was published by the respectable firm of Edward Arnold the following year, and there were several subsequent translations and editions.

As literary researcher Richard Dalby has pointed out, the book was very warmly received in Britain and also impressed other writers. John Dickson Carr, himself later an ingenious deviser of locked room puzzles, had his detective character Dr Gideon Fell acclaim Leroux's book as 'the best detective tale ever written'. Novelist Arnold Bennett, a frequent reviewer of crime novels, called it 'the most dazzlingly brilliant detective story I have ever read'. And Agatha Christie, who read the book with her sister Madge, recorded: 'we talked about it a lot, told each other our views, and agreed it was one of the best. We were (by then) connoisseurs of the detective story.' She added that Leroux had influenced her own early work.

Perhaps it should be no surprise that Leroux's book should be so successful amongst English language readers, apart from its obvious qualities. For Leroux himself was a keen Anglophile, and readily explained that he had learned from the work of Dickens, Kipling and H. G. Wells, as well as Conan Doyle and Poe. And even the French authors who influenced him most were also those well-loved by English readers, such as Alexandre Dumas and Jules Verne. All his life, Leroux was an extremely keen reader who amassed a large library, which he sometimes admitted distracted him from writing, although it would be hard to tell this from his prodigious output.

It was soon clear that publishers would demand more news of Joseph Rouletabille. Readers will discern at various points in this book a few tantalising references to an important influence on the young detective, a woman he remembers from his childhood who wore a distinctive scent. For Marcel Proust, it was the taste of the famous Madeleine cake that transported him to his golden days, in *À la recherche du temps perdu* (1913–27), but Leroux knew that our sense of smell is the most evocative yet elusive form of memory, and hints at its great significance for his character. We may guess at who the woman was, and also speculate about Rouletabille's origins and parentage, which are kept enigmatic throughout. However, the author – as if this book itself was not already complex and many-dimensioned enough – was clearly trailing clues here to his next book, the second Rouletabille adventure, *The Perfume of the Lady in Black*, which was serialised in France in 1908, published in book form there in 1909, by the Daily Mail again the same year, and as a book in Britain by Eveleigh Nash in 1911.

Leroux wrote over fifty further novels or collections of stories, including a handful featuring Joseph Rouletabille, involving encounters with the Russian royal family, adventures as a spy in World War I, foiling a German missile plot, defending himself against a charge of murder, further examples of the seemingly impossible crime, and the quest for a lost sacred book. If none of these ever quite repeated the success of *The Mystery of the Yellow Room*, the first adventure, that was not least because Leroux had set the standard so high. And it must be admitted that he did tend to indulge a fondness for the wildest of plots, so that sometimes the reader almost wonders if the author was doing it for a wager, or testing himself to see how far he could go.

Of course, the book that will always remain his most well-known is *The Phantom of the Opera* (also available from Wordsworth), published in 1910 in France and in 1911 in Britain, by Mills & Boon, when they were a more general imprint than now. This was the prime example of another facet of Leroux's writing career, which responded to the public's taste for the macabre and for tales of terror. Set in the grand surroundings of the Paris Opera House, with a thoroughly sinister yet not unsympathetically-depicted villain, and with all of the mysterious lure of the catacombs below, it was a masterpiece of dark glamour. Again drawing upon his experience as a journalist, Leroux maintained that his work was based upon a true story.

Though the book was at first only a moderate success – perhaps readers really wanted another Joseph Rouletabille adventure – its reputation soon grew. And of course it has been memorably portrayed in film and theatre. The classic silent film version of 1925, with Lon

Chaney in the title rôle, has never been bettered, but there have been excellent versions drawing on the story's weird allure, including with Claude Rains in 1943 and Herbert Lom in 1962, as well, of course, as the popular, long-running musical, originally with Michael Crawford. Leroux went on to write other work in the horror and supernatural vein, including tales of a vampire, soul stealing, and even – keeping right up to date – a killer robot.

For all the dark fearfulness of his most famous story, and all his remarkable ingenuity in devising the strangest crimes, all reports confirm that the author was a most amiable man, excellent company, generous, with a real interest in others (and not just to collect them as characters!) – as far removed from his villains and even the darker aspect of his tormented heroes as could be. Portly, bespectacled – he wore golden pince-nez – with a trim moustache and often portrayed with an affable grin, Leroux relished his success and never let his readers down.

Gaston Leroux died in 1927 in Nice, where he was supposed to be in retirement because of ill health. But it is likely that he never ceased writing, and numerous unpublished works were left at his death. Profligate, a lover of the good things in life, and also kindly open-handed, Leroux was always in need of money despite the huge success of his books. It's possible that his restless, fervent approach to his work partly weakened his health and contributed to a relatively early death. But we can still enjoy the fruits of his extraordinary life and imagination in his books, and in particular in his wonderful character of Joseph Rouletabille, the greatest French detective.

MARK VALENTINE

THE MYSTERY OF
THE YELLOW ROOM

Chapter 1

In which we begin not to understand

It is not without emotion that I begin to relate the extraordinary adventures of Joseph Rouletabille. Up till now he had so firmly opposed my doing so that I had given up hope of ever publishing one of the most remarkable detective stories of the past thirty years. I even imagine that the public would never have learnt the whole truth about the amazing case, known as the Mystery of the Yellow Room, with which my friend was so closely identified, if, on the recent nomination of the illustrious Stangerson to the rank of Grand Cross of the Legion of Honour, an evening journal, in an ignorant or malicious article, had not resuscitated a terrible drama which Joseph Rouletabille told me he wished to be for ever forgotten.

The Yellow Room! Who remembers the affair which caused so much ink to flow about thirty years ago? Things are forgotten so quickly in Paris. Have not the very name of the Nayves trial and the tragic story of young Ménaldo's death passed completely out of mind? Yet the public were so deeply interested at the time in the details of the trial, that a Ministerial crisis which occurred just then passed quite unnoticed. Now, the Yellow Room trial, which preceded the Nayves case by a few years, made far more commotion. The whole world puzzled for months over this obscure problem – one of the most obscure, to my knowledge, that ever challenged the perspicacity of our police, or taxed the conscience of our judges. Everybody tried to find the solution of the riddle. It was like a dramatic problem, with which both Europe and America became fascinated. In truth – I may say so, since there can be no question of the author's self-esteem in the matter, as I do nothing but transcribe facts on which some exceptional documents enable me to throw a new light – in truth, I do not think that in the domain of reality or imagination, or even among the inventions of Edgar Allan Poe and his imitators, anything to compare in mystery with the natural mystery of the Yellow Room can possibly be found.

What no one else could find out, Rouletabille, a youth of eighteen, then a junior reporter on a leading newspaper, succeeded in discovering. But when, at the Assizes, he gave the key to the whole case, he did not tell the whole truth. He told only so much of it as was necessary to explain the inexplicable and to ensure the acquittal of an innocent man. But the reasons he had for being reticent no longer exist, and my friend ought now to speak out fully. You are about to read the whole truth; and so without further preamble I shall now place before you the problem of the Yellow Room exactly as it was placed before the public on the day after the tragedy at the Château du Glandier.

On the 25th of October, 1892, the following note appeared in the latest news column of the *Temps*.

'A fearful crime has been committed at Glandier, on the border of the forest of Sainte-Geneviève, near Épinay-sur-Orge, at Professor Stangerson's. Last night, whilst the scientist was working in his laboratory, an attempt was made to murder Mlle Stangerson, who was sleeping in an adjoining room. The doctors will not answer for Mlle Stangerson's life.'

The sensation caused in Paris by this news may be easily imagined, for the public were already deeply interested in the work of Professor Stangerson and his daughter. They were the first to experiment in radiography, and the results of their studies were to lead M. and Mme Curie, later on, to the discovery of radium. Moreover, the professor was shortly going to read before the Academy of Sciences a sensational paper on his new theory – the Dissociation of Matter – a theory destined to shake the foundation of orthodox science, which has so long been based on the famous principle that nothing is destroyed and nothing created – and this paper was eagerly anticipated.

The next morning the newspapers were full of the tragedy. The *Matin*, among others, published the following article, entitled:

A SUPERNATURAL CRIME

We give the only details [explained the anonymous writer] we have been able to obtain concerning the crime at the Château du Glandier. The state of despair of Professor Stangerson, and the impossibilty of obtaining any information from the victim, have made our investigations and those of the police so difficult that, for the present, we cannot form the least idea of what took place in the Yellow Room, in which Mlle Stangerson, in her nightdress, was found lying on the floor in the agonies of death. We have, however, been able to interview Old Jacques – as he is called in the neighbourhood – an old servant in the Stangerson family. Jacques entered the Yellow Room at the same time as the professor. This room adjoins the laboratory, and both the laboratory and the Yellow Room are in a pavilion at the end of the park, about four hundred yards from the château.

'It was half-past twelve at night,' the old man told us, 'and I was in the laboratory where M. Stangerson was still at work when the thing happened. I had been cleaning and arranging a number of scientific instruments all evening, and was waiting for the departure of M. Stangerson before going to bed. Mlle Mathilde had worked with her father till midnight. Just as the twelve strokes of the hour had sounded on the cuckoo-clock in the laboratory, she rose, kissed M. Stangerson, and bade him good night. To me she also said, "Good night, Jacques!" as she pushed open the door of the Yellow Room. We heard her lock the door and shoot the bolt, so that I could not help laughing, and said to Monsieur: "There's Mademoiselle double-locking herself in. She must be afraid of 'the Good Lord's beast'!" Monsieur did not hear me, for he was thinking deeply, and just then I heard a fearful miawling, which I at once recognised as the cry of "the Good Lord's beast". It made me shiver. "Is that cat again going to keep us awake all night?" I said to myself; for I must tell you, sir, that to the end of October I live in the attic of the pavilion, right over the Yellow Room, so that Mademoiselle may not be left alone through the night at the end of the park. It is Mademoiselle's fancy to spend the spring, summer, and part of the autumn in the pavilion; she evidently finds it more cheerful than the château, as for the last four years – ever since the place was built – she has never failed to take up her lodging there in the early spring. When winter comes Mademoiselle returns to the château, for there is no fireplace in the Yellow Room.

'We had remained in the pavilion, then, M. Stangerson and I. We made no noise. He was seated at his desk. As for me, I was sitting on a chair, for I had finished my work, and I was watching him and thinking, "What a man! What brains! What knowledge!" I attach importance to the fact that we made no noise, for, on account of the silence, the assassin must have thought we had left the place. Then suddenly, while the cuckoo was sounding half-past twelve, there was a fearful scream in the Yellow Chamber. It was the voice of Mademoiselle, crying "Murder! Murder! Help!" Immediately afterwards revolver-shots rang out, and there was a great noise of tables and furniture being overthrown, as in the course of a struggle; and again we heard the voice of Mademoiselle screaming "Murder! Help! Father! Father!"

'As you may guess, we sprang up, and M. Stangerson and I threw ourselves at the door. But, alas! it was locked, strongly locked on the inside by Mademoiselle herself, and, as I told you, with key and bolt. We tried to force it open, but it was too solid. M. Stangerson was like a madman, and, truly, there was enough to make anyone mad, for we heard Mademoiselle still calling hoarsely, but now with a dying voice: "Help! Help!" M. Stangerson showered terrible blows on the door; he wept with rage and sobbed in his despair and helplessness.

'Then I had an inspiration. "The assassin must have entered by the window!" I cried. "I will go to the window!" and rushing from the pavilion, I ran like a lunatic.

'Unfortunately, the window of the Yellow Room looks on to the country outside, so that the park wall, which abuts on the pavilion, prevented me getting at the window. To reach it it was necessary to go out of the park. I ran towards the gate, and on my way met Bernier and his wife, the concierges, who were hastening to the pavilion, having evidently been attracted by the pistol-shots and our cries. In a few words I told them what had happened. I directed the concierge to join M. Stangerson at once, and told his wife to come with me and open the park gates. Five minutes later she and I stood before the window of the Yellow Room.

'The moon was shining brightly, and I saw quite clearly that the window had not been touched. Not only were the iron bars that protect it intact, but the shutters behind were closed exactly as I had closed them myself on the previous evening, and as I did every day, although Mademoiselle, knowing that I was tired and had much to do, had told me not to trouble myself, as she would close them herself. They were just as I had left them, fastened with an iron catch on the inside. The assassin, therefore, could not have entered that way, and could not possibly escape through there. But neither could I get in.

'It was awful – enough to turn one's brain! The door locked on the inside, and the shutters of the only window also fastened on the inside; and besides those shutters there were the iron bars, so close together that one could not have passed an arm between them. And Mademoiselle was still calling for help – or, rather, no; she had ceased to call. She was dead, perhaps. But I could still hear her father in the pavilion trying to break down the door.

'The concierge and I then ran back to the pavilion. The door, in spite of the furious attempts of M. Stangerson and Bernier to burst it open, was still holding firm. At length it gave way before our united and frenzied efforts, and then what did we see?

'I ought to tell you, by the way, that behind us the concierge woman was holding the laboratory lamp – a powerful lamp that lit the whole room.

'I must also tell you, sir, that the Yellow Room is quite small. Mademoiselle had furnished it with a fairly large iron bedstead, a small table, a commode, a washhand-stand, and two chairs. By the light of the big lamp we saw everything at a glance. Mademoiselle, in her nightdress, was lying on the floor in the midst of incredible disorder. The tables and chairs had been overturned, showing that there had been a violent struggle. Mademoiselle had certainly been dragged from her bed. She was covered with blood, and had terrible finger-nail marks on her throat – the flesh of her neck had been almost torn by the nails – and from a wound on the right temple a thin stream of blood was oozing, and made a little pool on the floor. When M. Stangerson saw his daughter in that dreadful state, he threw himself on his knees beside her, uttering a cry of despair. It was really pitiful to hear him. He ascertained that she still breathed, and devoted all his attention to her. As for us, we were searching for the wretch who had tried to kill our mistress, and I swear to you, sir, that if we had found him, it would have gone hard with him!

'But how was it to be explained that he was not there – that he had already escaped? It passes comprehension. There was nobody under the bed, nobody behind the furniture. All that we discovered were traces of his movements; blood-stained marks of a man's large hand on the walls and door; a big handkerchief red with blood and without any initials, an old cap, and many fresh footmarks on the floor – footmarks of a man with large feet, whose boot soles had left a sort of sooty impression. How had this man got in? How had he vanished? Don't forget, sir, that there is no chimney in the Yellow Room. He could not have escaped by the door, for it is narrow; and, besides, the concierge stood on the threshold with the lamp in her hand while her husband and I were searching for the assassin in this little bit of a square room, where it is impossible for anyone to hide. The door, which had been forced back against the wall, could not conceal anything behind it, as we at once found out. By the window, which was still secured in every way, with closed shutters and the iron bars untampered with, no flight had been possible. What then? Honestly, I began to believe in the Devil.

'Then all at once, on the floor, we discovered my revolver – yes, my own revolver! That brought me back to reality. The Devil would not have needed to steal my revolver to kill Mademoiselle. The man who had been there had first gone up to my attic and taken my revolver from the drawer where I kept it, and had used it afterwards against Mlle Mathilde. We ascertained, by counting the cartridges, that the assassin had fired two shots. When you come to think of it, sir, it was very lucky for me in those awful circumstances that M. Stangerson was in the laboratory when the crime occurred, and that he saw with his own eyes that I was with him, for otherwise, with this revolver business there is no telling what would not have happened. Very likely I should be already under lock and bar. The law wants nothing more to send a man to the scaffold!'

The editor of the *Matin* added to this interview the following note.

We have, without interruption, allowed Old Jacques to tell us roughly all he knows about the crime of the Yellow Room. We have reproduced his own words, only sparing the reader the continual lamentations with which he adorned his narration. It is quite understood, Old Jacques, quite understood, that you love your employers; you want them to know it, and never cease repeating it, especially since the discovery of your revolver. It is your right and we do not object. We should have liked to put some further questions to Old Jacques – Jacques Louis Moustier – but just as we were going to ask them he was sent for by the examining magistrate, who was carrying on his enquiries in the main hall of the castle. We found it impossible to gain admission to Glandier; and as for the 'Oak Grove', it is guarded by a wide circle of detectives and gendarmes, who are jealously examining all traces that can lead to the discovery of the assassin.

We should also have liked to question the concierges, man and wife, but they are not to be found. Eventually, we waited at a

roadside inn, not far from the gate of the château, for the departure of M. de Marquet, the examining magistrate of Corbeil. At
half-past five we saw him and his clerk, and before he entered his
carriage we were able to ask him the following questions: 'Can
you, M. de Marquet, give us any information as to the affair,
without inconvenience to the course of your inquiry?'

'Impossible!' was the reply. 'All I can say is that it is by far the
strangest affair I have ever known. The more we think we know
something, the further we are from knowing anything at all!'

We asked M. de Marquet to be good enough to explain his
meaning, and this is what he said – the importance of which no
one will fail to gather: 'If nothing is added to the material facts so
far established, I really fear that the mystery which surrounds the
abominable crime of which Mlle Stangerson has been the victim
will never be brought to light; but it is to be hoped, for the sake
of human reason, that the examination of the walls, ceiling, and
floor of the Yellow Room – an examination which I shall make
tomorrow, with the builder who erected the pavilion four years
ago – will convince us that one must never dispute the logic
of events. For the problem is this: we know how the assassin
gained admission. He must have entered by the door, and hid
himself under the bed, awaiting Mlle Stangerson. But how
did he leave? How did he manage to escape? That was the
problem. If no trap, no secret door, no recess or hiding-place,
no opening of any sort is found; if on sounding the walls – even
to the demolition of the pavilion – there is revealed no passage
practicable, not only for a human being, but for any being
whatsoever; if the ceiling shows no crack, if the floor hides no
tunnel, we shall really have to "believe in the Devil", as old
Jacques says.'

And the anonymous writer in the *Matin* mentions in this article –
which I selected as the most interesting of all those that were published that day on the mysterious case – the fact that the magistrate
laid stress on the words.

The article concluded with these lines:

We wanted to know what Old Jacques meant by the cry of the
Good Lord's beast. The landlord of the Castle Inn explained to
us that it is a particularly sinister cry which is made sometimes at
night by the cat of an aged woman in the district, known as Old
Mother Agenoux. This Mother Agenoux is a sort of saint, who

lives in a hut in the heart of the forest, not far from the grotto of Sainte-Geneviève.

The Yellow Room, the Good Lord's beast, Mother Agenoux, the Devil, Sainte-Geneviève, Old Jacques – here is an amazing and tangled crime which the stroke of a pickaxe in the wall of the pavilion may unravel for us tomorrow. Let us at least hope so, for the sake of human reason – to use the examining magistrate's words. Meanwhile, it is feared that Mlle Stangerson – who has not ceased to be delirious, and only pronounces one word distinctly, 'Assassin! Assassin!' – will not live through the night.

Finally, at a late hour, the same journal announced that the head of the Secret Police had sent a telegram to the famous chief-detective, Frédéric Larsan, who had been sent to London for an affair of stolen securities, ordering him to return to Paris immediately.

Chapter 2

In which Joseph Rouletabille appears for the first time

I remember as if it were yesterday the entrance of young Rouletabille into my room that morning. It was about eight o'clock, and I was still in bed, reading the article in the *Matin* about the Glandier crime.

But before going further I must introduce my friend to the reader.

I first knew Joseph Rouletabille when he was a young junior reporter. At that time I was a beginner at the Bar, and often met him in the ante-rooms of examining magistrates at the Law Courts, when I had gone to get a permit to visit the prisons of Mazas or St Lazare. He had, as they say in France, *une bonne bille* – a good ball of a head. It seemed to have been taken, round as a bullet, out of a box of billiard-balls; and for that reason, I presume, his colleagues of the Press – all enthusiastic billiard-players – had given him the nickname,* which he was to retain and eventually make famous. He was always red as a tomato, now gay as a lark, now grave as a judge. How was it that this boy – and he was only sixteen and a half years old when I saw him for the first time – had already managed to earn his living on the Press? It was what everybody who came into contact with him might have asked, had not the beginning of his career been so well known. At the time of the affair of the woman found cut up in pieces in the Rue Oberkampf – another forgotten affair – he had taken to the editor of the *Époque* – a paper then rivalling the *Matin* for rapid and complete news – the left foot, which was missing from the basket in which the lugubrious remains had been discovered. For a whole week the police had been vainly searching for this left foot, and Rouletabille had found it in a drain, where no one had thought of looking for it. To do this, he had engaged himself as a sewer-man, one of an extra gang engaged by the Administration of the City of Paris owing to serious damage caused by a sudden overflow of the Seine.

When the editor found himself in possession of the precious foot, and realised the string of intelligent deductions made by the lad

* Rouletabille = roll thy ball.

to discover it, he was full of admiration for so much detective skill in a brain of sixteen, and delighted at being able to exhibit in the 'morgue-window' of his paper the left foot of the victim of the Rue Oberkampf.

'With this foot,' he cried jocularly, 'I'll make a head' – *i.e.* leading – 'article.'

Then, having handed the ghastly parcel to the 'medico-legal expert' attached to the journal, he asked the youth, who was presently to become 'Rouletabille', what he would expect to earn as a junior reporter on the *Époque*.

'Two hundred francs a month,' the youngster replied modestly, dumbfounded by the unexpected proposal.

'You shall have two hundred and fifty,' said the editor. 'Only I want you to tell everybody that you have been on my paper for a month. Let it also be quite understood that it was not you, but the *Époque*, that discovered the foot of the woman of the Rue Oberkampf. With us, my young friend, the individual is nothing, the paper everything.'

He then dismissed the new reporter, but before the youth had reached the door called him back to ask his name. The other replied: 'Joseph Joséphin.'

'That's no name,' said the editor. 'But since you will not sign what you write, it is of no consequence.'

The beardless 'junior' speedily made himself many friends, for he was useful, and gifted with humour that delighted the most surly and disarmed the most envious among his colleagues. At the café frequented by the reporters before going to the Courts or to the Prefecture in search of the 'daily crime', he began to win a reputation as an unraveller of intricate affairs, which even reached the ears of the head of the Criminal Investigation Department. When a case was worth the trouble, and Rouletabille – who, by the way, was already known by this nickname – had been put on the scent by the editor, he often got the better of the most renowned detectives.

It was at the café that I became better acquainted with him. Barristers and journalists are not enemies – the first having need of advertisement, the last of information. We chatted, and I very soon felt a great sympathy for the young fellow. His intelligence was so wonderfully keen and original, and he had method and mental ability, too, such as I have never found in any other person.

Some time after this I was put in charge of the law news of the *Cri du Boulevard*. My entry into journalism could not but strengthen the ties which united me to Rouletabille. After a time, my new friend having undertaken a little judicial correspondence in the *Époque*, I was able occasionally to furnish him with the legal notions of which he stood in need.

Nearly two years passed in this way, and the more I saw of Rouletabille the more I loved him; for beneath his mask of joyous extravagance I had found him to be unusually serious and thoughtful. And on several occasions I, who was used to seeing him gay – and often a trifle too gay – found him plunged in the deepest sadness. When I tried to question him as to the cause of this change of humour, he merely laughed, but made no reply, and one day, when I asked him about his parents of whom he never spoke, he left me, pretending not to have heard what I said.

While things were in this state between us, the notorious affair of the Yellow Room happened – an affair which was not only to rank him as the first of newspaper reporters, but also to prove him to be the greatest detective in the world – a double rôle which it was not astonishing to find played by the same person, considering how the daily Press was already beginning to transform itself, and becoming what it almost is today – the gazette of crime.

Captious persons may complain of this; for myself, I regard it as an excellent thing, for we shall never have too many weapons, public or private, against criminals. Captious persons, however, contend that by daily devoting columns to crime, the Press finally inspires it. But we all know the people with whom one is never in the right.

Rouletabille, as I have said, entered my room that morning, the 26th of October, 1892. He was looking redder than usual; his eyes were protruding, his breath was short, and he appeared to be in a state of extreme excitement. He waved the *Matin* with a trembling hand, and cried: 'Well, my dear Sainclair, you've read – '

'The Glandier crime?'

'Yes; the Yellow Room! What do you think of it?'

'I think it must have been the Devil, or the Good Lord's beast, that committed the crime.'

'Be serious.'

'Well, I must confess that I really don't believe very much in assassins who make their escape through solid brick walls. I think Old Jacques did wrong to leave behind him the weapon with which the crime was committed, and, as he occupies the attic immediately above Mlle Stangerson's room, the architectural investigation ordered for

Friday by the examining magistrate will give us the key of the enigma, and we shall soon know by what natural trap or secret door the old fellow was able to slip in and out, and to return immediately to M. Stangerson in the laboratory without his absence being noticed. What else can I say? Of course, I'm only surmising.'

Rouletabille seated himself in an armchair, lit his pipe – which he was never without – smoked for a few minutes in silence – no doubt to calm the fever which visibly dominated him – and then replied in a tone of great irony: 'Young man, you are a barrister, and I have no doubt of your ability to save the guilty from conviction; but if you ever become a magistrate and go on the bench, how easy it will be for you to condemn innocent persons! You really are gifted, young man!'

For a while he smoked energetically, and then went on: 'No trap will be found, and the mystery of the Yellow Room will become more and more mysterious. That's why it interests me. The examining magistrate is right; nothing more strange than this crime will have ever been heard of.'

'Have you any idea of the way the assassin escaped?' I asked.

'None,' replied Rouletabille – 'none just now. But I have already certain ideas about the revolver. For instance, the revolver was not used by the assassin.'

'Good Heavens! By whom, then?'

'Well – by Mlle Stangerson.'

'I don't understand – or, rather, I have never understood,' I said.

Rouletabille shrugged his shoulders. 'Has nothing in the article in the *Matin* particularly struck you?'

'Nothing. Really, I have found the whole of the story equally strange.'

'What about the door being locked on the inside?'

'That's the only perfectly natural thing in the article.'

'Really! And the bolt?'

'The bolt?'

'The bolt – also inside the room – further fastening the door? Those are many precautions taken by Mlle Stangerson. To me it seems quite evident that she feared someone. She had, therefore, taken these precautions. She had even taken that revolver of Old Jacques's without telling him. No doubt she did not wish to alarm anyone, and least of all her father. What she dreaded took place, and she defended herself; there was a struggle, and she used the revolver skilfully enough to wound the assassin in the hand – which explains the impression on the wall and the door of the large, blood-stained hand of the man who was feeling for a means of exit from the room; but she did not fire soon enough to avoid the terrible blow she received on the right temple.'

'It was not with the revolver, then, that she was wounded on the temple?'

'The journal does not say it was, and, personally, I don't think it was – because it appears to me logical that the revolver was used by Mlle Stangerson against the assassin. Now, what was the weapon used by the murderer? The blow on the temple seems to show that the assassin wished to stun Mlle Stangerson – after he had unsuccessfully tried to strangle her. He must have known that the attic was inhabited by Old Jacques, and it was one of the reasons, I believe, why he used a silent weapon – a life-preserver, maybe, or a hammer.'

'All this does not explain how the assassin got out of the Yellow Room,' I observed.

'Certainly not,' replied Rouletabille, rising. 'And as that is the very thing that requires explanation, I am off to the Château du Glandier, and I came here to fetch you and take you there.'

'I?'

'Yes, dear friend, I want you. The *Époque* has definitely entrusted this case to me, and I must enlighten it as quickly as possible.'

'But in what way can I be of use to you?'

'M. Robert Darzac is at the Château du Glandier.'

'That's true. His despair must be boundless.'

'I must have a talk with him.'

Rouletabille said that in a tone that surprised me.

'Is it – do you think that there is something interesting in that quarter?' I asked.

'Yes.'

That was all he would say. He retired to my sitting-room, begging me to dress quickly.

I knew M. Robert Darzac, from having been of great service to him in a civil action while I was secretary to Maître Barbet Delatour. M. Robert Darzac, who was at the time about forty years of age, was a professor of physics at the Sorbonne. He was intimately connected with the Stangersons, for, after courting Mlle Stangerson assiduously for seven years, he was on the point of marrying her. She must have been about thirty-five, but was still remarkably good-looking.

While I was dressing I called out to Rouletabille, who was impatiently moving about in my sitting-room: 'Have you any idea as to the rank of the assassin?'

'Yes,' he replied; 'I believe him to be a well-connected person – but that, again, is only an impression.'

'What leads you to form it?'

'Well,' my friend replied, 'the greasy cap, the common handkerchief, and the marks of the rough boots on the floor.'

'I understand,' I said. 'One does not leave so many traces behind *when they express the truth*.'

'We shall make something of you yet, my dear Sainclair,' retorted Rouletabille.

Chapter 3

'A man has passed like a shadow through the shutters'

Half an hour later Rouletabille and I were on the platform of the 'Orleans' Station, awaiting the departure of the train which was to take us to Épinay-sur-Orge.

We noticed the arrival of the judicial Court of Corbeil, represented by M. de Marquet and his registrar. M. de Marquet had spent the night in Paris with the clerk, to watch the final rehearsal at the Scala of a little Revue, of which he was the author, under the pseudonym 'Castigat Ridendo'.

M. de Marquet was getting old. Generally he was extremely polite and good-tempered. Throughout his life he had had but one passion – that of dramatic art. During his magisterial career he was only interested in cases capable of furnishing him with materials for plays.

Though, thanks to his connections, he might have easily aspired to the highest judicial posts, he had really never struggled for anything but to achieve a success at the romantic 'Porte St Martin Théâtre' or at the pensive 'Odéon'. This noble ideal had led him to become examining magistrate of the small town of Corbeil, and to sign 'Castigat Ridendo' to a one-act play at the Scala.

On account of the mystery in which it was shrouded, the Yellow Room case was bound to appeal to so literary a mind. It interested him prodigiously, and he threw himself into it, less as a magistrate eager to know the truth than as an amateur of dramatic plots, who devotes his faculties entirely to mystery and intrigue, and who dreads nothing so much as reaching the end of the last act – the climax in which everything is explained.

Thus it was that at the moment of meeting him I heard M. de Marquet say to his registrar, with a sigh: 'Let us hope, my dear M. Maleine, this builder with his pickaxe will not destroy so wonderful a mystery.'

'Have no fear,' M. Maleine replied. 'His pickaxe may possibly demolish the pavilion, but it will leave our case intact. I have sounded the walls and studied the ceiling and floor, and I know all about them. I am not to be deceived. We need not fear anything; we shall discover nothing.'

Having thus reassured his chief, M. Maleine, with a discreet movement of the head, drew M. de Marquet's attention to us. The magistrate frowned, and, as he saw Rouletabille approaching him hat in hand, he sprang into one of the empty carriages, saying aloud to his registrar: 'Above all, no journalists!'

M. Maleine replied, 'I understand', and endeavoured to prevent Rouletabille from stepping into the compartment of the examining magistrate. 'Excuse me, gentlemen, this compartment is reserved.'

'I am a journalist engaged on the *Époque*,' said my young friend, with the utmost politeness and a number of salutations, 'and I have a word or two to say to M. de Marquet.'

'M. de Marquet is busy. His inquiry – '

'Ah, his inquiry, believe me, does not interest me! I am no mere reporter of petty events,' said Rouletabille, with an expression of utter contempt for the literature of the 'news' columns, 'but the dramatic critic of the *Époque*, and as I shall have this evening to give a little account of the Revue at the Scala – '

'Step in, please, Monsieur,' said the registrar courteously.

Rouletabille was already in the compartment. I followed him, and seated myself by his side. The registrar stepped in as well, and closed the carriage-door.

M. de Marquet looked severely at his clerk.

'Oh, Monsieur,' Rouletabille began, 'do not be angry with the young man. I know I joined you in spite of your instructions to him, but it is not with M. de Marquet that I desire to have the honour of speaking, but with "M. Castigat Ridendo". Allow me, as the dramatic critic of the *Époque*, to congratulate you.'

And Rouletabille, having first introduced me, introduced himself.

M. de Marquet, with a nervous gesture, was stroking his pointed beard. He explained to Rouletabille that he was too modest an author to desire that the veil of his pseudonym should be publicly raised, and that he sincerely hoped the enthusiasm of the journalist for the work of the playwright would not lead him to inform the world that Castigat Ridendo was no other than the examining magistrate of Corbeil.

Then he added, after a slight hesitation: 'The work of the author might be injurious to that of the magistrate. Especially in the provinces, far away from Paris, where the people are rather narrow-minded and conventional – '

'Please rely on my discretion,' Rouletabille exclaimed.

The train was now in motion.

'We're off!' said the magistrate, surprised at seeing us make the journey with him.

'Yes, Monsieur, Truth has started,' said Rouletabille, with a happy smile, 'on its way to the Château du Glandier. A fine case, M. de Marquet – a very fine case!'

'Very! In fact, an incredible, unfathomable, inexplicable affair. And my only fear, M. Rouletabille, is that journalists will interfere and try to explain it.'

This straight thrust went home to my friend.

'Yes,' he quietly replied, 'it is to be feared. Those journalists interfere in everything. As for me, Monsieur, I only address you because mere chance placed me on your way, and made me travel in your carriage.'

'Where are you going, then?' asked M. de Marquet.

'To the Château du Glandier,' replied Rouletabille, without flinching.

M. de Marquet was taken aback.

'You will not get in, M. Rouletabille.'

'Will you prevent me?' said my friend, already prepared for the fray.

'Certainly not. I am too fond of the Press and journalists to be in any way disagreeable to them; but M. Stangerson has given orders for his door to be closed against everybody, and it is well guarded. Not a journalist yesterday was able to get to the gate of Glandier.'

'So much the better,' Rouletabille retorted. 'I am in time.'

M. de Marquet bit his lips, and seemed decided to remain obstinately silent. From this new attitude he only relaxed a little when Rouletabille told him that we were going to Glandier for the purpose of shaking hands with an old and intimate friend, M. Robert Darzac, whom Rouletabille had perhaps met once in his life.

'Poor Robert!' he said. 'This dreadful affair may cause his death – he is so deeply in love with Mlle Stangerson.'

'The grief of M. Darzac is indeed painful to see,' M. de Marquet muttered, as if sorry to speak at all.

'But it is to be hoped that Mlle Stangerson will survive.'

'Let us hope so. Her father was telling me yesterday that if she were to die, he would soon join her in the grave. What an incalculable loss this would mean for science!'

'The wound on her temple is serious, is it not?'

'Evidently; and it is a miracle that it has not proved fatal. The blow was given with such tremendous force.'

'Then it was not with the revolver she was wounded?' said Rouletabille, glancing at me in triumph.

M. de Marquet appeared greatly embarrassed.

'I have said nothing, I don't want to say anything, and I shall not say anything.'

He then turned towards his registrar as if he no longer knew us.

But Rouletabille was not to be so easily shaken off. He moved nearer to the examining magistrate, and, showing him a copy of the *Matin*, which he drew from his pocket, said: 'There is one thing, Monsieur, which I may enquire of you without being indiscreet. You read the account given in the *Matin*? It is absurd, is it not?'

'Not in the least, Monsieur.'

'What! The Yellow Room has but one barred window, the bars of which have not been moved, and only one door, which had to be broken open – and the assassin was not found?'

'That's so, Monsieur – that's so. That's how the problem stands.'

Rouletabille said no more, but became absorbed in thought. A quarter of an hour passed in this way.

When he spoke again, he asked, addressing the magistrate once more: 'How was Mlle Stangerson's hair dressed that evening?'

'I don't see what you are aiming at,' replied M. de Marquet.

'It is a highly important point,' said Rouletabille. 'Her hair was parted in the middle, was it not? I am convinced that on that evening, the evening of the drama, she had her hair parted in the middle and covering both temples.'

'Then, M. Rouletabille, you are quite mistaken,' replied the magistrate. 'Mlle Stangerson that evening had her hair drawn up in a knot on the top of her head. It must be her usual way of dressing it. Her forehead was completely uncovered, I can assure you, for we have carefully examined the wound. There was no blood in the hair, and Mlle Stangerson's coiffure had not been touched since the crime was committed.'

'You are sure? You are quite sure that, on the night of the crime, she had not her hair arranged in bandeaux?'

'Perfectly sure,' the magistrate continued, smiling, 'for I remember the doctor saying to me, while he was examining the wound, "It is a great pity Mlle Stangerson was in the habit of dressing her hair in a loop above her forehead. If she had worn it low, the blow she received on the temple would have been lessened." But may I say that it seems rather strange that you should attach so much importance to this point.'

'Oh, if only she had her hair arranged in bandeaux!' said Rouletabille, with a gesture of discouragement. 'What a mystery! I *must* solve it.' He really looked desperate. 'And the wound on her temple is a terrible one?' he asked presently.

'Terrible.'

'With what weapon was it made?'

'That, my dear sir, is a secret of the investigation.'

'Have you found the weapon?'

The magistrate did not answer.

'And the wound in the throat?'

M. de Marquet informed us that the wound was such that, according to the doctors, if the assassin had pressed the throat a few seconds longer, Mlle Stangerson would have died of strangulation.

'The case, as reported in the *Matin*,' said Rouletabille, as keen as ever, 'seems to be more and more inexplicable. Can you tell me, Monsieur, what doors and windows there are in the pavilion?'

'There are five openings,' replied M. de Marquet, coughing once or twice, and giving way at last to the desire he felt to recount the whole of the fantastic mystery of the case he was investigating. 'There are five. First of all, the door of the vestibule, which is the only entrance to the pavilion. It is a door which is always automatically closed, and which cannot be opened, either from outside or inside, except by two special keys that are never out of the possession of either Old Jacques or M. Stangerson. Mlle Stangerson has no need for them, since old Jacques lodges in the pavilion, and during the daytime she never leaves her father. When they, all four, rushed into the Yellow Room, after breaking the door open, the door in the vestibule remained closed as usual, and, of the two keys for opening it, Old Jacques had one in his pocket, and M. Stangerson the other. As to the windows of the pavilion, there are four – the one window of the Yellow Room, the two windows of the laboratory, and the window of the vestibule. The window of the Yellow Room and those of the laboratory look on to the open country. The only window looking on the park is that of the vestibule.'

'It is by that window he escaped from the pavilion!' exclaimed Rouletabille.

'How do you know that?' asked M. de Marquet, fixing a strange look on my young friend.

'We'll see later how the assassin got away from the Yellow Room,' replied Rouletabille, 'but he must have left the pavilion by the vestibule window.'

'Once more, how do you know that?'

'How? Why, the thing is simple! As it is quite obvious that he could not escape by the door of the pavilion, it is obvious that he had to pass through a window, and it is indispensable, for him to pass, that there should be at least one window without iron bars outside. The window of the Yellow Room is secured by iron bars, because it looks out upon the open country; the two windows of the laboratory are evidently protected in a like manner for the same reason. Since the assassin got away, I conceive that he found a window that was not barred, and that must be the one of the vestibule, which opens on to the park – that is, into the interior of the estate. It doesn't require witchcraft to find that out.'

'Yes,' said M. de Marquet; 'but what you might have guessed is that this window, the only one which is not barred, has solid iron shutters. Now, these iron shutters remained fastened by their iron latch, and yet we have proof that the assassin made his escape from the pavilion by this very window. Traces of blood on the inside wall and on the shutters, and footprints on the ground – footprints which are entirely similar to those I found and measured in the Yellow Room – establish the fact that the assassin made his escape that way. But, then, how did he do it, seeing that the shutters remained fastened on the inside? He has passed like a shadow through the shutters. And, finally, the most bewildering part of it all is that it is impossible to form an idea as to how the criminal got out of the Yellow Room, or how he went through the laboratory to reach the vestibule, for he had to pass through there. Ah, yes, M. Rouletabille, it is altogether a fine case, a bewildering and fascinating puzzle. And the key to it will not be discovered for a long time, I hope.'

'What is it you hope, Monsieur?'

M. de Marquet corrected himself.

'I do not hope so; I think so. That is what I meant.'

'Could that window have been closed and refastened after the flight of the assassin?' asked Rouletabille.

'Of course, that is what seems quite natural to me at present, though inexplicable, for it would imply an accomplice – or even accomplices – and I don't see – ' After a short silence, he added: 'Ah, if Mlle Stangerson were only well enough today to allow of her being questioned!'

Rouletabille, following up his thought, asked: 'And what about the attic? There must be some opening in that attic!'

'Yes, I forgot all about the attic. There is a window – or, rather, skylight – in it, which, as it looks out on the open country, M. Stangerson had barred, like the other windows. These bars, as in the windows of the ground floor, have remained intact, and the shutters, which naturally open inwards, have remained closed. Besides, we have not discovered anything that could lead us to suspect that the assassin went through the attic.'

'It seems clear to you, then, Monsieur, that the assassin escaped – nobody knows how – by the vestibule window?'

'Everything goes to prove it.'

'I think so myself,' declared Rouletabille gravely. After a brief silence he continued: 'If you have not found any traces of the assassin in the attic – as, for example, dirty footmarks similar to those on the floor of the Yellow Room – you must come to the conclusion that it was not he who stole Old Jacques's revolver.'

'There are no traces in the attic other than those of Old Jacques himself,' said the magistrate, with a significant turn of the head; and he completed his thoughts by saying: 'Old Jacques was with M. Stangerson in the laboratory – and it was lucky for him. Now what part did his revolver play in the drama? It seems very clear that this weapon did less injury to Mlle Stangerson than to the assassin.'

Without replying to this question, which no doubt embarrassed him, M. de Marquet told us that two bullets had been found in the Yellow Room – one in the wall stained with the impression of a red hand – a man's large hand – and the other in the ceiling.

'Oh – oh! In the ceiling!' muttered Rouletabille. 'In the ceiling! That is most interesting! In the ceiling!'

He smoked for a while in silence, enveloping himself in clouds of smoke. When we reached Savigny-sur-Orge, I had to give him a tap on the shoulder to make him come out of his dream and step upon the station platform.

There the magistrate and his registrar bowed politely, and made us understand that they had seen quite enough of us; they then rapidly got into a trap that was awaiting them.

'How long does it take to walk to the Château du Glandier?' Rouletabille asked one of the railway-porters.

'From an hour and a half to an hour and three-quarters, easy walking,' the man replied.

Rouletabille, having looked up at the sky and found its appearance satisfactory, took my arm and said: 'Come on; I need a walk.'

'Well,' I asked, 'are things becoming less entangled?'

'Not a bit of it,' he said. 'The whole affair seems more entangled than ever! But to be frank, I have an idea.'

'What idea?'

'I can't tell anything just at present. My idea is one that involves the life or death of two persons at least.'

'Do you think there are accomplices?'

'I don't.'

We fell into silence. Presently he went on: 'It was a bit of luck, our falling in with the examining magistrate and his registrar. By the way, what did I tell you about the revolver?'

His head was bent down, he had his hands in his pockets, and he was whistling. After a while I heard him murmur: 'Poor woman!'

'Is it Mlle Stangerson you are pitying?'

'Yes; she's a noble woman, and worthy of being pitied! She is a great – a very great – character; and I fancy – I fancy – '

'You know her, then?'

'Not at all. I have never seen her but once.'

'Why, then, do you say that she is a woman of great character?'

'Because she has bravely faced the assassin; because she courage-ously defended herself; and, above all – oh, above all – because of the bullet in the ceiling!'

I looked at Rouletabille, and inwardly wondered whether he was not mocking me, or whether he had not suddenly gone out of his senses. But I soon saw that he had never been less inclined to joke, and the brightness of his keen and clever eyes assured me that he retained all his reason. Then, too, I was getting used to his broken way of talking, which most of the time left me puzzled as to his meaning, till suddenly, with a few clear and rapidly uttered sentences, he made his idea quite plain to me, and everything became quite intelligible. The words he had spoken, which had appeared to be void of sense, became so thoroughly logical, and his meaning so obvious, that I could not realise how it was I had not sooner understood him.

Chapter 4

'Amidst wild nature'

The Château du Glandier is one of the oldest castles in the Île-de-France, where so many famous buildings erected during the feudal days are still extant. Built right in the centre of a forest during the reign of Philippe le Bel, it stands a few hundred yards from the road which leads from the village of Sainte-Geneviève to Monthéry. Its mass of inharmonious structures is dominated by a keep. When the visitor has mounted the crumbling steps of this ancient keep, he reaches a little platform, where, in the seventeenth century, Georges-Philibert de Senquigny, 'Lord of Glandier, Maisons-Neuves, and other places', built the existing 'lanterne' in an abominable rococo style. One sees six miles away the proud tower of Monthéry – the keep and the tower which seem to tell each other across valley and plain the oldest legends of French history. The keep is supposed to contain the remains of Ste Geneviève, Paris's patron saint, and hard by are a well and a grotto dedicated to her.

In this place, which seems to belong entirely to the past, Professor Stangerson and his daughter settled down to prepare the science of the future. Its solitary position, in the midst of woods, had at once pleased them. They would have there no other witnesses of their labours and their hopes but old stones and grand oaks. Glandier – formerly Glandierum – was so called from the quantity of 'glands' (acorns) that in all times had been gathered at the spot. The district, mournfully notorious today, had fallen back – owing to the negligence of its owners – into the wild aspect of primitive Nature. Only the buildings buried there preserved the trace of strange changes. Every age had left its mark on them in some bit of architecture, with which was bound up the memory of some terrible event. Yet, such as it was, the castle, in which science had taken refuge, seemed quite a fitting scene for the mysteries of terror and death.

Having said this, I cannot refrain from making one further reflection.

If I have lingered a little over this description of Glandier, it is not because I have found a good opportunity for creating the atmosphere necessary for such scenes as are to be brought before the eyes of the reader; for, in truth, my first care in this narration will be to remain as simple as possible. I do not pretend to be an author – for an author is always something of a novelist. The mystery of the Yellow Room is full enough, as it is, of real tragic horror to do without the aid of literature. I am, and only desire to be, a faithful reporter. I have to tell the story – I place it in its own frame – that is all. It is only proper that you should know where the things happened.

To return to M. Stangerson. When he bought the estate, about fifteen years before the drama with which we are concerned took place, the Château du Glandier had for a long time been unoccupied.

Another old château in the neighbourhood, built in the fourteenth century by Jean de Belmont, was also abandoned, so that the region was practically deserted. A few small houses on the side of the road leading to Corbeil, and an inn, called the Castle Inn, which offered passing hospitality to wagoners, were about all that represented civilisation in this out-of-the-way place, which one would never have expected to find only a few miles from Paris.

But it was this very solitude which had finally determined the choice of M. Stangerson and his daughter.

M. Stangerson was already celebrated. He had just returned from America, where his works had made a great sensation. The book which he had published at Philadelphia on the *Dissociation of Matter by Electric Action* had aroused protestation throughout the whole of the scientific world. M. Stangerson was a Frenchman, but of American birth. Important legacy matters had kept him for several years in the United States, where he had continued work begun in France, but later he had returned to France in possession of a large fortune. This fortune was very welcome to him; for, though he might have made millions of dollars by exploiting two or three of his chemical discoveries concerned with new processes of dyeing, it was always repugnant to him to use for his own private gain the wonderful gift of invention which he had received from Nature. He did not think this gift was his. He owed it to mankind; and so, owing to this philanthropic view, all the products of his genius fell into the public domain.

If he did not try to conceal his satisfaction at coming into possession of this important fortune, which would enable him to devote himself to his passion for pure science, he had equally to rejoice, it seemed, for another cause. Mlle Stangerson was twenty years of age at the time when her father returned from America and bought the Glandier estate. She was exceedingly pretty, having in her both the Parisian grace of her mother – who had died in giving her birth – and all that fine vigour of American blood inherited from her father's father, William Stangerson. The latter, a citizen of Philadelphia, had been obliged to become a naturalised Frenchman, for family reasons, at the time of his marriage with a French lady – the lady who was to be the mother of the illustrious Stangerson. This explains the French nationality of the professor.

A charming blonde of twenty years of age, with blue eyes and a milk-white complexion, and radiant with health, Mathilde Stangerson was one of the most beautiful marriageable girls of either the Old or the New World. It was the duty of her father – in spite of the sorrow which a separation from her would cause him – to think of her marriage, and to feel glad that he would be able to give her a dowry. However that might have been, he nevertheless buried himself and his child at Glandier at the very moment when his friends were expecting him to introduce her to society. Some of them expressed their astonishment, but the professor replied to their questions: 'It is my daughter's wish. I can refuse her nothing. She chose Glandier herself.'

When she was questioned, the young girl calmly answered: 'Where could we work better than in this solitude?'

For Mlle Stangerson already assisted in the work of her father, though it could not then be supposed that her passion for science would lead her so far as to discourage all the suitors who presented themselves to her for more than fifteen years. However secluded the life led by the father and daughter, they had to appear at a few official receptions, and at certain times of the year in the drawing-rooms of two or three friends, where the fame of the professor and the beauty of Mathilde made a sensation. The extreme reserve of the young girl did not at first discourage suitors, but at the end of a few years they tired of the quest.

One only persisted with tender fidelity, and earned the name of 'perpetual fiancé', which he accepted with melancholy resignation. This was M. Robert Darzac. Mlle Stangerson was now no longer young, and it seemed likely that, if she had found no reason for marrying up to the age of five-and-thirty, she never would find one. But such an argument evidently found no acceptance with M. Robert Darzac, who continued to pay his court – if the delicate and tender affection which he ceaselessly bestowed upon this woman of five-and-thirty can be called courtship – in spite of her declared intention never to marry.

Suddenly, some weeks before the event with which we are concerned, a report – to which nobody attached any importance, so incredible did it sound – was spread about Paris that Mlle Stangerson had at last consented to marry M. Robert Darzac! And not until it was ascertained that M. Robert Darzac himself did not deny this hint of matrimony, did people slowly begin to see truth, or possibility, in the unlikely report. At last, however, M. Stangerson, as he was leaving the Academy of Science one day, declared that the marriage of his daughter to M. Robert Darzac would be celebrated privately in the Château du Glandier as soon as he and his daughter had put the finishing touches to the paper in which they were to condense all their labours on the 'Dissociation of Matter' – that is to say, on the return of matter to ether. The married couple would settle down at Glandier, and the son-in-law would lend his assistance in the work to which the father and daughter had devoted their lives.

The world of science had not had time to recover from the effect of this news, before it heard of the attempted assassination of Mlle Stangerson in the extraordinary circumstances which we have related, and which a visit to the château will now enable us to ascertain with greater precision.

I have purposely set down all these retrospective details, with which I was acquainted through my business relations with M. Robert Darzac, so that on crossing the threshold of the Yellow Room, the reader may now be as well informed as myself.

Chapter 5

*In which Joseph Rouletabille addresses to M. Robert Darzac
a few words which produce a mysterious effect*

We had been walking for several minutes, Rouletabille and I, along a wall enclosing the vast estate of M. Stangerson, and had already come within sight of the entrance gate, when our attention was drawn to a man half bent to the ground, who was so completely absorbed in what he was doing that he did not see us coming towards him. Now he stooped so low as to almost touch the ground; now he drew himself up, and attentively examined the wall; now he looked into the palm of his right hand, then walked away with long strides, then set off running, and again looked into the palm of his hand. Rouletabille by a gesture had brought me to a standstill.

'Hush! It is Frédéric Larsan at work! Don't let us disturb him.'

Joseph Rouletabille had a great admiration for the celebrated detective. I had never seen Frédéric Larsan before, but I knew him well by reputation.

The mysterious case of the 'gold ingots of the Paris Mint' which he had solved, and his discovery of the gang who had forced the safes in the vaults of the Universal Credit Bank, had made him popular. He was considered at the time – for Rouletabille had not yet given proof of his unique talent – to be the skilfullest unraveller of the most mysterious and complicated crimes. His reputation had extended throughout the world, and the police of London, Berlin, and even of America, often called him to their aid when their national inspectors and detectives found themselves at their wits' end. It was not surprising, therefore, that the head of the Sûreté, at the very outset of the Yellow Room mystery, should have wired 'Return immediately' to his precious subordinate, who had been sent to London in connection with a big case of stolen securities. Frédéric, who at the Sûreté was called the 'Great Fred', had made all speed, doubtless knowing by experience that if he were interrupted in his work, it was only because his services were urgently needed in another direction.

As Rouletabille said, Larsan that morning was 'already at work'. We soon found out in what manner.

What he was constantly looking at in the palm of his right hand was nothing but his watch, and he seemed to be counting minutes. Presently he turned back, and started to run once more, stopping only when he reached the park gate, where he again consulted his watch, and put it into his pocket; then shrugging his shoulder as if discouraged, he pushed the gate open, entered the park, closed and locked the gate, and, raising his head, perceived us through the bars. Joseph Rouletabille rushed forward, and I followed. Frédéric Larsan was waiting for us.

'M. Fred,' said Rouletabille, raising his hat, and showing the profound respect and admiration which, as a young reporter, he felt for the famous detective, 'can you tell me whether M. Robert Darzac is at present in the castle? Here is one of his friends of the Paris bar who would like to speak to him.'

'I really do not know, M. Rouletabille,' replied Larsan, shaking hands with my friend, whom he had several times met in the course of his most difficult inquiries. 'I have not seen him.'

'The concierges will be able to give us the information, no doubt?' said Rouletabille, pointing to the lodge, the door and windows of which were closed.

'The concierges will not be able to give you any information, M. Rouletabille.'

'Why not?'

'Because they were arrested half an hour ago.'

'Arrested!' cried Rouletabille. 'They, then, are the assassins?'

Frédéric Larsan shrugged his shoulders.

'When one cannot arrest the assassin,' he said, with an air of supreme irony, 'one can always indulge in the luxury of discovering accomplices.'

'Is it you who had them arrested, M. Fred?'

'No, no; not I. I have not had them arrested. In the first place, because – because I am pretty sure that they have nothing to do with the case, and also because – '

'Because of what?' asked Rouletabille eagerly.

'Because of nothing,' said Larsan, shaking his head.

'Because there are no accomplices,' whispered Rouletabille.

Frédéric Larsan started, and looked intently at Rouletabille.

'Aha! You have an idea, then, about this matter? Yet you have seen nothing, young man. You have not yet gained admission here.'

'I shall gain admission.'

'I doubt it. The orders are precise.'

'I shall gain admission if you let me see M. Robert Darzac. Do that for me! We are old friends, M. Fred. Please! Remember the fine story I wrote about you concerning the gold ingots case!'

Rouletabille's face was truly comic to watch. It expressed such an irresistible desire to cross that threshold beyond which some prodigious mystery had occurred. It appealed with so much eloquence, not of the lips and eyes only, but of all the features, that I could not refrain from bursting into laughter. Frédéric Larsan could retain his gravity no more than myself.

Meanwhile, behind the gate, Larsan calmly put the key in his pocket. I studied him.

He was a man of about fifty years of age. He had a fine head with hair turning grey, a colourless complexion, and firm profile. His forehead was high and bulging; his chin and cheeks were clean-shaven; his upper lip – without moustache – was finely shaped. His eyes were rather small and round, fixing on people a look that was at once searching and disquieting. He was of middle height and well built, and had an attractive and gentlemanly bearing. There was nothing of the vulgar detective about him. He was a great artist in his way; he knew it, and one felt that he had a high opinion of himself. His conversation pronounced him a sceptic – one disillusioned by experience. His strange profession had brought him into contact with so many crimes and villainies that it was only natural his 'feelings were hardened', to use Rouletabille's own expression.

Larsan turned his head at the sound of a vehicle, which had come from the château and reached the gate behind him. We recognised the trap which had conveyed the magistrate and his clerk from the station at Épinay.

'Well,' said Frédéric Larsan, 'you wanted to speak with M. Robert Darzac. There he is.'

The trap was already at the gate, and Robert Darzac was begging Frédéric Larsan to open it for him as he was pressed for time to catch the next train to Paris, when he recognised me. While Larsan was unlocking the gate, Darzac enquired what had brought me to Glandier at such a tragic moment. I then noticed that he was frightfully pale, and that his features expressed the deepest sorrow.

'Is Mlle Stangerson better?' I immediately asked.

'Yes,' he said, 'there is some chance they will save her. She *must* be saved.'

He did not add, 'or it will be my death,' but that end of the sentence trembled on his pale lips.

Rouletabille then intervened.

'You are in a hurry, Monsieur. Yet I must speak to you. I have something of the greatest importance to tell you.'

Frédéric Larsan interrupted.

'May I leave you?' he asked of Robert Darzac. 'Have you a key, or do you want me to lend you this one?'

'Thank you; I have a key, and will lock the gate.'

Larsan hurried off in the direction of the château, which towered majestically above us a few hundred yards away.

Robert Darzac was frowning, and already showing some impatience. I presented Rouletabille as an excellent friend of mine, but as soon as he learnt that the young man was a journalist, M. Darzac looked at me reproachfully, and saying he had to reach Épinay in twenty minutes, bowed, and whipped up his horse. But to my profound amazement Rouletabille had already seized the bridle and stopped the horse with a vigorous hand, while he pronounced this phrase, which was utterly meaningless to me: 'The vicarage has lost nothing of its charm, nor the garden of its brightness.'

These words had no sooner left the lips of Rouletabille than I saw Robert Darzac stagger. Pale as he was, he grew paler still. His eyes were fixed in terror on the young man, and he immediately stepped from the trap in an inexpressible state of agitation.

'Let us go!' he stammered. 'Let us go!' Then, suddenly, with a sort of fury, he repeated: 'Let us go, Monsieur! Let us go!'

And he started off along the road leading to the château, accompanied by Rouletabille, who still retained his hold of the horse's bridle. I said a few words to M. Darzac, but he did not answer me. I looked at Rouletabille questioningly, but he did not see me.

Chapter 6

In the depths of the oak grove

We reached the château, and as we approached it, saw four gendarmes pacing in front of a little door on the ground floor of the
keep. We soon learned that in a room on this ground floor, which
in mediaeval days served as a prison, Bernier and his wife, the
concierges, were confined.

M. Robert Darzac led us into the modern part of the castle
through a large door. Rouletabille, who had left the horse and trap in
the care of a servant, never took his eyes off Darzac. I followed his
look, and found that it was solely directed towards the gloved hands
of the Sorbonne professor. When we found ourselves in a small
sitting-room, furnished in old-fashioned style, M. Darzac turned to
Rouletabille, and said rather sharply: 'Speak! What do you want?'

The reporter answered in an equally sharp tone: 'I want to shake
hands with you.'

Darzac shrank back.

'What does it mean?'

He evidently understood what I then understood myself – that my
friend suspected him of the abominable attempt on the life of Mlle
Stangerson. He suddenly remembered the trace of the blood-stained
hand on the walls of the Yellow Room. I closely watched this man of
noble features, whose look, usually so straightforward, was, at this
moment, so strangely troubled. He held out his right hand, and,
pointing to me, said: 'You are the friend of M. Sainclair who once
rendered me a great service in a lawsuit, Monsieur, and I see no
reason for refusing to shake hands with you.'

Rouletabille did not take the extended hand. He said, lying with
the utmost audacity: 'Monsieur, I have lived several years in Russia,
where I have learned the usage of never shaking any but an un-
gloved hand.'

I thought the Sorbonne professor was going to give vent to his
rage, but, on the contrary, with an obvious and violent effort, he

calmed himself, took off his gloves, and presented his hands. There
was no scar on them.

'Are you satisfied?'

'No,' replied Rouletabille. 'My dear friend,' he said, turning to me,
'I must ask you to leave us alone for a moment.'

I bowed and retired, amazed at what I had just seen and heard. I
was at a loss to understand why M. Robert Darzac had not already
shown the door to my impertinent and stupid friend. I was, at the
time, angry with Rouletabille on account of his insulting suspicions,
which had led to the extraordinary glove incident.

For some twenty minutes I strolled in front of the château, trying
to link together the various events of that day, and not succeeding
in doing so. What was Rouletabille's idea? Was it possible that
M. Robert Darzac appeared to him as the criminal? How could
one think that this man, who was to have married Mlle Stangerson
in the course of a few days, had entered the Yellow Room to
assassinate his own fiancée? Besides, no explanation had so far
reached me as to how the criminal had been able to escape from the
Yellow Room; and so long as that mystery, which appeared to
me so inexplicable, remained unsolved, I thought it the duty of
everyone to refrain from suspecting anybody. And then, what
was the meaning of that seemingly senseless phrase, 'The vicarage
has lost nothing of its brightness,' which still rang in my ears? I
was anxious to rejoin Rouletabille and question him about that
mysterious sentence.

At that moment the young reporter came from the château, together with M. Robert Darzac, and, extraordinary to relate, I saw at
a glance that they were the best of friends.

'We are going to the Yellow Room. Come with us,' Rouletabille
said to me. 'By the way, old fellow, I'm keeping you with me all day.
We'll lunch together in the neighbourhood.'

'You'll lunch with me here, gentlemen – '

'No, thanks,' replied the young man; 'we'll lunch at the Castle Inn.'

'You'll fare very badly there. You'll not find anything.'

'Do you think so? Well, I hope to find something there,' Rouletabille replied. 'After luncheon we'll set to work again. I'll write my
article, and you'll be so good as to take it to the office for me.'

'Will you not return to Paris with me?'

'No, I shall stop here overnight.'

I turned toward Rouletabille. He spoke quite seriously, and M.
Robert Darzac did not appear to be in the least surprised. We were

passing by the keep, and heard wailing voices. Rouletabille asked:
'Why have these people been arrested?'

'It's partly my fault,' said M. Darzac. 'I remarked yesterday to
the examining magistrate that it was impossible to account for the
fact that the concierges had time to hear the revolver-shots, dress
themselves, and cover the distance which lies between their lodge
and the pavilion in the space of two minutes; for that is all the time
that elapsed between the firing of the shots and the moment when
they were met by Old Jacques.'

'That was certainly suspicious,' acquiesced Rouletabille. 'And they
were dressed?'

'That's just it. It seems so incredible. They were dressed – completely. Not a single garment was wanting. The woman wore clogs,
but the man had laced boots on – actually laced. Now, they declare
that they went to bed at half-past nine, as usual. On arriving this
morning, the examining magistrate brought with him from Paris a
revolver of the same kind as that used in the case of the crime, which
is not to be touched. He made the registrar fire two shots in the
Yellow Room with the doors and windows closed. We were with him
in the concierges' lodge and heard nothing; nothing *could* be heard
from there. The concierges have lied. There can be no doubt of it.
They were ready; they were already near the pavilion, waiting for
something. Of course, we do not accuse them of being the authors of
the crime, but their complicity is not improbable – M. de Marquet
had them arrested at once.'

'If they had been accomplices,' said Rouletabille, 'they would have
arrived dressed just anyhow – or, rather, they would not have arrived
at all. When people throw themselves into the arms of Justice with
so many proofs of complicity on them, it is because they are *not*
accomplices. I don't believe there are any accomplices in this affair.'

'Then why were they abroad at midnight? Let them say why.'

'They have certainly some reason for keeping silent. What that
reason is remains to be found. And even if they are not accomplices,
it may be important to know that reason. Everything that takes place
on such a night is important.'

We had just crossed an old bridge thrown over the Douve, and
were entering the part of the park called the Oak Grove. The oaks
there are centuries old. Autumn had already shrivelled their tawny
leaves, and their branches, black and twisted, looked like frightful
heads of hair entwined with reptiles, as the classic sculptors represent
the head of Medusa. This place, which Mlle Stangerson inhabited

part of the year because she found it cheerful, appeared to us sad and dreary. The soil was black and muddy from the recent rain and the decaying leaves; the trunks of the trees were black; even the sky above us, dull and overcast with heavy clouds, appeared in mourning.

It was in this desolate retreat that we came upon the white-walled pavilion. A strange building, indeed, without a window to be seen from where we stood. Only one little door marked the entrance to it. One might have thought it a tomb, a vast mausoleum in the depths of a wild forest. As we came nearer, we were able to make out its plan. The building got all the light it needed from the south – that is to say, from the open country. When the little door on the park was closed, M. and Mlle Stangerson must have found there an ideal prison in which to dwell amid their work and their dreams.

I will now give the plan of the pavilion. It had but one floor – the ground-floor – which was reached by a few steps, and above it an attic, with which we need not concern ourselves. It is, then, the plan of the ground-floor in all its simplicity which I here submit to the reader.

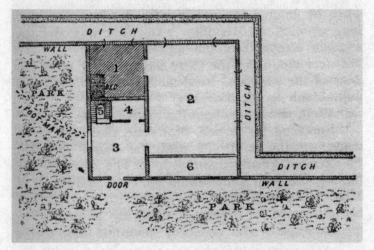

1. Yellow Room, with its one window and its one door opening into the laboratory.
2. Laboratory, with its two large barred windows and its two doors, one opening on to the vestibule, the other on to the Yellow Room.
3. Vestibule, with its unbarred window and door opening on to the park.
4. Lavatory.
5. Stairs to the attic.
6. Large and only fireplace of the pavilion, serving for the experiments of the laboratory.

This plan was drawn by Rouletabille himself, and I have ascertained that it was complete, and that there was not a line missing which might have led to the solution of the problem then set before Justice. With the plan and its description before him, the reader will know as much as Rouletabille knew when he entered the pavilion for the first time, and may wonder, as we did: 'In what way did the assassin escape from the Yellow Room?'

Before mounting the three steps leading up to the door of the pavilion, Rouletabille stopped, and said point-blank to M. Darzac: 'Well, and what about the motive of the crime?'

'Speaking for myself, Monsieur, there can be no doubt on the subject,' said the fiancé of Mlle Stangerson, greatly distressed. 'The marks of the fingers, the deep scratches on the chest and throat of Mlle Stangerson, show that the wretch who attacked her attempted to commit a dastardly crime. The medical experts who yesterday examined those marks declare they were made by the same hand as that of which the red impression has remained on the wall – an enormous hand, and much too large to enter my glove, Monsieur,' he added, with a bitter smile.

'Could not that red mark,' I interrupted, 'have been left by the hand of Mlle Stangerson, who, at the moment of falling, would have leant against the wall, and left on it, as she slipped, an enlarged impression of her blood-stained hand?'

'There was not a drop of blood on either of Mlle Stangerson's hands when she was found lying on the floor,' replied M. Darzac.

'It is quite certain, then,' I said, 'that it was Mlle Stangerson who was armed with the revolver of Old Jacques, since she wounded the hand of the assassin. Was she in fear of somebody or something?'

'Probably.'

'You don't suspect anybody?'

'No,' replied M. Darzac, looking at Rouletabille.

Rouletabille then said to me: 'I must tell you, my friend, that the inquiry is a little more advanced than M. de Marquet chose to tell us. It is not only known that the revolver was the weapon with which Mlle Stangerson defended herself, but the other weapon used to attack and strike Mlle Stangerson has been known from the first. It was, so M. Darzac tells me, a sheep's bone. Why is M. de Marquet surrounding this sheep's bone with so much mystery? Is it with the object of facilitating the investigation of the detectives? Probably. He imagines perhaps that its owner will be found among those in the criminal haunts of Paris, who are known to use this instrument of crime, the most terrible that nature has invented. But can one ever tell what may pass through the brain of an examining magistrate?' added Rouletabille, with contemptuous irony.

'A sheep's bone was found in the Yellow Room, then?' I asked.

'Yes, Monsieur,' said Robert Darzac, 'at the foot of the bed. But I beg you not to say anything about that sheep's bone, for we have promised M. de Marquet not to mention it.' I made a sign of approval. 'It is an enormous sheep's bone, the head of which – or, rather, the joint – was still red with blood from the wound inflicted on Mlle Stangerson. It is an old bone, and, according to appearances, must have been used for other crimes. So thinks M. de Marquet, who has had it taken to the Municipal Laboratory in Paris to be analysed. In fact, he thinks he has detected on this bone, not only the blood of the last victim, but other stains of dried blood, evidence of previous crimes.'

'A sheep's bone in the hands of a skilled assassin is a frightful weapon,' said Rouletabille – 'a weapon more useful and more sure than a heavy hammer.'

'The scoundrel has made that clear enough,' said M. Robert Darzac painfully. 'The joint of that sheep's bone fits the wound perfectly. My belief is that the wound would have been fatal had not the blow of the assassin been broken by the revolver of Mlle Stangerson. Wounded in the hand, he dropped the bone and fled. Unfortunately, the blow had been struck, and Mlle Stangerson, having first been nearly strangled, was stunned. If she had succeeded in wounding the man with the first shot of the revolver she might have escaped the blow. But she certainly seized the revolver too late; in the struggle the first shot deviated and lodged in the ceiling. It was only the second that took effect.'

M. Darzac then knocked at the door of the pavilion. My impatience to enter the place where the crime had been committed may easily be imagined. I was trembling with excitement, and, in spite of the great interest I took in the story of the sheep's bone, it irritated me to find that our conversation was becoming protracted, and that the door of the pavilion remained closed.

At last it was opened.

A man, whom I at once knew to be Old Jacques, stood on the threshold.

He appeared to be well over sixty years of age. He had a long white beard, and silvery hair on which he wore a flat Basque cap. He was dressed in a suit of brown velveteen, rather shabby and worn. He had clogs on his feet. He looked rather surly and cross, but his expression lightened as soon as he saw M. Darzac.

'Friends of mine,' our guide said simply. 'Anyone in the pavilion, Old Jacques?'

'I am not supposed to allow anybody to enter, Monsieur Robert; but, of course, the order does not apply to you. Besides, what do they mean by their secrecy? Those officials have seen everything there was to be seen, and taken enough sketches and drawn up enough reports – '

'Excuse me, Monsieur Jacques. Answer one question before anything else,' said Rouletabille.

'What is it, young man. If I can answer it – '

'Did your mistress that night wear her hair in "bandeaux"? You know what I mean – parted in the middle and covering part of the forehead – in the Madonna style?'

'No, young man. My mistress has never worn her hair in the way you mention, neither on that day nor on any other. She had her hair drawn up, as usual, so that one could see her beautiful forehead, pure as that of a new-born babe!'

Rouletabille grunted, and at once set about examining the door. He inspected the automatic fastening. He satisfied himself that it could never remain open, and that a key was required to open it.

Then we entered the vestibule, a small, well-lit room, paved with square red tiles.

'Ah! Here is the window by which the assassin escaped!'

'So they say, Monsieur – so they keep on saying! But if he had gone off that way we could not have helped seeing him. We are not blind, neither M. Stangerson nor I, nor the concierges they've put in prison! Why don't they put me in prison, too, on account of my revolver?'

Rouletabille had already opened the window, and was examining the shutters.

'Were these closed at the time of the crime?'

'Yes; fastened with the iron catch inside,' said Old Jacques; 'and I am pretty well certain that the murderer did not get out through them!'

'Are there any bloodstains?'

'Yes; there, on the stones outside. But what kind of blood?'

'Ah,' said Rouletabille, 'I can see the footsteps on the path there; the ground must have been very moist. I'll examine them presently.'

'Nonsense!' interrupted Old Jacques. 'The assassin did not go that way!'

'Indeed! Well, which way, then?'

'How do I know?'

Rouletabille was looking at everything, scenting everything. He went down on his knees, and rapidly examined the tiles in the vestibule. Old Jacques went on: 'Ah, you won't find anything, young man! Nothing has been found. Besides, everything is dirty now; too many persons have been here. They won't let me wash the floor. But on the day of the crime I had washed it thoroughly – I, Old Jacques; and if the assassin had passed there with his dirty feet, I should have seen it. He has left marks enough of his old boots in Mademoiselle's room.'

Rouletabille rose, and asked: 'When did you wash these tiles for the last time?' And he fixed his searching eyes on Old Jacques.

'Why, as I told you, on the day of the crime; about half-past five, while Mademoiselle and her father were taking a little walk before dining here, for they dined later in the laboratory. The next day the examining magistrate came and saw all the marks there were on the floor, as plainly as if they had been made with ink on white paper. But neither in the vestibule nor in the laboratory, which were as clean as a new sou, were the steps to be found – the steps of the man! Since they have been found near this window outside, he must have made his way through the ceiling of the Yellow Room into the attic, then cut a passage through the roof, and dropped to the ground right outside the vestibule window. But there's no hole either in the ceiling of the Yellow Room or in the roof of my attic, that's quite certain. So that, you see, nothing is known – nothing, no, nothing. And nothing will ever be known. It is a mystery of the Devil's own making.'

Rouletabille went down upon his knees again, almost in front of a small lavatory at the back of the vestibule. In that position he remained for almost a minute.

'Well?' I asked him when he got up.

'Oh, nothing very important; only a drop of blood!'

He then turned towards Old Jacques.

'When you began to wash the laboratory and the vestibule, was the vestibule window open?'

'No, Monsieur, it was closed; but after I had finished the washing of the floor, I lit some charcoal for Monsieur in the laboratory furnace, and as I lit it with old newspapers, there was some smoke; I opened the two windows in the laboratory and this one, to make a draught; then I shut those in the laboratory, and left the vestibule window open, and went out. When I returned to the pavilion this window had been closed, and Monsieur and Mademoiselle were already at work in the laboratory.'

'M. or Mlle Stangerson had, no doubt, shut it?'

'No doubt.'

'You did not ask them?'

'No.'

After a close scrutiny of the little lavatory and of the staircase leading up to the attic, Rouletabille – for *we* seemed no longer to exist – went into the laboratory. It was, I confess, in a state of great excitement that I followed him. Robert Darzac did not lose sight of my friend, but my eyes went straight to the door of the Yellow Room. It was closed, or, rather, pushed back towards the laboratory, and, as I immediately saw, partially shattered and out of use.

My young friend, who went about his work methodically, was silently studying the room in which we were standing. It was large and well lighted. Two big windows – almost bays – guarded by strong iron bars, looked out upon a wide extent of country. Through an opening in the forest they commanded a wonderful view down the length of the valley and across the plain to Paris, which could probably be seen on very clear and sunny days. But now there was nothing but mud on the ground, mist in the air, and blood in the room.

The whole of one side of the laboratory was occupied by a vast fireplace, with crucibles, furnaces, glass-bulbs and other instruments used for chemical experiments. There were tables loaded with phials, documents, and a small electrical machine – an apparatus, as M. Darzac informed me, used by Professor Stangerson to demonstrate the dissociation of matter under the action of solar light, etc.

Along the walls there were cabinets, with or without glass fronts, full of microscopes, special cameras, and an amazing quantity of chemical crystals.

Rouletabille was ferreting in the chimney. With the tip of his finger he searched the crucibles. Suddenly he drew himself up, holding a piece of half-consumed paper in his hand. He came to where we stood talking by one of the windows, and said: 'Keep that for us, M. Darzac.'

I bent over the piece of scorched paper which M. Darzac had just taken from the hand of Rouletabille, and read distinctly the following words – the only ones that remained readable:

' . . . . vicarage lost nothing charm, nor the gar of its brightness.'

Beneath there was a date: 'October 23'.

Twice since the morning these same senseless words had struck me, and for the second time I saw that they produced on the Sorbonne professor the same stunning effect. The first care of M. Darzac was to turn his eyes in the direction of Old Jacques. But the latter had not seen us, being busy near the other window. Then the fiancé of Mlle Stangerson tremblingly opening his pocket-book, put the piece of paper into it, and said, with a deep sigh: 'My God!'

Meanwhile Rouletabille had mounted into the chimney – that is to say, he had got up on the bricks of a furnace. He was attentively examining the chimney, which grew narrower as it rose, and which, at about three feet above him, was closed with sheets of iron fastened into the brickwork, and through which passed three small pipes, each six inches in diameter.

'Impossible to get in or out that way,' he said, jumping back into the laboratory. 'Besides, even if "he" had attempted it, he would have brought all that ironwork down to the ground. No, no; it is of no use looking there.'

Rouletabille next examined the furniture, and opened the doors of the cabinets. Then it was the turn of the windows, through which he declared no one could have possibly passed, and through which no one had passed or attempted to pass. At the second window he found Old Jacques still in contemplation.

'Well, Old Jacques,' he said, 'what are you staring at?'

'I'm watching the detective there. He is continually going round and round the lake. He's another who won't find out anything!'

'You don't know Frédéric Larsan, Old Jacques, or you wouldn't speak of him in that way,' said Rouletabille in a melancholy tone. 'If there is anyone here who will find the assassin, it is he.'

And Rouletabille heaved a deep sigh.

'Before they catch the criminal they'll have to find out how they lost him,' said Old Jacques stolidly.

At last we came to the door of the Yellow Room.

'Here's the door behind which something happened!' said Rouletabille, with a solemn accent that in any other circumstances would have been comic.

Chapter 7

In which Rouletabille makes investigations under the bed

Rouletabille, having pushed open the door of the Yellow Room, paused on the threshold, and said, with an emotion which I was only to understand much later: 'Ah, the perfume of the lady in black!'

The room was dark. Old Jacques wished to open the shutters, but Rouletabille stopped him.

'Did not the drama take place in total darkness?' he asked.

'No, young man, I don't think so. Mlle Stangerson always insisted on having a nightlight on her table, and it was I who lit it every evening before she went to bed. I was a sort of chambermaid, you must understand, when the evening came. The real chambermaid only came here in the morning. Mademoiselle worked so late.'

'Where did the table with the nightlight stand? Far from the bed?'

'Some way from the bed.'

'Can you put a match to the nightlight?'

'It is broken, and the oil in it was spilled when the table was upset. However, all the things in the room have been left just as they were. I have only to open the shutters, and you shall see for yourself.'

'Stop!'

Rouletabille went back into the laboratory, closed the shutters of the two windows there, and the door of the vestibule as well. When we were in complete darkness, he lit a wax vesta, gave it to Old Jacques, and told him to move to the middle of the room with it, to the place where the nightlight was burning that day.

Old Jacques, who was in his socks – he generally left his clogs in the vestibule – entered the Yellow Room with the vesta, and we vaguely perceived objects overthrown on the floor, a bed in one corner, and, in front of us to the left, the gleam of a looking-glass hanging on the wall near the bed.

Rouletabille said: 'That'll do. You may now open the shutters.'

'Don't come any farther,' Old Jacques said. 'You might make marks with your boots, and nothing must be disturbed or altered;

it is an idea of the magistrate, though he has nothing more to do in this room.'

He opened the shutters. The pale daylight entered from without, throwing a ghostly gleam on the saffron-coloured walls. The floor – for, although the laboratory and the vestibule were tiled, the Yellow Room had a flooring of wood – was covered with a yellow mat in one piece, which went over nearly the whole of the surface, going even under the bed and the washing-stand – the only pieces of furniture that remained on their legs. The round table, the bed-table, and two chairs had been overthrown. They did not prevent a large stain of blood being visible on the mat, made, as Old Jacques informed us, by the blood which had flowed from the wound on Mlle Stangerson's forehead. Besides this stain, drops of blood had fallen in all directions, following as it were the very plain traces of the footsteps – large and black – of the assassin. Everything led to the presumption that these drops of blood had fallen from the wound of the man who had, for a moment, pressed his red hand on the wall. There were other traces of the same hand on the wall, but much less distinct. They were quite obviously the marks of a man's large hand.

I could not help calling out: 'Look – look! This blood on the wall! The man who pressed his hand so heavily upon it in the darkness must certainly have believed that he was pushing at a door. That's why he pressed so hard, leaving on the yellow wallpaper a terribly accusing sign; for I don't think there are many hands of that sort in the world. It is big and strong, and the fingers are nearly all of the same length. As to the thumb, it is wanting; we have only the mark of the palm. And if we follow the track of this hand,' I continued, 'we see it, after leaving its imprint on the wall, grope along that side, feel for the door, find it, and then feel for the lock.'

'No doubt,' interrupted Rouletabille, chuckling. 'Only there is no blood either on the lock or on the bolt.'

'What does that prove?' I retorted, with an amount of logic of which I was quite proud. 'He probably pulled the bolt and opened the lock with his left hand, which would have been quite natural, supposing that his right hand was wounded.'

'He didn't open it at all!' said Old Jacques. 'We are not fools, I suppose! And there were four of us here when we burst open the door!'

I went on: 'What a queer hand! See what a queer hand it is!'

'It is quite normal,' said Rouletabille; 'only the imprint of it was distorted by its having slipped on the wall. The criminal must be a man of about five feet eight in height.'

'How do you find that out?'

'By the position of his red hand on the wall.'

My friend was concerned next with the mark of the bullet in the wall. This mark was a round hole.

'This bullet,' said Rouletabille, 'was fired straight – I mean, neither from above nor from below.' And he further remarked that it was a few inches lower on the wall than the red hand-print.

Rouletabille went back to the door and carefully examined the lock and the bolt, and satisfied himself that the door had certainly been burst open from the outside, for the lock and bolt were still on the door – one turned, and the other pushed in from the wall – the two sockets were nearly torn off, and only held in place by a screw or two.

The young reporter examined them; looked at both sides of the door; ascertained that the bolt could not be touched from the outside in any manner; that the key had been found in the inner side of the lock; and, finally, that, with the key in the lock, and on the inside, it was impossible to open that door from without with another kind of key. Having made sure of all these details and also that the door did not close automatically – that it was, in fact, the most ordinary of doors, fitted with solid lock and bolt, which had remained closed – he said at last: 'That's better!' Then, sitting down on the floor, he rapidly took off his boots.

The next thing he did was to rise and minutely examine the over-turned furniture. We watched him in silence. Old Jacques kept on saying, every time more ironically: 'Young fellow, you're giving yourself a great deal of useless trouble.'

Rouletabille raised his head.

'You speak the truth, Old Jacques,' he said; 'your mistress did not have her hair "in bandeaux" that evening. I was a fool to have believed that she did.'

And, supple as a serpent, he slipped under the bed. Old Jacques then remarked: 'Is it not amazing to think that the assassin was hidden under there? He must have been already under that bed at ten o'clock, when I came into this room to close the shutters and put a match to the nightlight, since neither M. Stangerson, Mlle Mathilde, nor I moved from the laboratory afterwards until the moment of the tragedy.'

Presently we heard Rouletabille asking from under the bed: 'At what time, M. Jacques, did M. Stangerson and Mlle Stangerson enter the laboratory?'

'At six o'clock.'

The voice of Rouletabille continued: 'Yes, *he* has been under here – that's certain. In fact, this is the only place where he could have hidden himself. Here, too, I find marks of his boots. When you entered, the four of you, did you look under this bed?'

'At once. We even drew it out of its place.'

'And between the mattresses?'

'There was only one mattress on the bed, and on that Mademoiselle was placed. The concierge and M. Stangerson immediately carried Mademoiselle on it into the laboratory. Under the mattress there was nothing but the spring-mattress – just the ordinary wire-netting – and that could not conceal anything or anybody. Remember, Monsieur, that there were four of us, and that nothing could fail to be seen by us, the room being very small and scantily furnished. Besides, all doors were locked behind us in the pavilion.'

'Perhaps he got away with the mattress,' I suggested – 'perhaps even inside the mattress! Everything is possible in such a mysterious case. Being so terribly upset, M. Stangerson and the concierge may not have noticed that they were carrying double weight. The thing is not impossible, especially if the concierge is an accomplice. I give you this idea for what it is worth; but it explains many things, and particularly the fact that the laboratory and the vestibule bear, neither of them, any footmarks such as those found in the room. When the mattress on which Mademoiselle was, was being transported from the laboratory to the château, a short pause may have been made near the window of the vestibule, and this would have allowed the man to escape.'

'What next – what next?' cried Rouletabille, deliberately laughing under the bed.

I felt rather vexed, and replied: 'No one can tell; everything seems possible.'

'The examining magistrate had the same idea, Monsieur,' said Old Jacques, 'and he carefully examined the mattress. He had to laugh at the idea, just as your friend is doing now; for whoever heard of a double-bottomed mattress! Besides, if there had been a man in the mattress, we should have perceived it.'

I had to laugh myself, and, indeed, the absurdity of my suggestion was afterwards apparent to me. But where did absurdity begin or end in this bewildering affair?

My friend was the only man capable of discovering the truth; and yet –

'I say!' he shouted from under the bed. 'This mat here has been moved out of place. Who did it?'

'We did, Monsieur!' Old Jacques exclaimed. 'When we couldn't find the assassin, we wondered whether there was a hole in the floor.'

'There is none,' replied Rouletabille. 'Is there a cellar?'

'No, there is no cellar. But that did not stop our searching, or prevent the examining magistrate and his clerk from studying the floor, board after board, as if there had been a cellar under it.'

The reporter then reappeared. His eyes were sparkling, his nostrils quivered. He remained on his hands and knees. I could not help comparing him in my mind to an admirable pointer on the scent of some wonderful game. And, indeed, he did scent the steps of a man – the man whom he had sworn to hand over to his chief, the Editor of the *Époque*, for it must not be forgotten that Rouletabille was a journalist.

Still on his hands and knees, he made his way to the four corners of the room, sniffing, so to speak, and going round every object in the place, around everything that we could see – which was not much – and around everything we could not see – which, it appeared, was considerable.

The washing-stand was a simple table standing on four legs. Nothing could possibly transform it into a hiding-place. There was no wardrobe, for Mlle Stangerson kept her outfit at the château.

The hands, and even the nose of Rouletabille travelled along the walls, which were constructed of solid brickwork. When he had done with the walls, and passed his nimble fingers over every portion of the yellow paper covering them, he turned to the ceiling, which he was able to touch by mounting a chair he had placed on the washing-stand, moving these ingeniously constructed steps from place to place. After he had finished the scrutiny of this ceiling, where he closely looked at the mark of the other bullet, he went to the window and examined the iron bars and shutters, all of which were solid and intact. At last he uttered a sigh of relief and satisfaction, and declared that now he was quite at ease.

'Well! do you realise now how thoroughly the unfortunate young lady was shut in when they tried to assassinate her, and when she was calling for help?' Old Jacques asked mournfully.

'She was!' said the young reporter, wiping the perspiration from his forehead. 'The Yellow Room was indeed as firmly closed as an iron safe!'

'Exactly,' I said, 'and that's just what makes this mystery the most puzzling I know of, even in the domain of imagination. In *The Murders in the Rue Morgue*, Edgar Allan Poe invented nothing like it. The place of the crime was sufficiently closed to prevent the escape of a man, but there was a window, through which a monkey – the author of the murders – could slip away; but here there is no question of an opening of any sort. With the door and the shutters fastened, and the window shut, as they were, a fly could neither enter nor get away.'

'In truth,' Rouletabille acquiesced, as he went on wiping his forehead, which perspired less on account of his recent bodily exertions than from the agitation of his mind – 'in truth, it is a very great, very fascinating and beautiful mystery.'

'The Good Lord's beast,' Old Jacques muttered – 'the Good Lord's beast herself, had she committed the crime, could not have escaped. Listen! Do you hear? Hush!'

Old Jacques was making a sign for us to keep silent, and, with his arm stretched out towards the forest, listened to something we could not hear.

'She is gone!' he said at length. 'I shall have to kill that beast. Her cry is too appalling. But it is the Good Lord's beast, and every night, they say, it goes to pray on the tomb of Ste Geneviève, and nobody dare touch her, for fear lest Mother Agenoux should cast an evil spell on them!'

'How big is that Good Lord's beast?'

'She is the size of a small retriever; she's a monster, I can tell you. Ah, I've more than once wondered whether it was not she that took our poor Mademoiselle by the throat with her claws! But the Good Lord's beast does not wear boots nor fire revolvers, nor has she a hand like that!' exclaimed Old Jacques, again pointing to the red hand on the wall. 'Besides, she would have been closed up in the room, and we should have seen her as well as we should have seen a man!'

'Obviously,' I said. 'At first, before we had seen the Yellow Room, I also wondered whether the cat of Mother Agenoux – '

'What! You too!' cried Rouletabille.

'And you?' I asked.

'Not for a moment! Ever since I read the article in the *Matin* I knew that no animal of any kind was the criminal. Now I swear that a fearful tragedy has been enacted here. . . . But you say nothing about the cap or the handkerchief found here, Old Jacques.'

'The magistrate took them, of course,' the old man answered hesitatingly.

The reporter said to him, very gravely: 'I have seen neither the handkerchief nor the cap, yet I can tell you what they are like.'

'You are very clever!' said Old Jacques, coughing and embarrassed.

'The handkerchief is a large one, blue, with red stripes, and the cap is an old Basque cap, like the one you are wearing now!'

'It is true; you must be a sorcerer,' said the old servant, trying to laugh, and not succeeding. 'But how do you know that the hand-kerchief is blue, with red stripes?'

'Because, if it had not been blue with red stripes, it would not have been found at all.'

Without giving any further attention to Old Jacques, my friend took from his pocket a piece of paper, opened a pair of scissors, bent over the foot-prints, placed the paper over one of them, and began to cut. In a short time he had a perfect pattern of it, which he handed to me, begging me not to lose it.

He then returned to the window, and, pointing to Frédéric Larsan, who had not left the side of the lake, asked Old Jacques whether the detective had, like himself, been working in the Yellow Room.

'No,' replied Robert Darzac, who had not pronounced a single word since Rouletabille had handed him the piece of scorched paper found in one of the crucibles. 'He pretends he doesn't need to examine the Yellow Room, that the assassin managed to escape from it in quite a natural way, and that he will this evening explain how he did it.'

Hearing M. Darzac talk in that way, Rouletabille turned pale – a most unusual thing.

'Has Frédéric Larsan actually found out the truth, which I am only beginning to guess at?' he murmured. 'Frédéric Larsan is a great man – a very great man – and I admire him. But what has to be done today is something better than the work of a detective, better than that which is taught by experience. The man who is to unravel this mystery will have to be logical – as logical as the fact that 2 plus 2 equals 4. He will have to "think it out from the right end".'

And the reporter rushed out, frantic at the thought that the great, the celebrated Fred might discover before him the solution of the problem of the Yellow Room.

I was able to overtake him on the threshold of the pavilion.

'Calm yourself, old fellow,' I said. 'Are you not satisfied with your progress?'

'I am,' he said to me, with a deep sigh of satisfaction. 'I am ex-tremely pleased. I have discovered many things.'

'Moral or material?'

'A few moral and one material. Take this one, for example.'

And rapidly he drew from his waistcoat pocket a folded piece of paper, which he must have put there while he was under the bed. In that folded paper there was a blonde hair of a woman.

Chapter 8

The examining magistrate takes the evidence of Mlle Stangerson

Five minutes later Joseph Rouletabille was bending over the footprints discovered in the park, under the vestibule window, when a man, who must have been a servant at the château, came towards us with hurried strides, and called out to M. Darzac, who was coming out of the pavilion: 'M. Robert, the magistrate is interrogating Mademoiselle.'

M. Darzac uttered a vague excuse, and set off running towards the château, the servant following him.

'If the lady speaks,' I said, 'matters will become interesting.'

'We must know,' said my friend. 'Let us go to the château.'

He drew me with him. But at the château a gendarme, stationed in the entrance-hall, denied us access to the stairs leading up to the first-floor. We had to wait.

Meanwhile, this is what passed in the victim's room.

The family doctor, finding that Mlle Stangerson was much better, but fearing a fatal relapse which would no longer permit of her being interrogated, had thought it his duty to inform the magistrate, who decided to proceed immediately with a brief interrogatory. At this interrogatory M. de Marquet, the Registrar, M. Stangerson, and the doctor were present. Later I procured the text of the interrogatory. Here it is in all its judicial dryness.

Question. Are you able, Mademoiselle, without too much fatigue, to give us a few necessary details of the frightful attack of which you have been the victim?

Answer. I feel much better, Monsieur, and I will tell you all I know. When I entered my room, I did not notice anything unusual.

Q. If you will allow me, Mademoiselle, I will ask questions and you will answer them. That will fatigue you less than making a long recital.

A. As you please, Monsieur.

Q. How did you spend the fatal day? I want you to be as minutely precise as possible. I would like to know all you did that day, if it is not asking too much of you.

A. I rose late, at ten o'clock, for my father and I had returned home late the previous night, having been to the dinner and reception given by the President of the Republic in honour of the Philadelphia Academy of Science. When I left my room at half-past ten my father was already busy in the laboratory. We worked together till mid-day. We then took half an hour's walk in the park, as we always do before lunch at the château. After luncheon, we took another walk for half an hour before returning to the laboratory. There we found my chambermaid, who had just cleaned out my room. I went into the Yellow Room to give her some important orders, and, directly afterwards, she left the pavilion, and I resumed my work with my father. At five o'clock we again went for a walk in the park, and had tea.

Q. Before leaving the pavilion at five o'clock did you go into your room?

A. No, Monsieur, but my father did. He went, at my request, to fetch me my hat.

Q. And he found nothing suspicious in the Yellow Room?

M. Stangerson. Positively nothing, Monsieur.

Q. It is almost certain that the assassin was not concealed under the bed at that time. When you went out, the door of the room had not been locked?

A. No; we had no reason for doing so.

Q. How long had you and M. Stangerson been absent from the pavilion?

A. About an hour.

Q. It was during that hour, no doubt, that the assassin got into the pavilion. But how? Nobody knows. True, footmarks have been found in the park – footmarks which go away from the vestibule window, but none have been found going to it. Did you notice whether the vestibule window was open when you went out?

A. I don't remember.

M. Stangerson. It was closed.

Q. And when you returned?

Mlle Stangerson. I didn't notice.

M. Stangerson. It was still closed. I remember it quite well, for I remarked aloud: 'Really, Old Jacques might have opened that window while we were away!'

Q. Strange, very strange! Remember, M. Stangerson, that Old Jacques, during your absence, and before going out, *had* opened it! Well, you returned to the laboratory at six o'clock. Did you resume work?

Mlle Stangerson. Yes, Monsieur.

Q. And you did not leave the laboratory from that hour until the moment when you entered your room?

M. Stangerson. Neither my daughter nor I, Monsieur. We were engaged in work that was so pressing we lost not a moment, neglecting everything else on that account.

Q. You dined in the laboratory?

A. Yes, for the same reason.

Q. Do you usually dine in the laboratory?

A. We rarely dine there.

Q. Could the assassin have known that you would dine in the laboratory that evening?

M. Stangerson. Really, I don't think so. It was only when we returned to the pavilion, at about six o'clock, that I decided to dine in the laboratory with my daughter. Just then my gamekeeper arrived, and detained me a moment, to ask me to accompany him on an urgent tour of inspection in a part of the woods which I have decided to thin. I had no time then, and put the thing off until the next day, and begged the gamekeeper, as he was going to the château, to tell the butler that we should dine in the laboratory. He left me to execute my order, and I joined my daughter, who was already at work.

Q. At what time, Mademoiselle, did you go to your room, while your father continued to work?

A. At midnight.

Q. Did Old Jacques enter the Yellow Room in the course of the evening?

A. Yes, to close the shutters and put a match to the nightlight.

Q. Did he notice anything suspicious?

A. He would have told us. Old Jacques is a good man, who is very fond of me.

Q. You affirm, Monsieur Stangerson, that Old Jacques afterwards remained with you all the time you were in the laboratory?

M. Stangerson. I am sure of it. I have no suspicion in that direction.

Q. When you entered your room, Mademoiselle, did you immediately shut the door and lock and bolt it? That was taking very great precaution, knowing your father and your servant were there. Were you in fear of something?

A. My father would be returning to the castle very soon, and Old Jacques would be going to bed. Besides, I *did* fear something.

Q. You were, indeed, so much in fear of something that you borrowed Old Jacques' revolver without informing him?

A. That is true. I didn't wish to alarm anybody, the less so since my fears might have been childish.

Q. What was it you feared?

A. I can hardly tell. For several nights lately I thought I heard, both in the park and out of the park, round the pavilion, unusual sounds – sometimes footsteps, at other times the cracking of branches. The night before the attack on me, when I had not gone to bed before three o'clock in the morning, on our return from the Élysée, I stood for a moment before my window, and I felt sure I saw shadows.

Q. How many?

A. Two, that moved round the lake; then the moon was hidden, and I lost sight of them. At this season every year I have generally returned for the winter to my apartment in the château, but this year I thought I would not leave the pavilion before my father had completed the résumé of his works on the 'Dissociation of Matter' for the Academy of Science. I did not wish that this important work, which was to have been finished in the course of a few days, should be impeded by a change in our daily habits. You can easily understand why I did not wish to mention my childish fears to my father, nor even to Old Jacques, who, I knew, would not have been able to hold his tongue. Knowing that he had a revolver in his room, I took advantage of his absence and borrowed it, placing it in the drawer of my bed-table.

Q. Have you, to your knowledge, any enemies?

A. None.

Q. You understand, Mademoiselle, that the elaborate precautions you took cause us some surprise?

M. Stangerson. Clearly, my child, such precautions were very strange.

A. No; I told you that for two nights I had been uneasy – very uneasy.

M. Stangerson. You should have told me of that. This terrible misfortune would have been avoided.

Q. When the door of the Yellow Room was locked, Mademoiselle, did you go to bed?

A. Yes; and, being very tired, I at once fell asleep.

Q. Was the nightlight still burning?

A. Yes; but it flickered feebly.

Q. Tell us, Mademoiselle, what happened afterwards.

A. I don't know whether I had been long asleep, but suddenly I awoke and uttered a loud cry.

M. Stangerson. Yes; a terrible cry – 'Murder!' It still rings in my ears.

Q. You uttered a loud cry –

A. A man was in my room. He sprang at me, seized me by the throat, and tried to strangle me. I was nearly stifled, when, suddenly, I was able to reach the drawer of my bed-table and grasp the loaded revolver which I had placed in it. At that moment the man had forced me to the foot of my bed, and was brandishing over my head a sort of mace. I fired. I felt a terrible blow on the head. It all happened, Monsieur, more rapidly than I can tell of it – and I know nothing more.

Q. Nothing? You have no idea how the assassin managed to escape from your room?

A. None whatever. I know nothing more. One does not know what happens when one is insensible.

Q. Was the man you saw tall or short?

A. I only saw a shadow, which appeared to me formidable.

Q. You cannot give us any description?

A. I know nothing more, Monsieur. A man threw himself upon me; I fired at him. I know nothing more.

Here ended the evidence of Mlle Stangerson. Joseph Rouletabille waited patiently for M. Robert Darzac, who soon appeared.

From a room near that of Mlle Stangerson he had heard the interrogatory, and came to report it to my friend with great accuracy, exhibiting a retentive memory and a tact which really surprised me. Thanks to the pencil-notes he had hastily taken, he was able to reproduce almost word for word the questions and the answers given.

Indeed, M. Darzac might have been taken for the secretary of my young friend, and acted in every way as if he had nothing to refuse him; or, better still, like someone who was working for him.

The fact of the closed window struck the reporter as it had struck the magistrate. Rouletabille asked Darzac to repeat once more the father's and the daughter's account of the way they had spent their time on the day of the drama. The circumstances of the dinner in the laboratory seemed to interest him in the highest degree, and he had it repeated to him three times, to make more sure that the gamekeeper was the only person who knew that the professor and his daughter were going to dine in the laboratory, and how he had come to know it.

When M. Darzac left off speaking, I said: 'That evidence does not much advance the problem.'

'It puts it back,' said M. Darzac.

'It throws light upon it,' said Rouletabille thoughtfully.

Chapter 9

Reporter and detective

We all three turned back towards the pavilion. At some distance from the building the reporter made us stop, and, pointing to a clump of bushes to the right, said: 'That's where the assassin came from when he entered the pavilion.'

As there were other similar clumps of bushes between the great oaks, I asked why the assassin should have chosen that one rather than any of the others. Rouletabille answered me by pointing to the path, which ran quite close to the thicket, and led to the door of the pavilion.

'That path,' he said, 'is gravelled, as you see. The man must have passed along it to go to the pavilion, as no traces of his steps have been found on the soft ground. He had no wings. He walked; but he walked on the gravel, which retained no impression of his boots. The gravel has, in fact, been trodden by many other feet, since the path is the most direct route between the pavilion and the château. As to the clump of bushes – formed by the sort of shrubs that don't prosper during the rough season, laurels and prickwood – it offered the assassin sufficient concealment till the moment came for him to make his way to the pavilion. It was while hidden in that clump of bushes that he saw M. and Mlle Stangerson, and then Old Jacques, leave the pavilion. Gravel has been spread nearly up to the window of the pavilion. The footprints of a man, parallel with the wall – marks which we saw a while ago – prove that he only needed to make one stride to find himself in front of the vestibule window, left open by Old Jacques. The man drew himself up by his hands and entered the vestibule.'

'After all,' I said, 'it is very possible.'

'Why this "after all"?' cried Rouletabille, growing suddenly angry. 'Why do you say in that tone "after all, it is possible"?'

I begged of him not to be angry, but he was already too much irritated to listen to me, and declared that he admired the prudent scepticism with which certain people (I!) approached the most simple problems, never daring to say 'That is so' or 'That is not so', so that their intelligence gave about the same results as if Nature had forgotten to supply the inside of their skull with a little grey matter! As I appeared vexed, my young friend took me by the arm, and admitted that he had not meant that for me, seeing that he held me in particular esteem.

'But,' he added, 'it is sometimes criminal not to reason with certainty when you are able to do so. If I did not reason as I have done in regard to this gravel,' he went on, 'I should have to reason with a balloon. My dear fellow, dirigible balloons are not yet sufficiently developed for me to take into consideration the possibility of an assassin falling from the clouds. Therefore, don't say that a thing is possible when it is impossible for it to be otherwise. We know now how the man entered by the window, and we also know the moment at which he entered. He did so during the walk of the professor and his daughter, at about five o'clock. The fact of the presence of the chambermaid – who had just cleared up the Yellow Room – in the laboratory at the very moment when M. Stangerson and his daughter returned from their walk at half-past one, permits us to decide that at half-past one the assassin was not under the bed in the room unless the chambermaid was his accomplice. What do you say to that, M. Darzac?'

M. Darzac shook his head, and said he was sure of the chambermaid's fidelity, and that she was a thoroughly reliable and devoted servant.

'Besides,' he added, 'at five o'clock M. Stangerson went into the Yellow Room to fetch his daughter's hat.'

'True; there's that as well,' said Rouletabille.

'That the man entered by the window at the time you say, I admit,' I remarked; 'but why did he shut the window, a fact which was bound to draw the attention of those who had left it open.'

'It may be that the window was not shut at once,' replied the young reporter; 'but, *if he did shut the window*, it was because of the bend in the gravel path, thirty yards from the pavilion, and because of three oaks that are growing at that spot.'

'What do you mean by that?' asked M. Darzac, who had followed us, and was listening with almost breathless attention to Rouletabille's words.

'I'll explain everything to you later on, Monsieur, when I judge the time to have come for doing so, but I don't think I've said anything of greater importance on this affair, if my hypothesis proves to be right.'

'And what is your hypothesis?'

'You shall never know if it doesn't turn out to be the truth. It is far too grave for me to mention, so long as it is only an hypothesis.'

'Have you, at least, any idea about the assassin?'

'No, Monsieur, I don't know who the assassin is; but fear nothing, M. Robert Darzac! I shall know!'

I could not but observe that M. Darzac was deeply moved, and I suspected that the affirmation of Rouletabille was not one that pleased him. Why, then, if he really feared that the assassin should be discovered, was he helping the reporter to discover him? My young friend seemed to have the same impression as myself, for he asked bluntly: 'It does not displease you, M. Darzac, that I should discover the criminal?'

'Oh! I would like to kill him with my own hands!' cried the fiancé of Mlle Stangerson, with a vehemence that amazed me.

'I believe you,' said Rouletabille gravely; 'but you have not answered my question.'

We were passing near the thicket of which the young reporter had spoken to us a minute before. I entered it, and pointed out to him evident traces of the movements of a man who had been hidden there. Rouletabille once more was right.

'Yes, yes,' he said. 'We have to deal with a human being, made of flesh and blood, who does not use any other means than those we use ourselves, and everything will be discovered in the end.'

He then asked me for the paper measurement of the other footprint which he had previously handed over to me, and applied it to a very clear footmark behind the shrubs. Then he rose and said: 'Of course!'

I thought he would now follow like a track the footmarks of the assassin in his flight from the vestibule window, but he led us far to the left, saying that it was useless ferreting in the mud, and that he was sure now of the road taken by the criminal.

'I know he went along the wall fifty yards away from the pavilion. Then he jumped over the hedge and across the ditch there, just opposite the little path leading to the lake. It is the nearest way of getting out of the estate and reaching the lake.'

'How do you know that he went to the lake?'

'Because Frédéric Larsan has not left the borders of it since the morning. There must be some curious indications there.'

A few minutes later we reached the lake.

It was a little sheet of marshy water, surrounded by reeds, on which floated some dead water-lilies' leaves. The great Fred must have seen us coming, but it is probable that we interested him very little, for he took hardly any notice of us, but continued to stir with his stick something we could not see.

'Look!' said Rouletabille. 'Here again are the footmarks of the fugitive. They skirt the lake at this place, return, and finally disappear just before this path, which leads to the high road to Épinay. The man continued his flight towards Paris.'

'What makes you think that,' I asked, 'since there are no footmarks on the path?'

'What makes me think that? Why, these footprints here, which I expected to find!' said Rouletabille, pointing to the sharply-defined imprint of an elegant boot. 'Look!' And he called to Frédéric Larsan.

'M. Fred, these elegant footmarks have been here ever since the discovery of the crime.'

'Yes, young man, and a careful note has been made of them,' replied Fred, without raising his head. 'You see, there are steps that come and steps that go back.'

'And the man had a bicycle!' the reporter exclaimed.

Then, after having looked at the marks of the bicycle, which followed, going and coming, the elegant footmarks, I thought I might intervene.

'The bicycle explains the disappearance of the big footprints of the assassin,' I said. 'The assassin, with his rough hobnailed boots, mounted a bicycle. His accomplice, the man with the elegant boots, had been acting for him.'

'No, no!' replied Rouletabille, with a strange smile. 'I have been expecting to find these elegant footprints ever since the beginning of the affair. I am pleased I have found them. They are the footmarks of the assassin.'

'Then there were two?'

'No; there was but one, and he had no accomplice.'

'Very good! Very clever!' said Frédéric Larsan.

'Look!' continued the young reporter, showing us the ground where it had been disturbed by big and heavy heels. 'The man seated himself there, and took off his hobnailed boots, which he had worn only for the purpose of misleading the police; then, taking them probably with him, he rose, with his own boots on, and went quickly to the high road, pushing his bicycle with his hand. He couldn't venture to ride it on this rough path. Besides, the lightness of the impression made by the wheels on the path, in spite of the softness of the ground, proves that what I say is right. If there had been a man on the bicycle the wheels would have sunk deeply into the soil. No, no, there was but one man there – the assassin – on foot.'

'Bravo, bravo!' Fred cried again, and, coming suddenly towards us, planted himself in front of M. Robert Darzac and said to him: 'If we had a bicycle here, we might demonstrate the correctness of the young man's reasoning, M. Robert Darzac. Do you know if there is one at the château?'

'No,' replied Darzac, 'there is not. I took mine to Paris four days ago, the last time I came to the château before the crime.'

'That is a pity,' replied Fred, in an extremely cold tone. Then, turning to Rouletabille, he said: 'If this goes on, you'll see that we shall both come to the same conclusion. Have you any idea as to how the assassin got away from the Yellow Room?'

'Yes,' my friend replied, 'I have an idea.'

'So have I,' said Fred, 'and it must be the same as yours. There are no two ways of reasoning in this affair. I am waiting for the arrival of my chief before offering my explanation to the examining magistrate.'

'Ah! The Chief of the Detective Department is coming?'

'Yes, this afternoon, for the confrontation in the laboratory before the magistrate of all those who may have played a part in the drama. It will be highly interesting. It is a pity you will not be able to be present.'

'I shall be present,' said Rouletabille confidently.

'Really! You're extraordinary for your age!' replied the detective, in a tone not wholly free from irony. 'You'd make a wonderful detective if you had a little more method; if you did not so much obey your instincts and the bumps on your forehead. I have noticed several times already, M. Rouletabille, that you reason too much. You do not allow yourself to be guided enough by observation. Tell me! What do you say to the blood-stained handkerchief and the red hand on the wall? I have only seen the handkerchief.'

'Bah!' said Rouletabille, slightly taken aback. 'The assassin was wounded in the hand by Mlle Stangerson's revolver.'

'Ah! A purely instinctive observation. Take care! You're too directly logical, M. Rouletabille. Logic will do you a bad turn if you use it indiscriminately. You are right when you speak of Mlle Stangerson's revolver. There is no doubt that the victim fired. But you are wrong when you say that she wounded the assassin in the hand.'

'I am sure of it!' cried Rouletabille.

Fred, imperturbable, interrupted him.

'Lack of observation, Monsieur – lack of observation again. The examination of the handkerchief, the numberless little round stains – impressions of drops of blood – which I find on the track of the footprints, at the moment when the foot touches the ground, prove to me that the assassin was not wounded at all. The assassin, M. Rouletabille, bled at the nose!'

The great Fred spoke most seriously. However, I could not refrain from uttering an exclamation.

The reporter looked gravely at Fred, who gravely looked at him. And Fred immediately came to a conclusion.

'The man, who was bleeding into his hand and handkerchief, wiped his hand on the wall. The fact is highly important, because there is no need of his being wounded in the hand for him to be the assassin.'

Rouletabille seemed to reflect deeply, and said: 'There is something much more dangerous, M. Frédéric Larsan, than the misuse of logic. It is the disposition of mind in certain detectives which makes them, in perfect good faith, twist this logic in aid of their preconceived ideas. You already have your idea about the assassin, M. Fred. Don't deny it. And it is necessary to your theory that the assassin should not have been wounded in the hand, for otherwise it would come to nothing. And so you have searched and found nothing else. It is a dangerous system – a dangerous system, M. Fred – to arrive at the proofs which one needs from a preconceived idea. That may lead you very much astray. Beware of judicial error, M. Fred; it is waiting for you.'

And, laughing a little, his hands in his pockets, Rouletabille fixed his cunning eyes on the great Fred.

Frédéric Larsan silently considered the youth who pretended to be a better detective than he, shrugged his shoulders, bowed to us, and moved quickly away, striking the stones on the path with his walking-stick.

Rouletabille watched his retreat, and then turned towards us, with a joyous and already triumphant expression.

'I shall beat him!' he exclaimed. 'I shall beat the great Fred, clever as he is! Rouletabille is smarter at the game than all the rest of them! The great Fred, the illustrious, tremendous, unique Fred, reasons like a child!'

And he danced a double-shuffle, but suddenly stopped. My eyes followed his eyes. They were fixed on M. Robert Darzac, who had turned ghastly pale, and was staring at the impression left by his feet alongside of the elegant footmarks. *There was no difference between them*!

We thought he was going to faint. His eyes, dilated with terror, avoided us, while his right hand, with a spasmodic movement, twitched at the beard that surrounded his honest, gentle, and despairing face. At length he regained his self-possession, saluted us, and left us, saying in a changed voice that he was obliged to return to the château.

'The deuce!' said Rouletabille.

He also appeared to be deeply concerned. He took from his pocket-book a piece of white paper, as I had before seen him do, and, with his scissors, cut out the shape of the elegant boot-marks that were on the ground. Then he applied this new paper pattern on the footprints of M. Darzac. It fitted perfectly. Rouletabille once more muttered: 'The deuce!'

Presently he added: 'Yet I believe M. Darzac to be an honest man.'

And he led me on the way to the Castle Inn, which we could see, less than a mile distant on the road, near a small clump of trees.

Chapter 10

'We shall have to eat red meat now'

The Castle Inn was rather modest in appearance; but I like those old inns, with their beams blackened with age and smoke, reminding one of the old coaching days. They belong to the past, they are linked with history, and make one think of the high road and its adventures.

I saw at once that the Castle Inn was at least two centuries old, perhaps older. Under its ancient and rustic signboard a man with a crabbed-looking face was standing on the threshold, apparently lost in dismal thought, if one were to believe the wrinkles on his forehead and on his knitted brow.

When we were quite close, he deigned to see us, and asked in a rather blunt and disagreeable manner if we wanted anything. He was obviously the ugly landlord of this pretty place. We expressed the hope that he would be good enough to let us have some luncheon, but he declared he had no provisions whatever, and that it would be impossible for him to satisfy us. As he spoke, he looked at us with unmistakable suspicion.

'You may take us in,' Rouletabille said to the fellow. 'We don't belong to the police.'

'I'm not afraid of the police; I'm not afraid of anybody,' the man replied.

I was already making a sign to my friend, giving him to understand that we should do better not to insist, but Rouletabille, who evidently wanted very much to enter the inn, slipped under the man's arm and stepped in.

'Come on,' he said, 'it's quite comfortable here!'

A great fire was blazing in the chimney, and we held out our hands to warm them, for the weather was rather chilly that morning. The room was fairly large. It was furnished with two heavy tables, a few stools, and a counter with rows of bottles of sirop and liqueur. On the mantelpiece the innkeeper's collection of earthenware pots and stone jugs was displayed.

'Here's a fine fire for roasting a chicken,' said Rouletabille.

'We have no chicken here,' the landlord replied – 'not even a miserable rabbit!'

'I know that,' said my friend, with an ironic smile. 'I know henceforth we shall have to eat red meat.'

I confess I did not in the least understand what Rouletabille meant. Why had he said to the landlord, 'We shall have to eat red meat'? Why did the innkeeper, as soon as he heard the words, swear terribly, then control himself and place himself at our disposal as obediently as Robert Darzac had done when he heard Rouletabille's magic words: 'The vicarage has lost nothing of its charm, nor the garden of its brightness'? Decidedly, my friend had the gift of making people understand him by the use of phrases wholly incomprehensible! I told him as much, and he smiled. I should have preferred that he should give me some explanation, but he had placed a finger on his lips, which evidently meant that he did not wish to speak, and also enjoined me to remain silent.

The landlord had pushed open a little side-door and called to somebody to bring him half a dozen eggs and a piece of beefsteak. The order was quickly executed, and there appeared at the top of the staircase a very pretty woman with beautiful blonde hair and large sweet eyes, who watched us with curiosity.

The innkeeper said to her roughly: 'Get out! And if the Green Man comes, don't let me see you about!'

She disappeared. Rouletabille took the eggs, which had been brought to him in a bowl, and the meat, which was on a dish, placed all carefully beside him in the chimney, unhooked a frying-pan and a grid-iron, and began to beat up our omelette before proceeding to grill our beefsteak. He further ordered of the man two bottles of the best cider, and seemed to take as little notice of the landlord as the landlord did of him. The man, however, looked sideways, first at Rouletabille, then at me, with obvious nervousness. He let us do our own cooking, and laid out the table near one of the windows.

Suddenly I heard him mutter: 'Ah, there he comes!'

His face changed, and his expression became one of fierce hatred. He went and glued himself to one of the windows, watching the road. There was no need for me to draw Rouletabille's attention to the fact; he had already left the omelette and joined the landlord at the window. I followed him.

A man, dressed entirely in green velveteen, wearing a huntsman's cap of the same colour, was advancing leisurely, smoking a pipe. He carried a gun slung over his shoulder, and showed in his movements an almost aristocratic ease. He must have been about five-and-forty years of age. He wore a pince-nez; his hair, as well as his moustache, was turning grey. He was remarkably handsome. As he passed by the inn, he seemed to hesitate, as if wondering whether he should enter, gave a glance towards us, took a few whiffs at his pipe, and then resumed his walk at the same nonchalant pace.

Rouletabille and I looked at our host. His flashing eyes, his clenched fists, his trembling lips, told us of his tumultuous feelings.

'He has done well not to come in here today!' he hissed.

'Who is that man?' asked Rouletabille, returning to his omelette.

'The Green Man,' growled the innkeeper. 'You don't know him? So much the better for you. He is not an acquaintance to make. He is M. Stangerson's gamekeeper.'

'You don't appear to like him very much,' said the reporter, pouring his omelette into the frying-pan.

'Like him! Nobody here likes him, Monsieur. He's one of those conceited fellows who have known better days, who have been rich – once. He hates everybody because he has been forced to become a servant to earn his living – for, after all, a gamekeeper is nothing but a servant – what do you say? Upon my word, one would think he is the master of Glandier, and that all the land and woods belong to him. He'll not allow a poor devil to eat a morsel of bread on the grass of the estate – *his* grass!'

'Does he often come here?'

'Too often. But I'll make him understand that I don't like the look of him. A month ago he didn't worry about us – the Castle Inn had never existed for him. He hadn't the time; he was far too busy then, courting the landlady of the Three Lilies at Saint-Michel. Now that he has done with her he wants to spend the time here. He's altogether a bad un – always after the girls. There's not an honest man that can bear him. Why, the concierges of the château themselves can't stand him – the Green Man!'

'Are the concierges of the château honest people, then, landlord?' asked Rouletabille.

'Call me Mathieu, that's my name. And, as true as my name is Mathieu, I believe them to be honest!'

'Yet they've been arrested?'

'What does that prove? But I don't want to interfere in other people's business!'

'And what do you think of the crime?'

'What? Of the attempt on the life of poor Mlle Stangerson? A good girl, I tell you, and dearly loved all around here! What do I think of the crime?'

'Yes, tell us your opinion.'

'Well, I think – nothing at all, and a lot of things. But that's no one's business!'

'Not even mine?' insisted Rouletabille.

The innkeeper looked at him sideways, and said gruffly: 'Not even yours!'

The omelette was ready. We sat down at table, and were silently eating, when the door was pushed open, and an old woman, dressed in rags, a staff in her hand, her head doddering, her white hair hanging loosely over her wrinkled forehead, appeared on the threshold.

'Ah, there you are, Mother Agenoux! It's a long time since we saw you last!' said our host.

'I've been very ill – very nearly dying,' said the old woman. 'Have you, by chance, anything for the Good Lord's beast?'

She entered the inn, followed by a cat larger than any I had ever imagined to exist. The beast looked at us, and mewed so dismally that I could not help shuddering. I had never before heard a cry so lugubrious.

As if he had been drawn by that cry, a man entered behind the old woman. It was the Green Man. He saluted us with a wave of the hand towards his cap, and seated himself at a table next to ours.

'Give me a glass of cider, Mathieu!' he said. As the Green Man had entered the innkeeper had started violently, but now – visibly – he checked his anger.

'I've no more cider. I've served the last bottles to these gentlemen,' he replied.

'Then give me a glass of white wine,' said the Green Man, without showing the least surprise.

'There's no more white wine left; there's nothing left!' said Mathieu, in a hollow voice.

'How is Mme Mathieu?'

The innkeeper clenched his fists, and I thought he would strike the Green Man. Then he said: 'She's all right, thanks!'

So the young woman with the large, tender eyes, whom we had just seen, was the wife of this loathsome and brutal rustic, who, to his physical shortcomings added that moral defect, jealousy.

Slamming the door behind him, the landlord left the room. Mother Agenoux was still there, leaning on her staff, her huge cat by her feet.

The Green Man asked her: 'Have you been ill, Mother Agenoux, that we haven't seen you for the last week?'

'Yes, Monsieur. I've only got up three times, and that was to go and pray to Ste Geneviève, our good patroness. The rest of the time I've been in bed. There was no one to nurse me but the Good Lord's beast.'

'She didn't leave you?'

'Leave me? No; neither by day nor night!'

'You are sure of that?'

'As I am sure of Paradise.'

'Then how was it, Mother Agenoux, that all through the night of the crime the cry of the Good Lord's beast was heard continuously?'

Mother Agenoux went and planted herself in front of the gamekeeper, and struck the floor with her staff.

'I know nothing about it!' she declared. 'But I'll tell you something. There are not two cats in the world that cry like this one. Well, on the night of the crime I, too, heard the cry of the Good Lord's beast outside; and yet she was on my knees, and didn't mew once! I swear it! I crossed myself when I heard that, as if I had heard the Devil!'

I looked at the gamekeeper while he was asking the last question, and I am much mistaken if I did not detect a mocking smile on his lips.

At that moment the noise of a sharp quarrel reached us – we even thought that we heard the dull sound of blows, as if somebody was being felled. The Green Man rose resolutely, and hurried to the door by the side of the fireplace. But that door was suddenly opened, and the landlord appeared, and said laughingly to the gamekeeper: 'Don't alarm yourself! It's only my wife; she has got the toothache! Here, Mother Agenoux, is some meat for your cat.'

He handed a small parcel to the old woman, who took it eagerly, and went out by the door, closely followed by the Good Lord's beast.

The Green Man asked: 'You'll not serve me?'

Mathieu no longer retained his passion.

'There's nothing for you here – nothing whatever! Clear out!'

The Green Man quietly refilled his pipe, lit it, bowed to us, and went out. He was no sooner on the threshold than Mathieu banged the door after him, and, turning towards us – his eyes bloodshot, and foaming at the mouth – he said hoarsely to us, shaking his clenched fist at the door he had slammed on the man he hated: 'I don't know who you are – you who come here and say, "We shall have to eat red meat now", but if you want to know, *that is the Assassin*!'

As soon as he had said that, Mathieu quitted us. Rouletabille returned to the fireplace, and said: 'Now let's grill our steak. How's the cider? It's a little sharp, but I rather like it!'

We saw no more of Mathieu that day, and deep silence reigned in the inn as we left it, having placed five francs on the table in payment for our meal.

Rouletabille at once took me on a three-mile walk round the estate of M. Stangerson. He stopped for ten minutes at the corner of a narrow road, which was quite black with soot, near to a charcoal-burner's hut in that part of the Ste Geneviève forest which is bordered by the road from Épinay to Corbeil. He told me that the assassin had certainly passed that way – accounting thus for the state of his rough boots – before entering the park and concealing himself in the little clump of trees near the pavilion.

'You don't believe, then, that the gamekeeper had anything to do with the crime?' I asked.

'We shall see that later on,' he replied. 'For the present moment I don't bother about the innkeeper's words. He spoke from hatred. It was not on account of the Green Man that I took you to the Castle Inn.'

Having said that, Rouletabille, using great precaution, glided – and I glided behind him – towards the little building, which, being near the park gate, was used as a lodge by the concierges who had been arrested that morning. With the skill of an acrobat he got into the maisonette by a sort of garret-window that had been left open, and returned ten minutes later, exclaiming: 'Of course!' – words which, in his mouth, meant a great deal.

Just as we were about to take the road leading to the château, there was a great commotion at the park gate. A carriage had arrived, and several persons were hastening from the château to meet it. Roule-tabille pointed out to me the gentleman who descended from it.

'There is the head of the Criminal Investigation Department – the Chief of the Sûreté,' he said. 'Now we shall see what Frédéric Larsan has up his sleeve, and whether he is really more clever than all the rest of us!'

The carriage of the Chief of the Sûreté was followed by three other vehicles filled with reporters, who also attempted to enter the park. But two gendarmes were stationed at the gate, with directions to admit no one. The Chief of the Sûreté calmed their impatience by promising to let the Press have that evening all the information he could give without inconveniencing the inquiry of the magistrate.

Chapter 11

In which Frédéric Larsan explains how the assassin was able to get out of the yellow room

Amongst a mass of papers – legal documents, memoirs, and newspaper-cuttings – which I possess relative to the Mystery of the Yellow Room there is one extremely interesting piece – an account of the famous interrogatory which took place that afternoon in the laboratory of Professor Stangerson, in the presence of the Chief of the Sûreté. This account is from the pen of M. Maleine, the registrar, who, like the examining magistrate, devoted his leisure moments to literary work. The document was to have been part of a book – never published – entitled, *My Interrogatories*. It was given to me by the registrar himself some time after the astounding *dénouement* of this case, which is unique in judicial records.

Here it is. It is not a mere transcription of questions and answers. The registrar often relates in it his personal impressions.

THE NARRATIVE OF THE REGISTRAR

We have been [writes the registrar], the examining magistrate and I, for a whole hour in the Yellow Room, in company with the builder who constructed the pavilion from plans drawn by Professor Stangerson himself. The builder had a workman with him. M. de Marquet had had the walls laid entirely bare – that is to say, he had had them stripped of the yellow paper which decorated them. Soundings with the pickaxe in different places had satisfied us that there was no opening of any kind. The floor and the ceiling had been minutely examined. We had discovered nothing – there was nothing to be discovered. M. de Marquet looked delighted, and never ceased repeating: 'What a case – what a case, gentlemen! You'll find we shall never discover how the assassin was able to get out!'

Suddenly M. de Marquet, who was beaming with joy because he was unable to solve the mystery, remembered that his duty was to try and solve it. He called to the officer in charge of the gendarmes.

'Go to the château,' he said, 'and request M. Stangerson and M. Robert Darzac to join me in the laboratory; also Old Jacques. And let your men bring the two concierges here.'

Five minutes later these people were all assembled in the laboratory. The Chief of the Sûreté, who had just arrived at Glandier, joined us at that moment. I was seated at the desk of Professor Stangerson, ready for work, when M. de Marquet made the following little speech – as original as it was unexpected.

'With your permission, gentlemen,' he said, 'as the usual kind of interrogatories give so little result, we will, for once, abandon the old system. I will not have you brought before me in turn individually. No; we will all remain here, as we are – M. Stangerson, M. Robert Darzac, Old Jacques, the two concierges, M. the Chief of the Sûreté, M. the Registrar, and myself. And we shall all be on the same footing. The concierges may for a while forget that they are prisoners. We are going to hold a conversation. I have called you together to confer. We are on the spot where the crime was committed, and what should we talk about if not about the crime? Let us talk about it, then, quite freely, with intelligence, or even with stupidity. Let us say anything that may pass through our minds. Let us speak without method – for method, so far, has not helped us much. We will trust to Chance – to Hazard. And now, let us begin!'

Then, as he passed near me, he said in a low voice: 'Eh? What do you think of that? What a scene! Could you have imagined that? I'll make a little play out of it for the Vaudeville Theatre.'

And he rubbed his hands with enjoyment.

I turned my gaze to M. Stangerson. The hope that had come to him from the latest reports of the doctors, who had declared that Mlle Stangerson might survive her wounds, had not effaced from his noble features the marks of the great sorrow that oppressed him.

This man had thought his daughter dead, and he had not yet recovered from the shock. His clear blue eyes expressed infinite sorrow. I had seen M. Stangerson on many occasions at public ceremonies, and from the first had been struck by the look in his eyes, for they seemed as pure as those of a child – dreamy eyes, with the sublime and immaterial look of the inventor or the madman.

At those functions his daughter was also to be seen, for the two were inseparable, it was said, and had shared the same labours for many years. The young lady, who was now five-and-thirty, but looked hardly thirty years of age, and was entirely devoted to science, still kept the admiration of all by her royal beauty; for she was without a wrinkle, and had conquered both time and love. Who could have told me then that I should one day find myself, with my papers, near the bed where she lay, and that I should hear her, almost expiring, tell us, with painful efforts, of the most atrocious and mysterious crime I ever heard of in my career? Who could have told me that I should find myself, that afternoon, before a despairing father, vainly trying to discover how his daughter's assailant had been able to escape from him? Of what use, then, are secret and persistent studies in an obscure retreat in the depth of woods, if they do not guarantee you against the great catastrophes of life and death, generally the lot of those only who lead the passionate and adventurous life of large cities?*

'Now, M. Stangerson,' said M. de Marquet rather pompously, 'kindly place yourself exactly where you were when Mlle Stangerson left you to enter her room.'

The professor rose, and, placing himself at about two feet from the door of the Yellow Room, said, in a voice that was without accent or emphasis – a voice which I can only describe as 'dead': 'I was here. Towards eleven o'clock, after having made a short chemical experiment at the furnaces of the laboratory, I moved my desk to this place, for Old Jacques, who spent all the evening in cleaning my apparatus, needed all the space behind me. My daughter worked at the same desk with me. When she rose, after kissing me, and bidding Old Jacques good-night, she had, in order to enter her room, to pass between my desk and the door, which was not easy. You may gather from this that I was very near the place where the crime was to be committed.'

'And that desk,' I asked, obeying, in thus mixing in the conversation, the express orders of my chief, 'what became of it as soon as you heard the cry of "Murder!" followed by the revolver-shots?'

Old Jacques answered: 'We pushed it back against the wall here, close to where it is at the present moment, so as to be able to get at the door at once.'

---

* I wish to remind the reader that I am merely transcribing the registrar's narration, and have changed nothing of its style.

I followed up my idea, to which, however, I attached only the importance of a mere supposition.

'Was the desk near enough to the door for a man, stooping low, to come from the room, slip under the desk, and pass out unnoticed?'

'You are forgetting,' M. Stangerson interrupted wearily, 'that my daughter had locked and bolted the door, that the door remained fastened, that we vainly tried to force it open from the very moment when the assassination began, that we were at the door while the struggle between the criminal and my poor child was going on, that the noise of it reached us, and that we heard my daughter's stifled cries while she was being strangled by the hands that have left their mark upon her throat. Rapid as the attack was, we were no less rapid, and rushed at once to the door which separated us from the tragedy!'

I rose from my seat, and once more examined the door with the greatest care. Then I returned to my place with a gesture of discouragement.

'Imagine,' I said, 'that the lower panel of this door could be removed without the whole door being necessarily opened, and the problem would be solved. But, unfortunately, this last hypothesis is untenable after an examination of the door – a solid and massive door of oak, made of one piece. That is plainly to be seen, in spite of the damage done to it by those who burst it open.'

'Yes,' said Old Jacques; 'it is an old and solid door that was taken from the château, and fitted here. They don't make doors like that nowadays. Why, it needed this iron bar to get the better of it; and there were four of us, for Mme Bernier, like the good woman she is, joined her efforts to ours. It's really a shame to think that she and her husband are prisoners now!'

Old Jacques had no sooner uttered these words than the tears and wailing of the concierges started afresh. I never saw more tearful prisoners; I was profoundly disgusted [*sic*]. Even admitting their innocence, I could not understand how they could show so little self-control in the face of misfortune. A firm attitude, in such moments, is better than any outpouring of tears and groans, which, in most cases, are feigned and hypocritical.

'Once more, enough of this snivelling!' cried M. de Marquet; 'and, in your own interest, tell us what you were doing under the window of the pavilion at the time your mistress was being attacked – for you were quite close to the pavilion when Old Jacques met you!'

'We were coming to the rescue,' they whined.

And, between two sobs, the woman burst out: 'Ah! if we only had the assassin, we should soon settle him!'

Again it proved impossible to get out of them two consecutive and rational sentences. They kept denying their guilt, and declaring, by Heaven and all the saints, that they were in bed when they heard the sound of the revolver-shot.

'It was not one, but two shots that were fired! You see, you are lying! If you heard one, you would have heard the other.'

'Really, Monsieur, it is only the second shot we heard. We must have been asleep when the first shot was fired.'

'Two shots were fired, that's true enough,' said Old Jacques. 'I know that all the chambers of my revolver were loaded. We have found two exploded cartridges and two bullets, and we heard two shots behind the door. Was not that so, M. Stangerson?'

'Yes,' replied the professor; 'there were two revolver-shots; the report of the first was rather dull, that of the second very loud and ringing.'

'Why do you persist in lying?' cried M. de Marquet, turning to the concierges. 'Do you think the police are as stupid as yourselves? Everything goes to prove that you were out of doors and near the pavilion at the moment of the tragedy. What were you doing there? You don't want to answer? Your silence proves your guilt. And, as for me,' he said, turning to M. Stangerson, 'I can only explain the escape of the criminal by the aid these two accomplices offered him. As soon as the door was forced open, and while you, M. Stangerson, were attending to your unfortunate child, the concierge and his wife facilitated the flight of the assassin, who, screening himself behind them, reached the vestibule window and sprang into the park. The concierge closed the window after him, and fastened the shutters, for, after all, those shutters could not have closed and fastened themselves. That is the conclusion I have arrived at. If any of you has any other idea, let him state it.'

M. Stangerson intervened.

'It was impossible! I do not believe in the guilt or complicity of my concierges, though I cannot understand what they were doing in the park at that late hour of the night. I say it was impossible, because Mme Bernier held the lamp, and did not move from the threshold of the room. I, as soon as the door was forced open, threw myself on my knees beside my daughter, and it was impossible for anyone to leave or enter the room by the door without passing over her body and disturbing me. It was impossible, because Old Jacques and Bernier had but to cast a glance round the room and under the bed, as I did myself on entering, to see that there was no longer anybody in the room except my daughter, who was lying prostrate on the floor.'

'What is your view of the matter, M. Darzac? You have not spoken yet,' said the magistrate.

M. Darzac replied that he had no opinion to express.

M. Dax, the Chief of the Sûreté, who, so far, had only listened and examined the place, at last deigned to open his lips.

'I think that, while we are waiting for the criminal to be arrested, we have to discover the motive for the crime. That would advance matters a little,' he said. Turning towards M. Stangerson, he continued in that cold tone of voice which I regard as indicative of firm intelligence and strength of character: 'Was not Mlle Stangerson shortly to have been married?'

The professor looked sadly at M. Robert Darzac.

'Yes; to my friend, whom I should have been happy to call my son – to M. Robert Darzac.'

'Mlle Stangerson is much better, and is rapidly recovering from her wounds? The marriage is simply delayed, is it not, Monsieur?' insisted the Chief of the Sûreté.

'I hope so.'

'What! Are you not sure?'

M. Stangerson did not answer. M. Robert Darzac appeared agitated, for I saw him pulling nervously at his watch-chain – nothing escaped me – M. Dax coughed, as did M. de Marquet, when he was embarrassed.

'You will understand, M. Stangerson,' he said, 'that in so perplexing a case we cannot afford to neglect anything. We must know all – even the smallest and most trivial fact concerning the victim. The most insignificant detail may prove important information. What is it that makes you doubtful, now we know that Mlle Stangerson is sure to recover, as to whether this marriage will take place? You said, "I hope so." That appears to me to imply a doubt. Why do you doubt?'

M. Stangerson made a visible effort.

'Yes, Monsieur,' he said at length, 'you are right. It is best that you should know a fact which, if I concealed it, might appear to be of importance. M. Darzac is sure to agree with me.'

M. Darzac, whose pallor at that moment was altogether abnormal, made a sign that he agreed with the professor. I concluded that if he only answered by a sign, it was because he was unable to speak.

'I must tell you, Monsieur,' continued M. Stangerson, 'that my daughter had sworn never to leave me, and held to her oath, in spite of all my prayers, for I have tried many times, as was my duty, to induce her to marry. We have known M. Robert Darzac many years. M. Darzac loves my daughter. I believed at one time that she loved him, since I had the joy recently of hearing from her lips that she at last consented to a marriage which I desired with all my heart. I am very old, Monsieur, and it was a blessing to know that when I am gone she would have at her side, to love her and continue our common labours, a man whom I love and esteem for his greatness of heart and for his science. Now, Monsieur, two days before the crime, for some unknown reason, my daughter suddenly declared to me that she would not marry M. Robert Darzac.'

A dead silence followed. It was a serious moment. M. Dax asked: 'Has Mlle Stangerson given you no explanation whatever? Has she not told you what her motive was?'

'She told me she was now too old to marry; that she had waited too long; that she had deeply reflected; that she esteemed, and even loved, M. Darzac, but it was better that things should remain as they were. She would be happy to see the bonds which attached us both to M. Robert Darzac drawn closer, but on the understanding that there should never be any more talk of marriage.'

'That is very strange,' muttered M. Dax.

'Very strange!' repeated my chief.

M. Stangerson, with a pale and icy smile, added: 'It is certainly not there that you will find the motive for the crime, M. Dax.'

'In any case, the motive was not theft,' said M. Dax impatiently.

'Oh, we were quite sure of that!' cried the examining magistrate.

At that moment the door of the laboratory was opened, and the officer in charge of the gendarmes entered, and handed a card to the examining magistrate. M. de Marquet read it, and uttered a half-angry exclamation: 'Well, what impudence!'

'What is it?' asked M. Dax.

'The card of a young reporter engaged on the *Époque* – Joseph Rouletabille is his name – with these words written on it: "One of the motives of the crime was robbery"!'

The Chief of the Sûreté smiled.

'Aha! Young Rouletabille! I've heard of him before. He is supposed to be rather ingenious. Let him come in, Monsieur.'

M. Joseph Rouletabille was allowed to enter. I had made his acquaintance in the train which that morning had brought us to Épinay-sur-Orge. He had entered our carriage almost in spite of me, and I had better at once say that his manners, his interference in a case which was a mystery to justice itself, had not commended him to me. I don't care for journalists. They are a sort of writers to be shunned like the plague. They think everything permissible, and they respect nothing. Grant them the least favour, allow them to approach you, and there is no annoyance you may not expect to come of it. This Joseph Rouletabille looked hardly twenty years old, and his insolence in daring to question us and discuss with us made him extremely objectionable to me. Besides, he had a way of expressing himself which showed clearly that he was mocking us. I know quite well that the *Époque* is a powerful newspaper, with which it is well to be on good terms, but it is also a paper that ought not to allow itself to be represented by half-fledged reporters.

M. Joseph Rouletabille entered the laboratory, bowed to us, and waited until M. de Marquet asked him to explain himself.

'You pretend, Monsieur, that you know the motive of the crime. That motive, against all evidence, is, you think, robbery?'

'No, Monsieur, I do not pretend that; I do not say that robbery was the motive of the crime, and I do not believe it was.'

'Then what is the meaning of this card?'

'It means that *one of the motives* for the crime was robbery.'

'What leads you to think so?'

'This! If you will be good enough to accompany me.'

And the young man begged us to follow him into the vestibule, and we did so. He led us towards the lavatory, and asked my chief to kneel beside him. This lavatory is lit by the glass door, and when the door was open the place was quite light. M. de Marquet and M. Rouletabille knelt down, and the young man pointed to a place on the tiles.

'The tiles of the lavatory have not been washed by Old Jacques for some time,' he said. 'That can be seen by the layer of dust that covers them. Now, observe at this place two large footprints and the black soot which everywhere accompanies the steps of the criminal. The soot, or ash, is nothing else than the charcoal dust that covers the path along which one has to pass to come straight through the forest from Épinay to Glandier. You know that at that place there is a small hamlet of charcoal-burners. Now, this is what the assassin must have done: he entered here in the afternoon, when there was no one in the pavilion, committed the robbery – '

'But what robbery? Where do you see any signs of robbery? What proves to you that a robbery was committed?' we all asked at once.

'What led me to suppose a robbery,' the journalist continued, 'was – '

'Was this!' interrupted M. de Marquet, still on his knees.

'Evidently,' said M. Joseph Rouletabille.

And my chief then explained that there was printed on the dust of the tiles the distinct mark of a heavy, rectangular parcel, and that the impression made by the cord around it was easily visible.

'You have been here before, then, M. Rouletabille, though I gave strict orders to Old Jacques, who was left in charge of the pavilion, not to allow anybody to enter?'

'Don't scold Old Jacques. I came here with M. Robert Darzac.'

'Ah, indeed!' exclaimed M. de Marquet discontentedly, casting a side-glance at M. Darzac, who remained still perfectly silent.

'When I saw the mark of the parcel by the side of the footprints I had no longer any doubt as to the robbery,' M. Rouletabille went on. 'The thief had not brought a parcel with him. He had here made that parcel of stolen objects, no doubt, and put it in this corner with the intention of taking it away when the moment should come for him to make his escape. He had also placed beside the parcel his heavy boots; for, look, there are no indications of steps leading to the marks left by the boots, and the bootprints are side by side, like boots at rest and containing no feet! That would account for the fact that the assassin, when he fled from the Yellow Room, left no trace of his steps either in the laboratory or in the vestibule. After having entered the Yellow Room in his boots, he took them off there, probably because he found them troublesome, or because he wished to make as little noise as possible. The marks made by him in going through the vestibule and the laboratory disappeared when Old Jacques washed the floors of those two places. Having taken off his boots, the assassin carried them in his hand from the threshold to the lavatory, and placed them there, for on the dust of the lavatory tiles there is no trace of bare feet nor stockings, nor of other boots. The man placed his boots beside the parcel – for the robbery had already been committed. The man then returned to the Yellow Room and slipped under the bed, where the mark of his body is perfectly visible on the floor, and even on the mat, which at that spot has been slightly moved from its place and creased considerably. Bits of straw also, freshly torn off, bear witness to the assassin's movements under the bed.'

'Yes, yes; we know all about that,' said M. de Marquet.

'This return of the robber under the bed,' continued Rouletabille, that astonishing boy-journalist, 'proves that robbery was not his only motive. Don't tell me that he hid himself there because he saw through the vestibule window M. and Mlle Stangerson about to enter the pavilion. It was much easier for him to climb up to the attic and wait there for an opportunity to get away, if his only purpose was flight. No, no; he wanted to be in the Yellow Room.'

Here the Chief of the Sûreté intervened.

'That's not at all bad, young fellow, and I congratulate you; for if we do not know yet how the assassin succeeded in getting away, we can already follow step by step his entry here, and we know what he did – he committed a robbery. But what has he stolen?'

'Some things that are extremely valuable,' replied the young reporter.

At that moment we heard a cry from the laboratory. We rushed there, and found Professor Stangerson, his eyes haggard, his limbs trembling, pointing to a sort of cabinet which he had opened, which we saw was empty.

At the same time he sank into the large armchair near his desk, and groaned: 'Once more I have been robbed!' And big tears rolled down his cheeks. 'Above all, do not say a word of this to my daughter. She would be more grieved than I am.' He heaved a deep sigh, and added in a heart-rending tone: 'After all, what does it matter, if only she lives?'

'She will live!' said M. Darzac, with deep emotion.

'And we will find the stolen objects,' said M. Dax. 'But what was in this cabinet?'

'Twenty years of my life,' replied the illustrious professor – 'or, rather, of our lives – the lives of my daughter and myself. Yes, our most precious documents, the most secret records of our experiments and researches for the last twenty years were in that cabinet. It is an irreparable loss for us, and, I venture to say, for Science. All the steps by which I have been able to arrive at the final proof of the destructibility of matter were there, carefully reported, labelled, and filed, and illustrated with sketches and photographs – all were there! The man who came wished to take all from me – my daughter and my work, my heart and my soul.'

And the great Stangerson cried like a child.

We stood round him in silence, deeply affected by his great distress. M. Robert Darzac, leaning on the armchair into which the professor had sunk, tried in vain to hide his tears – a sight which for a moment nearly made me sympathise with him, in spite of the instinctive repulsion with which his weird attitude and strange anxieties had inspired me.

M. Joseph Rouletabille, alone, as if his precious time and mission on earth did not permit him to dwell on the contemplation of human suffering, had very calmly gone up to the empty cabinet, and, pointing it out to the Chief of the Sûreté, broke the respectful silence with which we received the great scientist's despair. He gave us some explanations, of which we had no need, as to the way he had been led to believe that a robbery had been committed by the simultaneous discoveries he had made of traces in the lavatory, and of the emptiness of the precious cabinet in the laboratory. He had only gone rapidly through the latter room, but had at once been struck by the unusual shape of that cabinet, its solidity, the fact that it was made of iron – to be fireproof, no doubt – clearly indicating that it was intended for the preservation of objects to which the highest value and importance were attached, and, above all, that the key of such a precious cabinet had been left in the lock. 'One does not generally have a safe and leave it open.' Then this little key, with its brass head and complicated wards, had, it appeared, strongly attracted M. Rouletabille's attention.

M. de Marquet seemed greatly perplexed, as if he did not know whether he ought to be glad of the new direction given to the inquiry by the young reporter, or sorry that it had not been done by himself. In our profession we have to put up with these mortifications, and trample under foot our self-love, when the general good is in question. M. de Marquet conquered his feelings, and thought it right to add his compliments to those M. Dax had paid the young reporter.

Rouletabille simply shrugged his shoulders and said: 'I've done but little.' I should have liked to box his ears, especially when he added: 'You will do well, Monsieur, to ask M. Stangerson who ordinarily had possession of that key.'

'My daughter,' replied the professor. 'It never quitted her.'

'Ah, that changes the aspect of things, and does not agree with the theory of M. Rouletabille,' said my chief. 'If that key never quitted Mlle Stangerson, the assassin must that night have waited for her in her room for the purpose of stealing it from her, and the robbery could not have been committed until after the attack made on her life. But after the crime there were four persons in the laboratory! I can't make it out!'

And M. de Marquet repeated, with a desperate air, which must have meant in him the acme of delight – for he was never so pleased as when unable to solve a mystery: 'I cannot make it out at all.'

'The robbery,' said the reporter, 'could only have been committed before the attack upon Mlle Stangerson. I have special reasons to believe this. When the assassin entered the pavilion, he was already in possession of the brass-headed key.'

'That is impossible,' said M. Stangerson in a low voice.

'It is quite possible, Monsieur, and this proves it.'

The fiendish youth drew from his pocket a copy of the *Époque*, dated October 21 – I recall the fact that the crime was committed on the night between the 24th and 25th – and pointing to an advertisement, he read: ' "Yesterday a black satin reticule was lost in the Louvre Stores. It contained, amongst other things, a small brass-headed key. A handsome reward will be given to the person who found it. This person must write, *poste restante*, Bureau 40, to this address: M.A.T.H.S.N." Do not these letters suggest the name of Mlle Stangerson?' continued the reporter. 'The "key with a brass head" – is it not this key? I always read the advertisements. In my business, as in yours, Monsieur' – he turned here to my chief – 'one should always read the "personal" advertisements. Numberless intrigues are to be discovered there, and keys to intrigues. True, they have not always brass heads, but are none the less interesting. This advertisement in particular, because of the mystery with which the woman who had lost the key – not a very compromising object – surrounded herself, struck me very much. How she cared for that key! What a big reward she promised for its return! And I pondered over those six letters, M.A.T.H.S.N. The four first at once indicated to me a Christian name. "Math," I thought; that's evidently "Mathilde". But I could make nothing of the last two letters; so I threw aside the journal, and occupied myself with something else. Four days later, when the evening papers appeared with enormous headlines announcing the assassination of Mlle Mathilde Stangerson, the name Mathilde instinctively caused me to remember the letters in the advertisement. I had forgotten the two last letters, S.N. When I saw them again I could not repress a cry, "Stangerson!" I jumped into a cab, and rushed to the bureau No. 40, asking: "Have you a letter addressed to M.A.T.H.S.N.?" The clerk replied, "No"; and as I insisted, begged, and entreated him to search again, he said: "Are you playing off a joke, Monsieur? Yes, I had a letter with the initials M.A.T.H.S.N., but I gave it three days ago to a lady who came for it. You come today to claim the same letter, and the day before yesterday another gentleman claimed it with the same strange insistence. I've had enough of this mystification!" I tried to question the clerk as to the two persons who had already claimed the letter, but whether he wished to observe professional secrecy – he may have thought he had already said too much – or was irritated by what he took for a joke, he would not answer any of my questions.'

Rouletabille paused. We all remained silent. Each drew his own conclusions from the strange story of the *poste-restante* letter. It seemed, indeed, that we now held a solid thread, by the aid of which we should be able to follow up this extraordinary mystery.

M. Stangerson said: 'It appears almost certain that my daughter lost the key, and that she did not tell me of it in order to spare me all anxiety, and that she begged whoever had found it to write *poste restante*. She evidently feared that, by giving her address, enquiries would have resulted that would have apprised me of the loss of the key. It was quite logical, quite natural, for her to have taken that course, for I had already been robbed, Monsieur.'

'Where was that, and when?' asked the Chief of the Detective Department.

'Oh, many years ago, in America, at Philadelphia. Somebody stole from my laboratory the secret of two inventions that might have made the fortune of a whole nation. Not only have I never found out who was the thief, but I have never heard speak of the object of the robbery, doubtless because, in order to defeat the calculations of the person who had despoiled me, I myself offered those two inventions to the public, thus rendering the robbery of no avail. It is from that time that I have been very suspicious, and shut myself up systematically when I am at work. All the bars to these windows, the isolation of this pavilion, this cabinet, which I had specially constructed, this lock, this unique key – all these are the result of fears inspired by sad experience.'

'Very interesting,' declared M. Dax.

And then M. Rouletabille asked about the reticule. Neither M. Stangerson nor Old Jacques had seen it for several days, but a few hours later we were to learn from Mlle Stangerson herself that the reticule had either been stolen from her, or she had lost it; that things had occurred just as her father had stated to us; that she had gone to the Post Office No. 40 on October 23, and had received a letter which she declared was nothing but a vulgar joke, which she had immediately burned.

To return to our interrogatory – or, rather, to our conversation – I must state that, the head of the Sûreté having enquired of M. Stangerson under what conditions his daughter had gone to Paris on October 20 – the day on which the reticule was lost – we learned that she had gone there accompanied by M. Robert Darzac, who was not seen again at the château from that time to the day after the crime. The fact that M. Darzac was by her side in the Louvre Stores when the reticule disappeared could not pass unnoticed, and, it must be said, strongly awakened our interest.

This conversation between magistrates, accused, victim, witnesses, and journalist was coming to a close, when a truly theatrical sensation – an incident that could not displease my chief – was produced. The gendarmes came to announce that Frédéric Larsan requested to be admitted – a request that was at once complied with. The detective held in his hand a heavy pair of muddy boots, which he threw on the tiles of the laboratory.

'Here,' he said, 'are the boots worn by the assassin. Do you recognise them, Old Jacques?'

Old Jacques bent over them, and, thunderstruck, recognised a pair of old boots which he had some time back thrown into a corner of his attic. He was so taken aback as to be obliged to blow his nose to hide his agitation.

Then, pointing to the handkerchief in the old man's hand, Frédéric Larsan said: 'There's a handkerchief that bears an astonishingly close resemblance to the one found in the Yellow Room.'

'I know that well enough,' said Old Jacques, trembling. 'They are nearly alike.'

'Finally,' continued Frédéric Larsan, 'the old cap, found also in the Yellow Room, might formerly have covered the head of Old Jacques. All this, gentlemen, proves, I think, that the assassin wished to disguise his real personality. He did it in a very clumsy way, or so, at least, it appears to me, because we know for certain that Old Jacques is not the assassin, since he never left M. Stangerson. But suppose that M. Stangerson had not that night remained at his work so long; that, after parting with his daughter, he had gone back to the château, and Mlle Stangerson had been assassinated when there was no longer anybody in the laboratory, and when Old Jacques was sleeping in his attic, no one would have doubted that the servant was the assassin. He owes his salvation, therefore, to the drama having been enacted too soon, the assassin having, no doubt, from the silence in the laboratory, imagined that it was empty, and that the moment for action had come. The man, who was able to introduce himself here so mysteriously, and to take so many precautions against Old Jacques, was, there can be no doubt about it, someone extremely familiar with the house. At what time did he really introduce himself? In the afternoon? During the evening? I could not say. One who was thus familiar with the habits of persons in this pavilion must have entered the Yellow Room whenever he chose.'

'He could not have entered it when there were people in the laboratory!' said M. de Marquet.

'What do we know about it?' Larsan replied. 'There was the dinner in the laboratory, the coming and going of the servants in attendance. There was a chemical experiment being carried on between ten and eleven o'clock, and M. Stangerson, his daughter, and Old Jacques were engaged with the furnace in this corner of the high chimney. Who can say that the assassin – a man intimately connected with the house – did not take advantage of that moment to slip into the Yellow Room, after having taken off his boots in the lavatory?'

'It seems rather improbable,' said M. Stangerson.

'Granted. But it is not impossible. As to the escape, that's another thing. How did he escape? In the most natural way in the world.'

For a moment Frédéric Larsan paused. That moment seemed to us extremely long. We were waiting for his words with an eagerness only to be imagined.

'I have not been in the Yellow Room,' Larsan continued, 'but I take it for granted that you are sure that anyone could only have quitted the room by way of the door. It is by the door, then, that the assassin made his way out. As it cannot be otherwise, it must be so. He committed the crime, and then left by the door. At what moment? At the moment when it was most easy for him to effect his exit; at the moment when the matter becomes the least mysterious – so little mysterious, in reality, that there can be no other explanation. Let us consider the different "moments" which followed after the crime had been committed. There is the first moment, when M. Stangerson and Old Jacques are close to the door, ready to bar the way. There is the second moment, during which Old Jacques is absent for a while, and M. Stangerson stands alone before the door. There is the third moment, when M. Stangerson is joined by the concierge. There is the fourth moment, during which M. Stangerson, the concierge, and his wife, and Old Jacques are all before the door. There is the fifth moment, during which the door is burst open, and the Yellow Room invaded. The moment at which the flight is most explicable is the very moment when there is the smallest number of persons before the door. There is one moment when there is but one – that is the moment when M. Stangerson is alone before the door. Unless the complicity of silence of Old Jacques is admitted – which I do not believe, for he would not have left the pavilion to go and examine the window of the Yellow Room if he had seen the door opening and the assassin come out – the door was opened in the presence of M. Stangerson alone, and the man escaped. Here we must admit that M. Stangerson had powerful reasons for not arresting the assassin or causing him to be arrested, since he allowed him to reach the vestibule window, and since he closed it after him! That done, as Old Jacques would soon return, and it was necessary he should find things as he had left them, Mlle Stangerson, though horribly wounded, had still strength enough – and, no doubt, in obedience to the entreaties of her father – to refasten the door of the Yellow Room with both bolt and lock before sinking, nearly dying, on the floor. We do not know who committed the crime. We do not know the wretch of whom M. and Mlle Stangerson are the victims, but there is no doubt that they both know. This secret must be a terrible one for the father not to have hesitated to leave his daughter to die behind the door which she shut upon herself; terrible for him to have allowed the assassin to escape. But there is no other way in the world to explain the flight of the assassin from the Yellow Room!'

The silence which followed this dramatic and luminous explanation had in it something awful. We all of us felt pained for the illustrious professor, who was thus driven into a corner by the pitiless logic of Frédéric Larsan, and forced to confess the whole truth of his martyrdom, or to keep silent – a clearer and more terrible admission. We saw this man – a very monument of sorrow – raise his head with a gesture so solemn that we bowed our heads to it, as at the sight of something sacred. He then pronounced these words, in a voice so loud that it seemed to exhaust him: 'I swear on the head of my suffering child that I never for an instant quitted the door of her room from the moment I heard her cry for help; that that door was not opened while I was alone in the laboratory; and, finally, that when we entered the Yellow Room – my three domestics and I – the assassin was no longer there. I swear I do not know the assassin!'

May I mention that, in spite of the solemnity of M. Stangerson's words, we little believed in his denial? Frédéric Larsan had shown us the truth, and it was not soon to be abandoned.

When M. de Marquet declared that the conversation was at an end, and as we were about to leave the laboratory, Joseph Rouletabille, the young reporter, the mere boy, approached M. Stangerson, took him by the hand with the greatest respect, and I heard him say: 'I believe you, Monsieur.'

* * *

I here close the quotation which I thought it necessary to make from the narrative of M. Maleine, Registrar at the Tribunal of Corbeil. I need not tell the reader that all that passed in the laboratory was faithfully and immediately reported to me by Rouletabille himself.

Chapter 12

Frédéric Larsan's stick

It was not until 6 p.m. that I prepared to leave the château, taking with me the article hastily written by my friend in the little sitting-room which M. Robert Darzac had placed at our disposal. The reporter was to sleep at the château, availing himself of the inexplicable hospitality of M. Robert Darzac, to whom M. Stangerson, in those sad moments, left the care of all the domestic affairs. Nevertheless, he insisted on accompanying me to the station at Épinay. As we crossed the park, he said to me: 'Frédéric is really a very able fellow, and has not belied his reputation. You know how he came to find Old Jacques's boots? Near the spot where we noticed the elegant bootmarks and the disappearance of the rough ones, there was a rectangular hole, freshly made in the moist ground, indicating that a stone had evidently been removed. Larsan searched for that stone without finding it, and quickly concluded that it had been used by the assassin to sink the old boots in the lake. The deduction was excellent, as the success of the search proved. It had escaped me, but it is fair to say that my mind was turned in another direction, for, because of the extraordinary number of false traces left by the assassin, and the measure of the black footprints corresponding with that of Old Jacques's boots – which I had established, without his suspecting it, on the floor of the Yellow Room – it had become perfectly clear to me that the assassin had sought to turn suspicion on to the old servant. That is precisely what made me say to Jacques that, a cap having been found in the fatal room, it was bound to be similar to his. It further allowed me to give him the description of the stained handkerchief, as resembling one that I had seen him use. Up to this point Larsan and I agree, but no further; and the duel between us is going to be terrible, for, though in good faith, he is working up an error, which I shall have to fight against *with nothing*.'

I was surprised at the profoundly grave accent with which my young friend pronounced the last words.

He repeated: 'Yes, terrible, terrible! But is it really fighting with nothing, this fighting with one's wits as weapon?'

We were then passing the back of the château. Night had come. A window on the first floor was partly open. A feeble light came from it, as well as some sounds that arrested our attention. We went on until we reached the side of a door that was situated just under the window. Rouletabille, in a low tone of voice, made me understand that it was the window of Mlle Stangerson's room. The sounds which had attracted our attention ceased, then started again for a while, and we heard stifled sobs. We were only able to catch these words, which reached us distinctly: 'My poor Robert!'

Rouletabille whispered in my ear: 'If we only knew what was being said in that room, my inquiry would soon be finished.'

He looked about him. The darkness of the evening enveloped us; we could not see much beyond the narrow lawn, bordered by trees, which ran behind the château. The sobs had ceased.

'As one cannot hear anything, one may at least try to see,' said Rouletabille.

And, making me a sign to deaden the sound of my steps, he led me across the path to the trunk of a tall birch-tree, whose white shape was visible in the darkness. This birch stood exactly in front of the window in which we were so much interested, its lower branches on a level with the first floor of the château. From the top of these branches one might see what was passing in Mlle Stangerson's room, and such was Rouletabille's idea, for, enjoining me to remain silent, he clasped the trunk with his vigorous arms and climbed up. I soon lost sight of him amid the branches, and there was a great silence.

In front of me the open window remained lighted, and I saw no shadow move across it.

I listened, and presently from above me these words reached my ears: 'After you!'

'After you, pray!'

Two persons were talking together right above my head, exchanging terms of civility! I was amazed, but still more so when there appeared presently on the smooth trunk of the tree two human forms that quietly reached the ground. Rouletabille had climbed up alone, and had returned – two!

'Good evening, M. Sainclair!'

It was Frédéric Larsan. The detective had already occupied the post of observation, when my young friend had hoped to be alone.

Neither the one nor the other took any notice of my astonishment, however. I thought I could understand that from their observatory they had witnessed a scene of tenderness and despair between Mlle Stangerson, lying on her bed, and M. Darzac, on his knees by her pillow. Already each appeared to have drawn different conclusions from what they had seen. It was easy to guess that the scene had strongly impressed the mind of Rouletabille in favour of M. Robert Darzac, while to the mind of Larsan it attested nothing but perfect hypocrisy, acted with great art by the fiancé of Mlle Stangerson.

As we reached the park gate Larsan stopped us.

'My stick!' he cried. 'I left it back there, near the tree.'

And he quitted us, saying that he would rejoin us directly.

'Did you notice Frédéric Larsan's stick?' the young reporter asked me as soon as we were alone. 'It is quite a new one, which I have never before seen him use. He seems to take great care of it. It never leaves him. One would say he was afraid lest it should fall into the hands of strangers. Before today I have never seen Frédéric Larsan with a stick. Where has he found that stick? It is not natural that a man who has never before used a walking-stick should, the day after the crime of Glandier, never move a step without one. On the day of our arrival at the château, directly he saw us, he put his watch in his pocket and picked up his stick from the ground. I was wrong, perhaps, not to have attached more importance to that movement.'

We were now out of the park. Rouletabille had become silent. His thoughts were certainly still dwelling on the subject of Frédéric Larsan's new cane. I had proof of that when, as we neared Épinay, he said to me: 'Frédéric Larsan arrived at Glandier before me. He began his inquiry before me. He has had time to discover things and find things about which I know nothing. Where did he find that cane?'

Then he added: 'It is probable that his suspicion – more than his suspicion, his reasoning – about Robert Darzac's guilt has led him to lay his hand on something palpable. Can it have been this cane? Where the deuce can he have found it?'

At Épinay, as I had to wait twenty minutes for the train, we entered a small inn. Almost immediately the door reopened behind us, and Frédéric Larsan made his appearance, brandishing the famous stick.

'I have found it!' he said gaily.

We all three seated ourselves at a table. Rouletabille never moved his eyes from the cane. He was so absorbed that he did not notice a mysterious sign made by Larsan to a railway clerk, a very young man whose chin was adorned with a tiny blonde and ill-kept beard. The young man rose, paid for his drink, and went out. I should not myself have attached any importance to that sign if it had not been brought back to my mind some months later by the reappearance of the fellow at one of the most tragic moments of this story. I then learned that the young man was an assistant of Larsan's, told off to watch the movements of travellers at the station of Épinay-sur-Orge; for Larsan neglected nothing which he thought might be useful to him.

I again turned my eyes to Rouletabille.

'I say, M. Fred,' he exclaimed, 'since when have you taken to a walking-stick? I've always seen you walking with your hands in your pockets.'

'It is a present that was made to me,' replied the detective.

'Recently?' Rouletabille insisted.

'No; it was given to me in London.'

'Of course; you have just come from London, M. Fred. May I look at your stick?'

'Why, certainly.'

Fred handed the stick to Rouletabille. It was a large yellow bamboo cane, with a hooked handle and a gold mount.

Rouletabille, having examined it minutely, returned it to Larsan, with a bantering expression on his face, saying: 'That's amusing! They presented you in London with a French stick.'

'Possibly,' said Fred imperturbably.

'Read the mark here, in tiny letters: "Cassette, 6A Opéra".'

'The French often have their washing done in London,' said Fred; 'why should the English not buy their sticks in Paris?'

When Rouletabille had seen me into the train, he said to me: 'Remember the address!'

'Yes – "Cassette, 6A Opéra". Rely on me; you shall have a line tomorrow morning.'

That evening, on reaching Paris, I saw M. Cassette, dealer in walking-sticks and umbrellas, and wrote to my friend.

'A man, unmistakably answering to the description of M. Robert Darzac – same height, slightly stooping, putty-coloured overcoat, bowler hat – purchased a cane similar to the one in which we are interested, on the evening of the crime, at about eight o'clock. M. Cassette has not sold another such cane during the past two years. Fred's cane is new. It is clear enough that his is the one recently purchased at Cassette's. It was not he who purchased it, since he was in London at the time. Like you, I think that he found it somewhere about M. Robert Darzac. But if, as you say, the assassin was in the Yellow Room from five or even six o'clock, and the tragedy was not enacted until towards midnight, the purchase of this stick gives an irrefutable alibi for M. Robert Darzac.'

Chapter 13

'The vicarage has lost nothing of its charm, nor the garden of its brightness'

A week after the occurrence of the events I have related – on November 2, to be accurate – I received at my domicile in Paris the following telegraphic message.

COME TO GLANDIER BY THE EARLIEST TRAIN. BRING REVOLVERS. FRIENDLY GREETINGS. – ROULETABILLE.

I have already said, I think, that at that period I was a young barrister, and, like all beginners, had very few cases. I went to the Law Courts rather for the purpose of familiarising myself with my professional duties than for the defence of the 'widow and orphan'. I felt, therefore, no surprise at Rouletabille disposing of my time in that way. Moreover, he knew how much I was interested in his journalistic adventures in general, and, above all, in the Glandier case. I had not heard for a week of the progress of that mysterious affair, except by innumerable paragraphs in the newspapers, and by the very brief notes of Rouletabille in the *Époque*. Those notes had divulged the fact that old traces of human blood had been found on the sheep's bone, as well as fresh traces of the blood of Mlle Stangerson; the old stains belonging to other crimes, probably dating years back.

It may be easily imagined that the affair engaged the attention of the Press throughout the world. No crime had perplexed the general public so much. It appeared to me, however, that the judicial inquiry made very little progress, and I should have been very pleased with the receipt of my friend's invitation to rejoin him at Glandier, had not the despatch contained the words: 'Bring revolvers.'

That worried me a great deal. If Rouletabille telegraphed to me to take revolvers, it was because he foresaw that there would be occasion to use them. Now, I confess it without shame, I am no hero. On the other hand, here was a friend, evidently embarrassed, calling upon me to go to his aid. I did not hesitate very long; and, after assuring myself that the only revolver I possessed was properly loaded, I hurried towards the 'Orleans' Station. On the way I remembered that Rouletabille wanted not one, but two revolvers. I therefore went to a gunsmith's and bought an excellent weapon, which I decided to offer my friend.

I hoped to find him at the station at Épinay, but he was not there. However, a trap was waiting for me, and I soon reached Glandier. Nobody was at the gate, and it was only on the threshold of the château that I met the young man. He greeted me in a friendly manner, and embraced me, enquiring warmly as to the state of my health.

When we were in the little sitting-room which I have mentioned before, Rouletabille made me sit down, and said: 'It's all going wrong.'

'What's going wrong?'

'Everything!'

He came nearer and whispered: 'Frédéric Larsan is working with all his might against M. Robert Darzac.'

This did not surprise me, since I had seen the fiancé of Mlle Stangerson turn pale before his own footprints. However, I at once observed: 'What about that cane?'

'It is still in the hands of Frédéric Larsan, who never puts it down.'

'But does it not supply an alibi for M. Darzac?'

'Not the least in the world. Gently questioned by me, M. Darzac denied having, on that evening or on any other, purchased a cane at Cassette's. Anyway,' said Rouletabille, 'I'll not swear to anything, for M. Darzac has such strange silences that one does not know exactly how to take what he says.

'To the mind of Frédéric Larsan, this cane must appear a piece of damning evidence.'

'In what way? Owing to the time at which it was bought, it couldn't have been in the possession of the assassin.'

'The time won't trouble Larsan; he is not obliged to adopt my theory, which begins by introducing the assassin into the Yellow Room between five and six o'clock. What prevents him from making him enter between ten and eleven o'clock at night? At that very time M. and Mlle Stangerson, helped by Old Jacques, were engaged in making an interesting chemical experiment in the part of the laboratory occupied by the furnaces. Larsan will say that the assassin slipped between them, however unlikely this appears. He has already given the examining magistrate to understand so much. When one looks closely into it, the idea of Larsan is absurd, seeing that the "familiar", if there is one, must have known that the professor was going to leave the pavilion presently, and that it was necessary for him – the "familiar" – to put off doing anything till after the professor's departure. Why should he have risked crossing the laboratory while the professor was in it? And besides, when should he have entered the Yellow Room?'

'All these points have to be elucidated before Larsan's fanciful idea can be admitted. I am not going to waste my time over it, for I have an irrefutable theory, which won't permit of my troubling about this mere fancy. Only, as I am obliged to keep silent, and Larsan sometimes speaks, everything might, in the end, seem to turn against M. Robert Darzac – were I not there,' added the young reporter proudly. 'For there are against M. Darzac other things far more crushing than the story of the stick, which remain incomprehensible to me – the more incomprehensible as Larsan does not in the least hesitate to let M. Darzac see him with that stick, which is supposed to have been Darzac's. I understand many things in Larsan's theory, but I do not yet understand the stick affair.'

'Is Larsan still at the château?'

'Yes; he hardly ever quits it. He sleeps there, as I do, at the request of M. Stangerson, who has done for him what M. Robert Darzac has done for me. Accused by Frédéric Larsan of knowing the assassin, and of having allowed him to escape, M. Stangerson is affording his accuser every facility for arriving at the discovery of the truth, just as M. Darzac is doing for me.'

'But you are persuaded of M. Darzac's innocence?'

'For a moment I believed in the possibility of his guilt. That was when we arrived here for the first time. The time has now come to tell you what passed between M. Darzac and me.'

Here Rouletabille interrupted himself, and asked me if I had brought the weapons. I showed him the two revolvers. Having examined them, he said, 'All right!' and handed them back to me.

'Shall we need them?' I asked.

'Probably this evening. We shall spend the night here – you don't mind?'

'Not at all,' I said, with a grimace that made Rouletabille laugh.

'Come,' he said, 'this is no time for laughing. Let us talk seriously. You remember the phrase which was the "Open Sesame" of this château mystery?'

'Yes,' I said, 'perfectly. "The vicarage has lost nothing of its charm, nor the garden of its brightness." It was again that very phrase you found on the half-burned piece of paper among the ashes in the laboratory.'

'Yes; at the bottom of the paper the flame had spared the date – October 23. Remember this date, it is highly important. I am now going to tell you about that curious phrase. On the evening before the crime – that is to say, on the 23rd – M. and Mlle Stangerson went to a reception at the Élysée; I know this, because I saw them there myself. I was there in my professional capacity, having to interview one of the savants of the Academy of Philadelphia who was being entertained that night. I had never before seen either M. or Mlle Stangerson. I was seated in the room adjoining the Hall of Ambassadors, and, tired of being jostled by so many people, I had fallen into a vague reverie, when I scented near me the perfume of the "lady in black".

'You will ask me what is the perfume of the "lady in black". Be satisfied to know that it is a perfume of which I am very fond, because it was that of a lady who was extremely kind to me when I was a child. The lady who was that evening scented with the perfume was dressed in white. She was wonderfully beautiful. I couldn't help rising and following her. An old man held her arm under his, and, as they passed, I heard voices say: "Professor Stangerson and his daughter". Thus I learned who it was I was following.

'They met M. Robert Darzac, whom I knew by sight. Professor Stangerson, accosted by Mr Arthur William Rance, one of the American savants, seated himself in the great gallery, and M. Darzac led Mlle Stangerson into the conservatory. I still followed. The weather was very mild; the garden doors were open. Mlle Stangerson threw a *fichu* over her shoulders, and I saw that it was she who begged M. Darzac to go with her into the garden. I followed farther, interested by the agitation plainly exhibited in the bearing of M. Darzac. They strolled slowly by the wall near the Avenue Marigny. I took the central alley, walking parallel with them, and then crossed over for the purpose of getting nearer to them. The night was dark, the grass deadened the sound of my steps. They had stopped under the flickering light of a gas-jet, and appeared both to be bending over a paper held by Mlle Stangerson, reading something which deeply interested them. I stopped, enveloped in darkness and silence.

'Neither of them saw me, and I distinctly heard Mlle Stangerson repeating, as she was refolding the paper: "The vicarage has lost nothing of its charm, nor the garden of its brightness." It was said in a tone at once so mocking and so desperate, and was followed by a burst of laughter so nervous, that I think the phrase will never cease to sound in my ears. But yet another phrase was pronounced, this time by M. Darzac: "Shall I have to commit a crime, then, to win you?" He was in a singularly agitated state. He took the hand of Mlle Stangerson, and held it for a long time to his lips, and I thought from the movement of his shoulders that he was weeping. Then they went away.

'When I returned to the great gallery,' Rouletabille continued, 'I saw no more of M. Darzac, whom I was not to see again until after the crime at Glandier. But I saw Mlle Stangerson, her father, and the delegates from Philadelphia. Mlle Stangerson stood near Mr Arthur William Rance, who was talking with much animation, his eyes during the conversation glowing with singular brightness. Mlle Stangerson, I thought, was not even listening to what he was saying, her face expressing total indifference. Mr Rance is a red-faced man, a whisky-drinker probably. After M. and Mlle Stangerson had gone, he went to the buffet, and never left it. I joined him there, and rendered him some little service in the midst of the pressing crowd. He thanked me, and said he was returning to America three days later – that is to say, on the 26th, the day after the crime. I talked with him about Philadelphia. He told me he had lived there for five-and-twenty years, and that it was there he had met the illustrious Professor Stangerson and his daughter. Then he took to drinking champagne again, and I thought he would never leave off. When he was very nearly drunk I left him.

'Such was my experience that evening. For some reason, during the night I couldn't help thinking of the Stangersons and you may imagine what effect the news of the assassination of Mlle Stangerson produced on me, with what force recurred to me the memory of those words pronounced by M. Robert Darzac: "Shall I have to commit a crime to win you?" It was not this phrase, however, that I repeated to him when we met here at Glandier. That phrase about the vicarage and the bright garden, which Mlle Stangerson had appeared to read from a paper in her hand, sufficed to open to us the gate of the château. Did I think at the time that M. Darzac was the assassin? I do not believe I ever really thought so. At that time I had not any serious idea or suspicion. I had so little evidence to go upon. But I needed M. Darzac to prove to me at once that he had not been wounded in the hand.

'When we were alone together I told him how I had chanced to overhear a part of his conversation with Mlle Stangerson in the garden of the Élysée, and when I told him I had heard the words, "Shall I have to commit a crime, then, to win you?" he was greatly troubled, but certainly much less than he had been when hearing me repeat the phrase about the vicarage. What threw him into a state of real consternation was to learn from my lips that the day on which he was to meet Mlle Stangerson at the Élysée was the very day on which she had gone during the afternoon to the Post Office No. 40 in search of the letter, which was, perhaps, the one they read together that night in the garden of the Élysée, which ended with the words: "The vicarage has lost nothing of its charm, nor the garden of its brightness!" That supposition was confirmed by the discovery I made, as you remember, in one of the furnaces of the laboratory, of a fragment of that letter dated October 23. The letter had been written, and taken away from the post office on the same day.

'There can be no doubt that, on returning from the Élysée that night, Mlle Stangerson had tried to destroy this compromising paper. It was in vain that M. Darzac denied that the letter had anything whatever to do with the crime. I told him that in an affair so mysterious as this he had no right to hide from justice the incident of the letter; that I was personally convinced it was of considerable importance; that the desperate tone in which Mlle Stangerson had pronounced the phrase about the vicarage, that his own tears, and the threat of a crime which he had expressed after the letter was read, left me no room for doubt. M. Darzac became more and more agitated, and I determined to take advantage of the effect my words had produced on him.

' "You were on the point of being married, Monsieur," I said negligently, and without looking at him, "and suddenly that marriage becomes impossible, because of the author of that letter, since, as soon as you have read it, you speak of a crime being necessary for you to win Mlle Stangerson. Therefore, there is someone between you and her, someone who forbids her to marry you, someone who kills her – or attempts to kill her – so that she should not marry!"

'And I concluded this little speech with these words: "Now, Monsieur, you have only to give me the name of the assassin!"

'I had, without being fully aware of it, said something which was terrible to him; for, when I again turned towards him, I saw his face distorted with anguish. His forehead was bathed in perspiration, and terror lurked in his eyes.

' "Monsieur," he said to me, "I am going to ask something from you which may appear madness, but in exchange for which I would readily give my life. You must not speak before the magistrate of what you saw and heard in the garden of the Élysée – neither before the magistrates nor before anyone in the world. I swear to you that I am innocent, and I feel that you believe me; but I would rather pass for being guilty than see the suspicions of the law fasten on that phrase, 'The vicarage has lost nothing of its charm, nor the garden of its brightness.' The law must know nothing about that sentence. Monsieur, I leave it in your hands; but forget that evening at the Élysée. A hundred other ways are open to you that will lead to the discovery of the criminal. I will open them for you. I will help you. Do you wish to take up your quarters here; to appear here as a master; to take your meals, sleep here? Watch my actions, the actions of everyone here? You shall do at Glandier as if you owned it, Monsieur; but forget the evening at the Élysée!" '

Rouletabille paused to take breath. I now understood the extraordinary attitude of M. Robert Darzac towards my friend, and the facility with which the young reporter had been able to settle down at the château. My curiosity could not fail to be excited by all I heard. I asked Rouletabille to tell me more about the whole affair. What had happened at Glandier during the past week? Had not my friend told me that there were now against Darzac circumstances far more terrible than that of the stick found by Larsan?

'Everything seems to turn against him,' my friend replied, 'and the situation is becoming exceedingly grave. M. Darzac does not appear to be much concerned about it, but he is wrong. Nothing interests him but the health of Mlle Stangerson, which was daily improving, when something occurred that is still more mysterious than the mystery of the Yellow Room!'

'Impossible!' I cried. 'What could be more mysterious than the mystery of the Yellow Room?'

'Let us first return to M. Darzac,' said Rouletabille, calming me. 'I was just telling you that everything is turning against him. The elegant boot-marks found by Frédéric Larsan appear to be really the footprints of the fiancé of Mlle Stangerson. The marks made by the bicycle may have been made by *his* bicycle. This point has been verified. Ever since he had that bicycle he had left it at the château. Why should he have taken it to Paris at that particular time? Was he ceasing to go to the château? Was the breaking off of his marriage terminating his relations with the Stangersons?

Professor Stangerson, his daughter, and M. Darzac himself declare that those relations were to continue unchanged. What, then?

'Frédéric Larsan, however, believes that it was all over between M. Darzac and the Stangersons. From the day when M. Darzac accompanied Mlle Stangerson to the Louvre Stores until the day after the crime, the ex-fiancé did not return to Glandier. It must also be remembered that Mlle Stangerson lost her reticule containing the key with the brass head while she was in M. Darzac's company. From that day to the evening at the Élysée the Sorbonne professor and Mlle Stangerson did not see one another, but they might have written to one another. Mlle Stangerson went to the Post Office No. 40 in search of a *poste-restante* letter, which Larsan believes to have been from Robert Darzac, for, knowing, of course, nothing of what took place at the Élysée, Larsan is led to believe that it was M. Darzac himself who stole the reticule and the key in order to force Mlle Stangerson's consent by getting possession of her father's most valuable papers – papers which would have been restored to him on condition that the marriage engagement was fulfilled.

'All this would have been a very doubtful and almost absurd supposition, as Larsan himself admitted to me, but for another thing, much more serious. In the first place, there is something which, so far, I have been unable to explain. It would seem that it was M. Darzac himself who, on the 24th, went to the post office and asked for the letter which Mlle Stangerson had called for and received on the previous day. The description of the man who made the application tallies in every respect with the appearance of M. Darzac, who, in answer to the questions put to him by the examining magistrate, denies that he went to the post office. I believe him, for, even admitting that the letter was written by him – which I do not think is the case – he knew that Mlle Stangerson had already called for and received it, for he had seen that very letter in her hands in the garden at the Élysée. It was not he, then, who called at the Post Office No. 40 on the 24th to ask for a letter which he knew to be no longer there.

'To me it seems evident that it was somebody greatly resembling him, and it must be the thief of the reticule, who in the letter demanded something from the owner of the reticule, Mlle Stangerson – something which was not sent to him. He must have been amazed at the failure of his demand, hence his application at the post office to learn whether the letter he had sent with the letters M.A.T.H.S.N. on the envelope had been delivered to the person to whom it was addressed. Finding that, although it had been claimed, his request had not been granted, he had become furious. What was he asking for? Nobody but Mlle Stangerson knew this. The next day it was reported that she had been assassinated during the night, and the following morning I discovered that the professor had, at the same time, been robbed by means of the key referred to in the *poste-restante* letter. It seems that the man who went to the post office to enquire for the letter is the assassin. Now, Frédéric Larsan has argued in that way, and the argument seems logical enough – only he applies it to M. Darzac. Needless to say, the examining magistrate, Larsan, and myself have done our best to obtain from Post Office No. 40 precise particulars of the person who went there on October 24. But nothing has been learned as to where he came from or where he went. We know nothing about him beyond the description which makes him resemble M. Darzac – nothing.

'I inserted the following advertisement in the leading journals: "A handsome reward will be given to the cabman who drove a fare to the Post Office No. 40 about ten a.m. on October 24. Apply at the Office of the *Époque*, and ask for M. R." There has been no application. After all, the man may have walked to the post office; but as he was most likely in a hurry, there was a chance that he might have taken a carriage. I have been pondering over this problem night and day. Who is the man who so strongly resembles M. Darzac, and is found buying the cane which has fallen into the hands of Frédéric Larsan?

'The most serious point of it all is that M. Darzac, who was due, at the very same time when his double called at the post office, to deliver a lecture at the Sorbonne, did not deliver it. One of his friends replaced him. When I questioned him as to how he spent the time, he tells me that he went for a walk in the Bois de Boulogne! What do you think of this professor, who gets another to do his work while he goes to the Bois de Boulogne for a walk? Further, I must tell you that, although M. Darzac says he went for a walk during the morning of the 24th, he is totally unable to say what he did on the night between the 24th and the 25th. When Frédéric Larsan asked him for information on this point, he quietly replied that it was no business of his how he spent his time in Paris, whereupon Fred threatened that he would find out, without the aid of anybody.

'All this seems to give some kind of basis to the great Fred's hypothesis – the more so that the fact of Robert Darzac being in the Yellow Room might be established, and thus corroborate the detective's explanation how the assassin made his escape. M. Stangerson, in that case, would have allowed him to get away, in order to avoid a frightful scandal! It is this very hypothesis that I believe altogether wrong, which is going to mislead Frédéric Larsan, though that would not altogether displease me, were the life of an innocent person not at stake. But tell me, is that hypothesis really misleading Frédéric Larsan?'

'Perhaps he is right!' I exclaimed, interrupting Rouletabille. 'Are you sure that M. Darzac is innocent? It seems to me that all these are most unfortunate coincidences.'

'Coincidences,' my friend retorted, 'are the worst enemies of truth.'

'What does the examining magistrate think of the affair?'

'M. de Marquet hesitates to charge M. Darzac in the absence of any direct evidence. Not only would he have public opinion wholly against him, to say nothing of the University, but, above all, M. and Mlle Stangerson. Mlle Stangerson adores M. Robert Darzac. Little as she was able to see the assassin, it would be hard to make the public believe that she would not have recognised him if he had been the aggressor. We know that the Yellow Room was very dimly lit, but a night-light, however small it may be, gives some light, remember. That, my friend, is how things stood when three days – or, rather, three nights – ago an incredible thing occurred.'

Chapter 14

'I expect the assassin this evening'

'First of all,' said Rouletabille, 'I must show you over the château, to enable you to understand – or, rather, to demonstrate to you – that it is impossible to understand. I myself believe that I have found what everybody else is still searching for – how the assassin escaped from the Yellow Room without complicity of any sort, and without Mlle Stangerson having anything to do with it. But so long as I am not sure of the personality of the assassin I cannot say what my theory is – only that I believe it to be correct, and in any case perfectly natural and quite simple. As to what took place three nights ago in this château, it seemed to me for twenty-four hours absolutely inconceivable, and yet the result I deduce from it is so absurd that I would almost prefer the obscurity of the inexplicable.'

The young reporter then invited me to go with him, and we walked round the château together. Dead leaves rustled under our feet – the only sound I heard. One might have thought that the château had been deserted. Those old stones, the stagnant water in the ditches surrounding the keep, the desolate earth covered with the rubbish of the past summer, the black skeletons of the trees – all gave this dreary spot, haunted by a wild mystery, the most sombre appearance. As we were passing round the keep we met the Green Man, the game-keeper, who did not salute us, but passed by as if we had not existed. As on the day when I had seen him for the first time through the window of the Castle Inn, he had his gun slung at his back, his pipe in his mouth, and his pince-nez on his nose.

'A queer customer!' muttered Rouletabille.

'Have you spoken to him?' I asked.

'Yes; but nothing is to be got out of him. He answers only with growls, shrugs his shoulders, and walks away. He ordinarily lives on the first floor of the keep – a big room that was formerly used as an oratory. He lives in great seclusion, never goes out without his gun, and only makes himself agreeable to women. He is handsome and well groomed, and the women for four leagues round are all setting their caps at him. For the moment he is only paying attention to Madame Mathieu, whose husband is keeping a lynx-eye upon her in consequence.'

After passing the keep, which stands at the extremity of the left wing, we went back to the château. Rouletabille, pointing to a window which I recognised as one of the windows of Mlle Stangerson's apartments, said to me: 'If you had been here two nights ago, at one o'clock in the morning, you would have seen me at the top of a ladder preparing to enter the château by that window.'

As I expressed some astonishment at this piece of nocturnal gymnastics, he begged me to pay great attention to the exterior arrangement of the château, after which we went back into the building.

'I must show you the first floor of the château – the right wing – which is where I am lodged,' said my friend.

In order to make quite clear the position of the different rooms, I give a plan of the first floor of that right wing of the château, drawn by Rouletabille the day after the occurrence of the phenomenon of which I am about to tell.

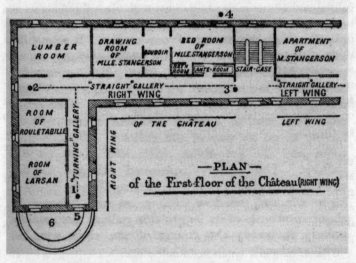

1. Spot at which Rouletabille placed Frédéric Larsan.
2. Spot at which Rouletabille placed Old Jacques.
3. Spot at which Rouletabille placed M. Stangerson.
4. Window by which Rouletabille entered.
5. Window found open by Rouletabille when he left his room. All the other doors and windows were shut.
6. Terrace surmounting a projecting room on the ground-floor.

Rouletabille motioned me to follow him up a flight of stone stairs, which on the first floor ended in a landing. From this landing one could pass to the right or left wing of the château by a gallery. This gallery, high and wide, extended the whole length of the building, and was lit from the front of the château facing the north. The rooms, with windows looking to the south, opened out of the gallery. Professor Stangerson inhabited the left wing of the building; Mlle Stangerson had her apartments in the right wing.

We entered the gallery to the right. A narrow carpet, laid on the waxed floor, which shone like glass, stifled the sound of our steps. Rouletabille asked me in a low voice to walk carefully as we passed Mlle Stangerson's door. Her apartments consisted of her bedroom, an ante-room, a small bathroom, a boudoir, and a drawing-room. One could pass from one to another of these rooms without having to go by way of the gallery. The drawing-room and the ante-room alone had doors on the gallery. The gallery continued straight to the eastern end of the building, where it was lit by a high window (window No. 2 on the Plan). At about two-thirds of its length this gallery met another gallery following the course of the right wing at right angles.

To make all this quite clear, we shall call the gallery leading from the landing to the eastern window the 'straight gallery', and that at the end of it, at right angles to it, the 'turning gallery'. It was at the meeting-point of these two galleries that Rouletabille had his room, adjoining that of Frédéric Larsan. The doors of both these opened on to the turning gallery, whilst the doors of Mlle Stangerson's apartments opened into the straight gallery. [*see the plan*]

Rouletabille pushed open the door of his room, and after we entered closed it, and even fastened the bolt.

I had not had time to glance round when he uttered a cry of surprise, and pointed out to me on a small table a pince-nez.

'What is that doing here?' he wondered. 'What is this pince-nez doing on my table?'

I should have been puzzled to answer him.

'Unless,' he said – 'unless it – unless it is what I have been search-ing for – unless it is a pince-nez for a long-sighted person!'

He eagerly seized it, his fingers caressing the convexity of the glasses, and then he looked at me with a terrifying expression on his face.

'Oh! oh!'

That exclamation he repeated again and again, as if his thoughts had suddenly turned his brain.

He rose, and, putting his hand on my shoulder, laughed like one demented as he said: 'That pince-nez will drive me mad, for the thing, mathematically speaking, is possible, but, humanly speaking, it is impossible – or then – or then – '

There came two light knocks on the door. Rouletabille partly opened it, and a head looked in. I recognised Mme Bernier, whom I had seen when she was being taken to the pavilion to answer the questions of the magistrate, and I was astonished, for I thought that she was still under lock and key. She said, in a very low tone of voice: 'In the crack of the floor!'

Rouletabille replied 'Thanks!' and the woman disappeared. He again turned towards me, after having carefully refastened the door. Then he uttered words which had no meaning to me, and as he spoke his eyes were haggard.

'If the thing is mathematically possible, why should it not be humanly possible? But if it is humanly possible, the affair is formidable!'

I interrupted him in his soliloquy.

'The concierges are at liberty, then?' I asked.

'Yes, I have had them set free. I need trustworthy persons. The woman is thoroughly devoted to me now, and the concierge would give his life for me. And since the pince-nez has glasses for a long-sighted person, I shall need the assistance of persons ready to die for me!'

'Oho!' I said. 'You seem to be speaking earnestly. When will the occasion occur?'

'Tonight, for I forgot to tell you, my friend – *tonight I expect the assassin.*'

'What! You mean this? You expect the assassin tonight? You know him, then?'

'Perhaps I know him! But I should be mad to affirm categorically at this moment that I know him, for the mathematical clue which I have of the assassin gives a result so frightful, so monstrous, that I hope it is still possible I am mistaken. Oh, I hope so, with all my heart!'

'How – since you did not know the assassin five minutes ago – can you say that you expect him tonight?'

'Because I know that he must come!'

Rouletabille filled his pipe very slowly and lit it, and this presaged a most captivating recital. At that moment someone was walking in the gallery, passing before our door. Rouletabille listened. The sound of the footsteps died away in the distance.

'Is Frédéric Larsan in his room?' I asked, pointing to the partition.

'No, he is not there,' my friend answered. 'He went to Paris this morning, still on the scent of Darzac, who also went off to Paris. All that will turn out very badly. I foresee that within a week M. Darzac will be arrested. The worst of it is that everything seems to go against him – events, facts, people. Not an hour passes without bringing some new evidence against him. The examining magistrate is overwhelmed by it, and sees nothing else. I cannot blame him, in the circumstances.'

'Yet Frédéric Larsan is not new at the game,' I said.

'I thought,' said Rouletabille, with a slightly contemptuous twist of the lips – 'I thought he was much cleverer. Of course, he is no fool. I had, indeed, a good deal of admiration for him before I knew his methods. They are deplorable. He owes his reputation solely to his cunning, but he lacks philosophy; the mathematics of his conceptions are very poor.'

I looked at Rouletabille, and could not help smiling on hearing this boy of eighteen talking about a man of fifty, who had given proofs of being the finest detective in Europe, as if he were a lad of fifteen.

'You smile,' he said; 'you are wrong! I swear to you that I will outdo him, and in a striking fashion! But I must make haste about it, for he has a colossal start – a start given him by M. Robert Darzac, which tonight will be increased still more. Think of it! Every time the assassin comes to the château M. Robert Darzac, by a strange fatality, is away from it, and flatly refuses to give any account of the employment of his time.'

'What do you mean – "every time the assassin comes to the château"?' I cried. 'Has he returned, then?'

'Yes, during that famous night, when the phenomenon occurred.'

I was at last going to hear about that phenomenon which Rouletabille had mentioned several times during the last half-hour without giving me any explanation. But I had learned never to press Rouletabille when he spoke, for he spoke only when the fancy took him, or when he judged it to be useful, and cared much less for my curiosity than for making a complete résumé for himself of any important event in which he was interested.

Presently, with short, rapid phrases, he apprised me of things so fantastic that, in truth, they made me feel as if I had lost the power of thinking, and even common sense itself. I was utterly bewildered. Indeed, the phenomena of that still unknown science called hypnotism, for example, are not more inexplicable than the disappearance of the body of the assassin at the very moment when four persons touched him! I speak of hypnotism as I would of electricity – the nature and laws of which are still practically unknown to us – because at the time it appeared that the affair could only be explained by the inexplicable – that is to say, by an event outside known natural laws. And yet, if I had had Rouletabille's brain, I should, like him, have had the presentiment of the 'natural' explanation, for the most remarkable point about the different mysteries of Glandier is undoubtedly the natural manner in which Rouletabille explained them. But who could have boasted then, and who, indeed, could boast today, of a brain like Rouletabille's? I have never seen on any other person's forehead extraordinary bumps such as he had, with the exception perhaps, of Frédéric Larsan's, although one had to look at the great detective very closely to notice the bumps, whilst Rouletabille's were prominent, and struck the eyes at once.

I have, among the papers that were handed to me by the young reporter after the case was over, a notebook of his, in which there happens to be a complete account of the 'phenomenon of the disappearance of matter' in the case of the assassin, and the reflections to which it gave rise in my young friend's mind. It is preferable, I think, to submit to the reader that account than to continue to reproduce my conversation with Rouletabille, for I would not like in such a faithful narrative to add a single word that was not the expression of the strictest truth.

Chapter 15

The trap

[extract from the Notebook of Joseph Rouletabille]

'Last night – the night between October 29 and 30' [writes Roule-tabille] – 'I woke towards one o'clock in the morning. Sleeplessness, or noise outside? The cry of the Good Lord's beast rings out with fearful loudness at the end of the park. I rise and open my window. Cold wind and rain; thick darkness and silence. I close the window again. Again that uncanny cry in the distance. I hastily slip on a pair of trousers and a coat. Outside the weather is awful. No one would turn even a cat out in it. Who, then, is imitating the mewing of Mother Agenoux's cat so close to the château? I seize hold of a cudgel – the only weapon in my possession – and, without making any noise, open my door.

'I am now in the gallery. A lamp with a reflector lights it perfectly. The flame of that lamp flickers; there is a draught; I feel it. I turn round. Behind me a window is open – the window at the extremity of the "turning gallery", where Larsan's and my room are – the gallery I call "turning" to distinguish it from the "straight" gallery, on which the apartment of Mlle Stangerson opens. These two galleries meet each other at right angles. Who has left that window open, or who has just opened it? I go to the window, and lean out. Four feet below there is a sort of verandah over the semicircular projection of a room on the ground-floor. One could at need jump from the window on to the verandah, and then drop into the main court of the château. Whoever entered that way had evidently not the key of the entrance-hall door. But why should I imagine that nocturnal gymnastic scene on account of an open window which has, perhaps, been left open by the negligence of a servant? I close it again, smiling at the facility with which I can build up a whole drama on the suggestion of an open window!

'Again the cry of the Good Lord's beast! Then silence. Then rain has ceased to beat on the window. All are asleep in the château. I walk with infinite precaution on the carpet of the gallery. On reaching the corner of the straight gallery, I put my head forward and peep out cautiously. In that gallery there is another lamp with a reflector, which illuminates clearly the three armchairs there and the pictures hanging on the wall. What am I doing here? Never has the château been quieter. Perfect silence reigns. What is the instinct that urges me towards Mlle Stangerson's room? Why does a voice within me cry, "Go on, to the door of Mlle Stangerson's room"? I look down upon the carpet on which I am treading, and see that my steps are being guided towards the room of Mlle Stangerson by the marks of steps that have already gone there! Yes, on the carpet are traces of muddy footsteps, and they lead to Mlle Stangerson's room! Horror! horror! I recognise instantly in those footprints the impression of the elegant boots, the footprints of the assassin! He has come, then, from the outside on this abominable night. If one can descend from the gallery by way of the window and the verandah beneath, one can also enter by the same way.

'The assassin is there, in the château, for there are no marks of returning footsteps. He entered the château by the open window at the extremity of the turning gallery; he passed Frédéric Larsan's door and mine; he turned to the right into the straight gallery, and entered the room of Mlle Stangerson. I am standing before the door of her ante-room; it is half-open. I push it without making the least noise. I am now in the ante-room. There, under the door of her room, I see a streak of light. I listen. No sounds – not even those of breathing. Ah, if I could only know what is passing in the silence behind that door! I examine the door. I find it is locked, and the key on the inner side. And to think that the assassin is, perhaps, there! He must be there! Will he escape this time? All depends on me. It needs a cool brain, and, above all, I must make no wrong move! I must see into that room. Shall I enter it by Mlle Stangerson's drawing-room? But if I do so I shall have to cross her boudoir, and the assassin would escape by the gallery door – the very door in front of which I am standing now.

'Tonight no crime has yet been committed, for there is total silence in the boudoir, where two servants, acting as nurses, are spending the night, and will remain until Mlle Stangerson is thoroughly restored to health.

'As I am almost sure that the assassin is there, why not at once raise the alarm? The assassin may, perhaps, escape, but I may thus save the life of Mlle Stangerson. What if the assassin tonight is not an assassin? The door has been opened to allow him to enter – by whom? – and it has been refastened – by whom? Mlle Stangerson every night shuts herself up in her apartment with her nurses. Who turned the key of that room to admit the assassin? The nurses? Two faithful servants – the old chambermaid and her daughter Sylvia? It is very unlikely. Besides, they sleep in the boudoir, and Mlle Stangerson – very nervous and prudent, M. Darzac told me – sees to her own safety, since she is able to move about her room, which I have not yet seen her quit. This nervousness and prudence on her part, which had struck M. Darzac, had given me also food for reflection. At the time of the crime of the Yellow Room there can be no doubt that she expected the assassin. Was she again expecting him? Who opened the door to the man who is there? Was it herself? She is bound to dread his coming. What extraordinary reasons can she have to be thus compelled to open the door to him? Ah, what would I not give to know!

'If there is such silence behind the door, it is, no doubt, because there is need for it. My intervention might do more harm than good. How can I tell? Nothing assures me that my intervention might not in a minute bring about a crime. Ah, to see and to know, without breaking that silence!

'I leave the ante-room, turn to the left, and go down the stairs. I am now in the entrance-hall, and as silently as possible make my way to the little room on the ground-floor where Old Jacques has been sleeping since the attack made at the pavilion.

'I find him dressed, his eyes wide open, almost haggard. He does not seem surprised to see me. He tells me he got up because he heard the cry of the Good Lord's beast, and also footsteps in the park close to his window. He then looked through that window, and a short while ago saw a black phantom pass by. I ask him whether he has a weapon. No, he no longer has one, since the examining magistrate took his revolver from him. We go together by a little back door into the park, and steal along the château to a point just below the window of Mlle Stangerson's room.

'There I place Old Jacques against the wall, ordering him not to move; then, taking advantage of a moment when the moon is hidden by a cloud, I walk to a place opposite the window, but out of the patch of light which comes from it – for the window is half-open. For what purpose? By way of precaution? As a means of escape in the event of someone suddenly entering the room? Anyone jumping from that window would run no small risk of breaking his neck! But the assassin may have had a rope? He is sure to have thought of everything. Oh, to know what is passing in that silent room! I return to Old Jacques, and whisper one word in his ear: "Ladder!" I thought at first of the tree which a week ago I used as a look-out, but I immediately saw, from the way the window was opened, I should not be able to see from the tree anything that was happening in the room. Besides, I want not only to see, but to hear, and to act.

'Old Jacques is greatly agitated, almost trembling. He disappears for a moment, and returns without the ladder, but making frantic signs to me to rejoin him quickly. When I get near him he gasps: "Come!"

'He leads me round the château to the keep. Arrived there, he says: "I went in search of my ladder in the lower room of the keep, which the gardener and I use for lumber. The door was open and the ladder gone. On coming out, there's where I caught sight of it by the moonlight."

'And he was pointing to the other end of the château, to a ladder resting against the stone buttresses supporting the verandah, under the window which I had found open. The projection of the verandah had prevented my seeing it. With the ladder it was quite easy to enter the turning gallery of the first-floor, and I had no longer any doubt of its having been the way taken by the unknown man.

'We run to the ladder, but just as we reach it Old Jacques draws my attention to the door of the little semicircular room, situated under the verandah, at the extremity of the right wing of the château. That door was ajar. Old Jacques pushes the door open a little farther, and looks in.

' "He's not there!" he whispers.

' "Who is not there?"

' "The gamekeeper!" With his lips once more to my ear, he adds: "You know that the gamekeeper lives in this room, for they are repairing the keep!"

'And again he points to the half-opened door, the ladder, the verandah, and the window in the turning gallery, which a short while ago I closed myself.

'What were my thoughts? Had I time to think? I felt more than I thought.

'Evidently, if the gamekeeper is up there in the room – I say if, because just at present, besides the ladder and the fact that the gamekeeper's room is empty, I have no ground to suspect him – if he is there, he has been obliged to use the ladder, and enter by that window; for, behind the room where he lives now, there is that of the butler and his wife, the cook, and farther back the kitchens, which make it impossible for him to reach by that way the front hall and staircase of the château. If it is the gamekeeper who went up there, it must have been easy for him to go yesterday evening under some pretext into the gallery, and fix the window in such a manner that it only needed to be pushed open from the outside for him to jump into the gallery. The fact of the unfastened window singularly narrows the field of search for the discovery of the assassin's personality. He must belong to the house, unless he has an accomplice, which I do not believe – unless – unless Mlle Stangerson herself saw that that window was not fastened on the inside. But, then, what could be the frightful secret which would compel her to remove the obstacles separating her from the assassin?

'I seize hold of the ladder, and we return to the back of the château. The window of Mlle Stangerson's room is still ajar; the curtains are drawn, but do not join, and allow a bright stream of light to pass and fall upon the path at our feet. Under the window I plant my ladder. I am almost sure that I have made no noise. And while Old Jacques remains at the foot of the ladder, I mount it very softly, my stout stick in my hand. I hold my breath. I lift my feet and place them on the rungs with the greatest care. Now a great cloud discharges itself in a fresh downpour. It is lucky for me! I shan't be heard at all!

'Suddenly I hear the sinister cry of the Good Lord's beast. I stop climbing. It seems to me to come from somewhere behind me, only a few yards away. If the cry is a signal. If some accomplice of the man has seen me on my ladder! Perhaps it calls the assassin to the window! Perhaps –

'Heavens! The man is at the window! I feel his head above me. I hear him breathe, and I cannot look at him. The least movement of my head, and I am lost! No; he goes. He has seen nothing. I feel, rather than hear him moving on tiptoe in the room, and I climb up a few more rungs. My head reaches to the level of the window-sill; my forehead rises above it; my eyes see between the two curtains.

'A man is there, seated at the little desk of Mlle Stangerson. He is writing. His back is turned to me. A candle is before him, but as he is bent over it the light throws shadows which give him a deformed appearance. I see nothing but a monstrous, stooping back.

'A bewildering fact! Mlle Stangerson is not there! Her bed has not been laid upon! Where, then, is she sleeping? Doubtless in the next room, with her nurses. A mere supposition. Joy of finding the man alone. Calmness of mind for preparing the trap.

'But who is this man, writing there before me, seated at this desk as if he were at home? If there were not the footprints of the assassin on the carpet in the gallery, the open window, and the ladder beneath that window, I might be led to believe that this man has a right to be there, and that he is there naturally, for ordinary reasons which I do not yet know. But there is no doubt that this mysterious person is the man of the Yellow Room, the man who made a terrible attempt on the life of Mlle Stangerson, the man she has not dared to denounce. Ah, to see his face, to surprise him, to capture him!

'If I spring into the room at this moment he will escape through the ante-room or by the door on the right which opens into the boudoir; then he will run through the drawing-room, reach the gallery, and I shall lose him. Now I have him. Another five minutes and I shall secure him better than if I had him in a cage! What is he doing there alone in Mlle Stangerson's room? What is he writing? To whom is he writing? [I descend and lay the ladder on the ground.] Old Jacques follows me. We re-enter the château. I send Old Jacques to wake M. Stangerson. He is to await me in the professor's room, and say nothing precise to him before I come. I have to go and awaken Frédéric Larsan. That's very annoying. I would have liked to work alone – to discover everything, and arrest the assassin under the very nose of Larsan fast asleep! But Jacques and M. Stangerson are old men, and I am not yet fully developed. I should not be strong enough, perhaps. Larsan is used to dealing with ruffians, with whom one has to wrestle, whom one throws to the ground – and who rise afterwards with handcuffs on their wrists. Larsan opens the door of his room. His eyes are swollen with sleep. He is ready to send me to the devil, for he doesn't in the least believe in my "junior reporter's fancies". I have to assure him that the man is there.

' "That's very strange," he says. "I thought I left him this afternoon in Paris!"

'He dresses himself in haste, and arms himself with a revolver. We steal quietly into the gallery.

' "Where is he?" Larsan asks.

' "In Mlle Stangerson's room."

' "And Mlle Stangerson?"

' "She is not in her room."

' "Let's go there."

' "Don't go there! The man, on the least alarm, will escape! He has three ways by which he may do so – the door, the window, the boudoir where the nurses are!"

' "I'll shoot him!"

' "And if you miss him – if you only succeed in wounding him? He'll escape again! Besides, he is certainly armed! No; let me arrange this, and I will answer for all!"

' "As you like," he replied, with fairly good grace.

'Then, after satisfying myself that all the windows of the two galleries were thoroughly secure, I placed Frédéric Larsan at the end of the turning gallery in front of the window which I had found open and had closed.

' "On no account," I said to Fred, "must you stir from this post till I call you. The chances are that the man will return to this window, and try to escape this way when he is pursued, for it is here he made his entrance and prepared for his flight. You have a dangerous post."

' "What will be yours?" asked Fred.

' "I shall spring into the room, and 'beat him up' towards you."

' "Take my revolver," said Fred, "and I'll take your stick."

' "Thanks," I said; "you are a good fellow!"

'I took it from him. I was going to be alone with the man who was writing in the room, and was really glad to have the revolver.

'I quitted Fred, having posted him at the window (No. 5 on the Plan), and went, still with the greatest precaution, to M. Stangerson's room in the left wing of the château. I found him with Old Jacques, who had faithfully obeyed my instructions, confining himself to telling his master to dress as quickly as possible. In a few words I explained to M. Stangerson what was happening. He also armed himself with a revolver, followed me, and we all three went quickly into the gallery. All this had taken about ten minutes. The professor wished to jump upon the assassin at once and kill him. I made him understand that, above all, he must not, in his desire to shoot him, miss him and let him escape.

'When I had sworn to him that his daughter was not in the room, and ran no danger, he controlled himself, and allowed me to direct the whole affair. I told M. Stangerson and Old Jacques that they should only come to me when called, or when I fired my revolver, and I sent Old Jacques to place himself before the window at the end of the straight gallery (No. 2 on the Plan). I chose that place for Jacques because I thought that the assassin, when tracked out of the room, would fly through the gallery towards the window which he had left open, and at once seeing at the angle of the two galleries that the window was guarded by Larsan, would pursue his course along the straight gallery. There he would encounter Old Jacques, who would prevent his jumping out of the window there into the park. Under this window there was a sort of buttress, while all the other windows in the galleries were at such a height above the ditches surrounding the château that it was almost impossible to jump from them without breaking one's neck. All the doors and windows, including those of the lumber-room at the end of the straight gallery, as I had rapidly assured myself, were firmly secured.

'Having thus indicated to Old Jacques the post he had to occupy, and having seen him take up his position, I placed M. Stangerson on the landing at the head of the stairs, not far from the door of his daughter's ante-room. Everything led me to suppose that when I came upon the assassin in the room he would fly by way of the ante-room rather than the boudoir where the women were, and the door of which must have been closed by Mlle Stangerson herself if, as I thought, she had taken refuge in the boudoir for the purpose of avoiding the assassin who was coming to see her. In any case, the man had to return to the gallery, where somebody was waiting for him at every possible egress.

'On reaching the gallery, he sees M. Stangerson on his left. He veers to the right towards the turning gallery, the way of his prepared flight. At the intersection of the two galleries he sees at once on his left, as I have explained, Frédéric Larsan at the end of the turning gallery, and opposite him Old Jacques at the end of the straight gallery. M. Stangerson and myself run behind him. He is ours! He can no longer escape us!

'The plan I had formed seemed to me the best, the surest, the most simple. It would, no doubt, have been simpler still if we had been able to place somebody behind the door of Mlle Stangerson's boudoir, which opened out on her bedroom. We should then have been in a position to besiege the two doors of the room in which the man was, but we could not penetrate the boudoir except by way of the drawing-room, the door of which had been locked on the inside by the anxious care of Mlle Stangerson. It was out of the question. But even if I had had the free arrangement of the boudoir, I should have held by the plan I have explained, because any other plan of attack would have separated us at the moment of the struggle with the man, whilst my plan united us all for the attack at a spot which I had selected with almost mathematical precision – the intersection of the two galleries.

'Having thus placed my people, I again went out of the château, hurried to my ladder, and, replacing it against the wall under the window of Mlle Stangerson's room, climbed up, revolver in hand.

'If there are readers who smile at so many precautionary measures, I refer them to the mystery of the Yellow Room and to all the proofs we had of the fantastic cunning of the assassin. Further, if there be readers who think my explanations needlessly minute at a time when they should be completely carried away by the rapidity of movement, decision, and action, I answer them that I wished to report here, at length and completely, all the details of a plan of attack conceived and executed as rapidly as it is slow in the narrative. This slowness and accuracy are necessary in order that nothing may be omitted from the narrative of the conditions under which the strange phenomenon was produced, and, until some natural explanation of it is forthcoming, it seems to me to prove, even better than the theories of Professor Stangerson, the dissociation of matter – I will even say the *instantaneous* dissociation of matter.'

Chapter 16

Phenomenon of the dissociation of matter
[extract from the Notebook of Joseph Rouletabille – continued]

'I am again near the window-sill' [continues Rouletabille], 'and again my head is above it. Between the curtains, the arrangement of which has not changed, I prepare to look, and am curious to know in what attitude I shall find the assassin. If only he has his back still turned towards me! If only he is still seated at the desk, and writing! But perhaps – perhaps he is no longer there? Yet, how could he have fled? Have I not possession of his ladder? I collect all my coolness and self-control. I raise my head still higher; I look. He is there! I see again his monstrous back, deformed by the shadow thrown by the candle – only he is no longer writing, and the candle is not on the desk. It is on the floor now, over which he is bending. A queer position, but it serves me.

'I breathe again. I climb a few more rungs. I am at the top of the ladder. With my left hand I take hold of the banister-rail. At the moment of success I feel my heart beat wildly. I place my revolver between my teeth. My right hand is now also holding on to the banister-rail. One jump, and I should be on the window-ledge. I hope the ladder won't – Alas! I am obliged to press on it heavily in order to raise myself, and hardly have my feet quitted the top rung when the ladder sways under me. It grates on the wall and falls, but already my knees are touching the stone, and by a lightning move-ment I pull myself over.

'But the assassin has been even quicker than I. He has heard the noise of the ladder against the wall. I saw the monstrous back of the man rise suddenly. He turned. I saw his face. Did I really see it? The candle on the floor only really lit his legs. Above his waist there was nothing but shadow and darkness. I saw a man with long hair and beard – a man with mad-looking eyes, a pale face framed by large whiskers. Their colour was red – at least, I think so, for it was very difficult to see properly, and, besides, I only had a glimpse of him. I did not know the man. That was the main impression I received from that face in the dim light in which I saw it. I did not know the face, or, at least, I did not recognise it.

'Ah! Now for rapid action! I had to be the wind, the hurricane, lightning itself! But, alas! there were some necessary movements to be made, and while I was making them – my knees on the window-ledge, my feet on the floor – the man, who had seen me at the window, had bounded to his feet, rushed – as I foresaw he would – to the door of the ante-room, had opened it, and fled. But I was already behind him, revolver in hand, shouting "Help!"

'Like an arrow I had darted across the room, but I had been able to notice a letter on the table. I almost overtook the man in the ante-room, for it took him a second or two to open the door and pass into the gallery. He banged the door on me, but I had wings, and was in the gallery only a few feet behind him. He had taken, as I supposed he would, the gallery on his right, the road he had prepared for his flight. "Help, Jacques! Help, Larsan!" I shouted.

'He could not escape us! I raised a shout of joy, a savage yell of victory. The man reached the junction of the two galleries hardly two seconds before M. Stangerson and I, and the meeting which I had calculated and prepared – the fatal shock which must inevitably take place at that spot – took place. We all met at the crossing-place, M. Stangerson and I coming from one end of the straight gallery, Old Jacques coming from the other end of the same gallery, and Frédéric Larsan coming from the turning gallery. But the man was not there!

'We looked at each other with stupid eyes, with terrified eyes, in face of this impossibility, of this "unreality". The man was not there!

' "Where is he? Where is he?" we all asked together.

' "He could not have escaped!" I cried in a fit of temper, for my anger was greater than my terror.

' "I actually touched him!" Frédéric Larsan exclaimed.

' "He was there! I felt his breath on my face!" cried Old Jacques.

' "We were touching him!" M. Stangerson and I repeated.

'And once more we all said, like maniacs, "Where is he? Where is he? Where is he?"

'We raced madly along the two galleries, we visited doors and windows. They were closed – hermetically closed. No one could have opened them, since we found them all shut. Besides, would not the opening of a door or window by this man whom we were hunting, without our having noticed it, have been more inexplicable still than his disappearance?

' "Where is he? Where is he?" He cannot have got away by a door, or a window, or any other means.* He could not have passed through our bodies.

'I confess that, on the moment, I felt "done for", for the gallery was well lighted, and there was neither trap nor secret door in the walls, nor any sort of hiding-place. We moved the armchairs and looked behind the pictures. Nothing! nothing! We would have looked inside the flowerpots if there had been any.'

* When this mystery, thanks to Rouletabille, was explained, in a perfectly natural way, by the help alone of the young man's prodigious logic, we were forced to realise that the assassin had not got away either by a window, a door, or by the stairs – a fact which the Law refused to admit.

Chapter 17

The mysterious gallery
[extract from the Notebook of Joseph Rouletabille – continued]

'Mlle Mathilde Stangerson appeared at the door of her ante-room.'
[continues Rouletabille in his notebook] 'We were near her door, in
the gallery, where the incredible phenomenon had just happened.
There are moments when one feels one's brain melting, as it were,
gradually away. A bullet in the head, a fractured skull, the seat of
logic crushed, reason shattered – all this is, no doubt, comparable
with the sensation which was exhausting – nay, "emptying" – me.

'Happily, Mlle Stangerson appeared. I saw her, and it was a divers-
ion from my chaotic state of mind. I inhaled the perfume of the lady
in black. Dear lady in black, whom I shall never see again! Ten years
of my life – half of my life, even – I would gladly give to see her again!
Alas! I only come across – and that very rarely – her perfume, or a
perfume similar to that, which reminds me of the past, and takes me
back to the little visitors'-room in the school of my youth!*

'It was this sharp reminder of the dear perfume which made me go
to the lady, dressed entirely in white, and so pale – so pale, so beautiful – standing near the mysterious gallery. Her gorgeous golden
hair, gathered up at the back of her neck, left visible the red star on
her temple, the wound that nearly caused her death. When I had
only just begun to "think out this affair from the right end", I
concluded that on the night of the mystery of the Yellow Room Mlle
Stangerson wore her hair in "bandeaux". But before I had been in the
Yellow Room, how could I have thought otherwise?

'And now, since the occurrence in the mysterious gallery, I no
longer think. I stand there, stupid, before the apparition, pale and

---

* When he wrote this Rouletabille was eighteen years of age, yet he spoke of his
youth! I have conscientiously reproduced his narrative, but wish to warn the
reader that the episode of the "perfume of the lady in black" has nothing to do
with the "Mystery of the Yellow Room." It is not my fault if, in the document I
am merely transcribing, Rouletabille details certain reminiscences.

lovely, of Mlle Stangerson. She is clad in a dressing-gown of dreamy white. One might take her for a sweet phantom. Her father takes her in his arms and kisses her passionately, as if he were recovering his lost child. She has been in danger, and he might easily have lost her again. He dare not question her. He draws her into her room. We follow them, for we want to know. The door of the boudoir is open. The terrified faces of the two nurses look towards us. Mlle Stangerson enquires the meaning of all the stir.

' "It's all very simple," she says. Very simple, indeed! She says the idea occurred to her not to sleep that night in her room, but in the boudoir with the nurses. She locked the door of the boudoir herself, for since the night of the crime she has felt sudden fears. What could be more likely?

'But who can imagine why on that particular night when "he" was to come, she, by mere chance, determined to shut herself in with the two women? Who can imagine why she does not now accept her father's offer to sleep in the drawing-room? Who can understand why the letter which a few moments ago I saw on the table in this room is no longer there? He who does understand all this will probably say: "Mlle Stangerson knew that the assassin was coming – she could not prevent his coming again – and she warned no one because the assassin had to remain unknown – above all, unknown to her father, unknown to all but to M. Robert Darzac." Yes, M. Darzac must know him now – perhaps knew him before. One should remember the phrase in the Élysée Garden: "Shall I have to commit a crime, then, to win you?" Against whom that crime, if not against the obstacle, against the assassin? One should always remember the words of Darzac in answer to my question: "Would it displease you that I should discover the assassin?" "I would kill him with my own hand!" And I replied: "You have not answered my question." Which was true. Indeed, indeed, M. Darzac knows the assassin so well that, whilst wishing to kill him himself, he fears lest I should discover him. He has assisted me in my inquiry only for two reasons – in the first place, because I forced him to; and, further, because she would be better guarded.

'I am in the room – in her room. I look at her, and I also look at the place where the letter was just now. She has taken possession of it. The letter was obviously for her – obviously. Ah, how she trembles! She trembles at the fantastic story told her by her father of the presence of the criminal in her room, and of the chase after him. But it is evident, it is quite plain, that she is not wholly satisfied by the assurance given her, until she is told that the assassin, by some incomprehensible means, by magic, has been able to escape.

'Then there is silence. Such a silence! We are all standing there looking at her – her father, Larsan, Old Jacques, and I. What thoughts are being woven in silence around her? After the mystery of the mysterious gallery, after the amazing and yet real presence of the assassin in her room, it seems to me that all our thoughts – from those labouring in the cranium of Old Jacques to those which were dawning in the brain of M. Stangerson – might all be expressed in these words to her: "Oh, you who know the mystery, explain it to us, and we shall be able to save you, perhaps!" Oh, how I long to save her – from herself and from that other! I cannot help crying as I watch her. Yes, my eyes fill with tears before so much misery, with so much concealed.

'She is there – she with the perfume of the lady in black. At last I see her in her room – in that room where she would never admit me; in that room where she remains ever silent. Since the fatal hour of the Yellow Room we have hung about this invisible and dumb woman to learn what she knows. Our desire, our will to know must be one more torment to her. Who can tell us that, if we do learn, the knowledge of her mystery would not be the signal for a tragedy more terrible than those which have already taken place? Who can tell us that it would not mean her death? Yet she nearly died, and we knew nothing – or, rather, there are some of us who know nothing. But I – if I knew "who", I should know all. Who – who? Not knowing "who", I must remain silent out of pity for her. For there is no doubt that she knows how he escaped from the Yellow Room, and yet keeps her secret. Why should I speak? When I know "who", I will speak to him – to him!

'She looks at us now, as if from afar – as if we were not in the room. M. Stangerson breaks the silence. He declares that henceforth he will not quit his daughter's room. In vain she tries to oppose his resolution; M. Stangerson firmly holds to his purpose. He will instal himself there, this very night, he says; then, thoughtful of the health of his daughter, he reproaches her for having left her bed. Now he talks to her as if she were a little child. He smiles at her; he hardly knows what he says or does. The illustrious professor is losing his head. We are more or less in the same state of mental collapse. Suddenly Mlle Stangerson says, "Father, father!" in a tone of such tender and intense distress that he bursts into a fit of sobbing. Old Jacques blows his nose, and Frédéric Larsan is obliged to turn aside to hide his emotion. For myself, I am done; I cannot think; I am unable to feel. I am thoroughly disgusted with myself.

'It is the first time that Frédéric Larsan has found himself face to face with Mlle Stangerson since the attack in the Yellow Room. Like me, he had insisted on being allowed to question the unfortunate lady; but he had not, any more than myself, been received. To him, as to me, the same answer had always been given: Mlle Stangerson was too weak to see us; the interrogatories of the examining magistrate fatigued her enough, as it was, etc. There was evidently the intention not to assist us in our researches, which never surprised me, but always astonished Frédéric Larsan. It is true that he and I had a totally different conception of the crime.

'They weep, and I still repeat to myself: "Save her – save her in spite of herself, without compromising her, without allowing him to speak! Who is 'he'? Who is the assassin? Take him and shut his mouth!" But M. Darzac has made it clear that, to shut his mouth, the man must be killed! That is the logical conclusion to be drawn from Darzac's words. Now, have I the right to kill the assassin of Mlle Stangerson? No; but let him only give me the chance! If only just to see whether he is really a creature of flesh and blood! Just to see his dead body, since we cannot capture him alive!

'Ah, how can I make this woman, who does not even look towards us, who is wholly absorbed by her fear and by the distress of her father, understand that I am capable of doing anything to save her? Yes, yes; I will once more attempt to "think out the affair from the right end", and I will work wonders!

'I move towards her. I would speak to her; I would entreat her to have confidence in me; I would, in a few words, make her understand – she and I alone – that I know how the assassin escaped from the Yellow Room, *that I have guessed the motives of her secret*, and that I pity her with all my heart. But she already makes a sign, begging us to leave her alone. She is weary; she needs immediate rest. M. Stangerson asks us to go back to our rooms, thanks us, dismisses us. Frédéric Larsan and I bow to him, and, followed by Old Jacques, we return to the gallery. I hear Larsan murmur: "Strange – very strange!" He makes a sign to me to enter his room. At the door he turns towards Old Jacques and asks: "You clearly saw him, did you not?"

'"Who?"

'"The man."

'"Saw him? I should think I did! He had a big red beard and red hair."

'"That's how he appeared to me," I said.

' "And to me also," said Larsan.

'The great Fred and I are alone now, talking in his room. We discuss the matter for an hour, turning it over and viewing it from every side. From the questions he asks me, from the explanations he gives, it is clear to me that, in spite of his eyes, in spite of my eyes, in spite of everyone, he is persuaded that the man disappeared by some secret passage in the château.

' "For he knows the château well," Larsan says to me – "he knows it thoroughly well."

' "He is a rather tall man, well built."

' "He is as tall as he wants to be," he murmurs.

' "I understand," I say. "But how do you account for his red hair and beard?"

' "Too much beard and too much hair – they are false," Fred explains.

' "That's easily said. You are always thinking of Robert Darzac. Can you not free yourself from that idea? I am certain Darzac is innocent."

' "So much the better. I hope he is. But everything combines to condemn him. You've noticed the marks on the carpet? Come and have a look at them."

' "I have seen them. They are the marks of the elegant boots, the same as were to be seen on the side of the lake."

' "Can you deny that they are those of Robert Darzac?"

' "No; but one may be mistaken."

' "Have you noticed that those footprints only go in one direction – that they are going to Mlle Stangerson's room, but do not return thence? When the man came from the room, pursued by us all, he left no footprints behind him!"

' "The man, perhaps, had been in her room for hours, and the mud on his boots had time to dry. Then he glided with such rapidity on the points of his toes! We saw him running, but we did not hear his steps."

'Suddenly I break off this useless chatter, void of reason, and unworthy of us. I make a sign to Larsan to listen.

'There is someone shutting a door below!

'I rise. Larsan follows me. We go down to the ground-floor. We step outside. I lead Larsan to the little semicircular room under the verandah, beneath the window of the turning gallery. I point to the door, now closed, but open a short while ago. A strip of light is visible under it.

' "The gamekeeper!" Fred exclaims.

' "Come on!" I whisper.

'Having decided – I know not why – to believe the Green Man the culprit – though I am not very sure of my own belief – I go to the door and rap smartly at it.

'Certain readers may think that this return to the gamekeeper's door is made rather late – that our first duty, after having found that the assassin had escaped us in the gallery, was to search everywhere else, around the château, and in the park.

'If such an objection is made, all I can answer is that the assassin had disappeared from the gallery in such a fantastic way that we really thought he was no longer anywhere! He had eluded us when our hands were outstretched to seize him – when we were almost touching him. No longer had we any ground for hoping that we could clear up the mystery of the night and the park. Besides, the disappearance of the man had almost maddened us.

'As soon as I rapped at the door it was opened, and the gamekeeper quietly asked us what we wanted. He was undressed, and ready to go to bed. The bed had not yet been disturbed.

'We entered.

' "Not yet gone to bed?" I said.

' "No," he replied bluntly; "I've been making a round of the parks and the woods. I am only just back, and I am sleepy."

' "Look here," I said, "a little while ago there was a ladder close by this window."

' "What ladder? I didn't see any ladder! Good night, gentlemen!"

'And he simply put us out of the room. When we were outside I looked at Larsan. He was impenetrable.

' "Well?" I said.

' "Well?" he repeated.

' "Does this not give you some new ideas?"

'There was no mistaking his ill-humour. On re-entering the château I heard him mutter: "It would be strange – very strange indeed – if I had been mistaken to that extent."

'And these words he said, as I thought, to me rather than to himself. Then he added: "In any case, we shall soon know what to think. Dawn will bring the light." '

Chapter 18

Rouletabille has drawn a circle between the two bumps on his forehead
[extract from the Notebook of Joseph Rouletabille – continued]

We parted on the threshold of our rooms after shaking hands in a melancholy sort of way. I was glad to have awakened some suspicion of being wrong in that original mind – extremely intelligent, but anti-methodical. I did not go to bed. I awaited the coming of day-light, and then went down to the front of the château. I walked round it, and examined every trace of footsteps coming towards it or going from it. But they were so mixed and confused that I could make nothing of them. Here I may remark that I do not, as a rule, attach undue importance to the external signs of a crime.

The method that consists of marking down the criminal from his footprints is altogether primitive. There are so many footmarks that are identical. One may use them as an indication, but they can never be considered as absolute proofs. However, I went in a disturbed state of mind into the deserted court of honour, and looked at all the footprints I could find there, seeking for some indication from which I might consider the events of the mysterious gallery.

Ah, to 'think it out from the right end!' Desperately I sat down upon a stone. What have I been doing for the last hour, if not the most elementary work of the ordinary detective? I have been court-ing error like any cheap inspector, about some footmarks which may make me say what they please – which will make me think as they please!

I find myself even more absurd, with less intelligence than those detectives invented by modern novelists. Oh, you story-detectives, who erect mountains of nonsense out of one footprint on the sand, or out of the impression of a hand on a wall! Their methods lead them to get innocent persons convicted – and you, Larsan, are nothing but one of those detectives, after all!

You have been able to convince the examining magistrate, the Chief of the Sûreté himself, and everybody else. You need only one more piece of evidence. Fool! You are still in want of the very first! All evidence supplied by the senses only is no proof. I, too, am inclining to superficial clues, but only so far as they may come within the 'circle traced out by the right end of my judgment'. This circle has often been very small indeed. But, small as it was, it was at the same time wide, for it contained nothing but the truth. Yes, yes; obvious signs have never been anything to me but servants; they never were my masters. They never made me that monstrous thing, a thousand times worse than a blind man – a man who cannot see straight. That is why, my dear Frédéric Larsan, I shall triumph over your error and your "instinctive" methods.

How stupid, how weak of me! Here I am, stooping over the ground, searching the mud for footprints. All this because, during the night, there happened in the mysterious gallery an event which did not seem to come within the 'circle of my judgment'!

Come, lift up your head, Rouletabille, my friend; it is impossible that the event of the mysterious gallery should be outside that 'circle'. You know it – you know it! Raise your head, then, press with your two hands the bumps on your forehead, and remember that when you formed that circle in your brain, like a geometrical figure on a sheet of paper, you began to 'think things out from the right end'.

Now go on; return to the mysterious gallery, relying on the 'right end of your judgment', as Frédéric Larsan leans upon his cane, and you will soon prove the great Fred nothing but a fool.

JOSEPH ROULETABILLE

October 30th, noon

As I thought, so I acted. My head on fire, I returned to the gallery, and without finding there anything more than I had seen last night, the 'right end of my judgment' told me a thing so dreadful that I had to pull myself together for fear of collapsing.

I shall, indeed, need strength now to unfold those further developments that I see in the ever-widening compass of my brain.

JOSEPH ROULETABILLE

October 30th, midnight

Chapter 19

Rouletabille invites me to lunch at the Castle Inn

It was not until much later that Rouletabille handed me the note-book in which the story of the phenomenon in the mysterious gallery had been put down by him at length on the morning following that enigmatical night.

The day when I rejoined him in his room at Glandier he told me, with full details, all that the reader now knows, including the employment of his time during the few hours he had spent in Paris that week, where he learned nothing that could be of any use to him.

The event of the mysterious gallery had occurred in the night between October 29th and 30th – that is to say, three days before my return to the château. It was on November 2nd, then, that I went back to Glandier, summoned by the telegram from my friend, and bringing the two revolvers with me.

All the time he was speaking he had fingered the convexity of the glasses of the pince-nez which he had found on the table, and I saw by the joy which he took in working with those long-sighted glasses that they must constitute one of those clues he could foresee within 'the circle of his judgment'. That strange and unique way of his, of expressing himself in strange terms, but equal to his thoughts, no longer surprised me; but one often needed to know what was in his mind to understand the words he used, and it was not easy to read Joseph Rouletabille.

The 'mind' – the faculty of thinking – of this boy of eighteen was one of the most remarkable things I have ever observed. Rouletabille went about without suspecting the astonishment, the bewilderment, which he met with wherever he went. I am sure that he did not in the least dream of the original and singular quality of his mind; and, like a person who is unconscious of the eccentricity of his appearance, he was at his ease wherever he happened to be. Yet his reasoning was so rapid, so accurate, so powerful in its simplicity that everyone marvelled.

When he had finished his story, Rouletabille asked me what I thought of it. I replied that his question greatly embarrassed me. He then begged me to try, in my turn, to 'think it out from the right end'.

'Well,' I said, 'it seems to me that the starting-point of my argument would be this: there can be no doubt that the assassin whom you pursued was in the gallery at a certain moment – '

I paused.

'Having begun so well, you ought not to be stopped so soon!' he exclaimed. 'Come, make a little effort!'

'I'll try. Since he was in the gallery, and disappeared from it without passing through any door or window, it must have been that he got away by some other opening.'

Joseph Rouletabille looked at me with pity, smiled negligently, and did not hesitate long before telling me that I reasoned like a child – or like Frédéric Larsan.

Rouletabille had alternate periods of admiration and contempt for the great Fred. Sometimes he would say, 'He is really clever!' sometimes he would growl, 'What a fool!' And his opinion depended – I often noticed it – upon whether the discoveries of Frédéric Larsan tallied with his reasoning, or contradicted it. It was one of the weak points in the character of this strange youth.

We had risen. He led me into the park. Just as we entered the court of honour, and were making for the gate, the sound of shutters thrown back against the wall made us turn our heads, and we saw at a window on the first-floor of the château the red, clean-shaven face of a man I did not know.

'Hallo!' muttered Rouletabille. 'Arthur Rance!'

He dropped his head, quickened his pace, and I heard him say between his teeth: 'Was he in the château last night? What has he come here for?'

When we had gone some distance from the château I asked my friend who this Arthur Rance was, and how he came to know him. He recalled to me his talk of that same morning, and reminded me that Mr Arthur William Rance was the American from Philadelphia with whom he had so freely clinked glasses at the Élysée reception.

'But was he not to have left France almost immediately?' I asked.

'Undoubtedly, and that's why I am so surprised at finding him still, not only in France, but at Glandier, of all places! He did not arrive this morning, and he did not arrive last night. He must have arrived before dinner, then! Why did not the concierges inform me?'

I remarked to my friend, with reference to the concierges, that he had not yet told me what he had done to set them at liberty.

It so happened that we were close to their lodge. On the threshold Bernier and his wife were watching us coming. A kind smile lit their happy faces. They did not appear to have retained any angry recollection of their imprisonment. My friend asked them at what time Arthur Rance had arrived. They answered that they did not know he was at the château. He must have called on the previous evening, but they had not opened the gate for him, because Mr Rance, being a great walker, and not wishing a carriage to be sent to meet him, was accustomed to alight at the station of the little hamlet of St Michel, whence he came on to the château through the forest. He reached the park by the grotto of Ste Geneviève, over the little gate of which he climbed, and thus found himself in the park.

As the concierges spoke, I saw Rouletabille's face cloud and exhibit a certain discontent – no doubt, discontent with himself. Evidently, he was rather vexed that, having worked so much on the spot – having so minutely studied the people and things at Glandier – he had yet to learn that Arthur Rance was accustomed to come to the château.

Much annoyed, he demanded an explanation.

'You say that Mr Arthur Rance often comes here? When did he last come?'

'We couldn't say exactly,' replied Bernier, 'seeing that we could know nothing while they were keeping us in prison; also, if the gentleman, when he comes to the château, does not pass through the gate, neither does he when he leaves.'

'Do you know when he came for the first time?'

'Oh, yes, monsieur! Nine years ago!'

'He was in France nine years ago, then?' said Rouletabille. 'But this time, how often has he come to Glandier, as far as you know?'

'Three times.'

'When did he come last, so far as you know?'

'About a week before the crime in the Yellow Room.'

Rouletabille again asked – this time of the woman: 'In the interstice in the floor?'

'In the interstice in the floor,' she replied.

'Thanks,' said Rouletabille. 'Get ready for tonight.'

He pronounced those words with a finger on his lips, to command discretion and silence.

We left the park, and walked towards the Castle Inn.

'Do you take your meals at this inn?' I asked.

'Sometimes.'

'But you also take your meals at the château?'

'Yes; Larsan and I are served, sometimes in my room, sometimes in his.'

'M. Stangerson has never invited you to his table?'

'Never.'

'Your presence in the château does not displease him?'

'I don't know. In any case, he does not act as if we were in his way.'

'He does not question you?'

'Never. His mind is still in a turmoil. He has not yet got over the astounding events of the Yellow Room. Remember, he stood at the door behind which his daughter was being assassinated. He broke open the door, and did not find any assassin. That kind of thing would upset anybody's mental balance. The professor is persuaded that as he at the time could not discover anything, there is no reason why we should discover anything now. But he has made it a duty, ever since Larsan's words about him, not to oppose what he calls our "illusions".'

Rouletabille was now once more lost in his reflections. At last he realised my presence, and told me how he had liberated the two concierges.

'I went recently,' he said, 'to M. Stangerson, taking with me a piece of paper, on which I asked him to write the following words: "I promise, whatever they may confess, to keep in my service my two faithful servants, Bernier and his wife", and to sign this paper. I explained to the professor that if he signed this, I would be able to make the concierges speak out, and I also declared that I was convinced they had nothing to do with the crime. He had shared this opinion from the first. The examining magistrate presented the signed document to the Berniers. They spoke. They said what I was certain they would say as soon as they were sure they would not lose their situation.

'They confessed that they poached on M. Stangerson's estate; that they were out poaching on the night of the crime, and happened to be near the pavilion at the moment when the attempt was made on Mlle Stangerson's life. The few rabbits they secured by poaching they sold to the landlord of the Castle Inn, who served them to his customers or sent them to Paris. That was the truth, and I had guessed it from the first. Do you remember what I said on entering the inn the first time? "We shall have to eat red meat now!" Those words I had heard in the morning, when we arrived at the park gate; and you also heard them, but you did not attach any importance to them. You recollect that, just as we reached that gate, we stopped to look at a man who was running along the wall, every moment consulting his watch. That man was Frédéric Larsan, who was already at work. Now, behind us, the landlord of the Castle Inn, standing on the steps of the inn, was saying to somebody inside, "We shall have to eat red meat now!"

'Why that "now"? When one is, as I am, in search of the most mysterious truth, one cannot afford to allow anything of what one sees or hears to escape. One has to find the meaning of everything. We had arrived in an out-of-the-way place which had been upset by a crime. Common sense led me to consider every word spoken around me as being a possible reference to the event of the day. "Now" meant to me "since the crime". From the very beginning of my inquiry, therefore, I sought to find a connection between that phrase and the drama. We went to lunch at the Castle Inn. I bluntly repeated the words, and saw, by Mathieu's surprise and trouble, that I had not, as far as he was concerned, exaggerated the importance of the phrase.

'I had, at the time, learned that the concierges had been placed under arrest. Mathieu spoke of them as of true friends whom one regrets. A very simple association of ideas formed in my mind, and I thought, "Now that the concierges are arrested, we shall have to eat red meat!" No more concierges, no more game. How was I led to think particularly of game? Very simply. The hatred expressed by Mathieu for M. Stangerson's gamekeeper – a hatred which, he pretended, was shared by the concierges – led me gently to the idea of poaching. Now, since the concierges could not have been in bed at the moment of the drama – which was perfectly obvious – why were they abroad that night? For the drama? I was not disposed to think so, and I already imagined, for reasons which I shall tell you later, that the assassin had no accomplice, and that the whole drama is a mystery between Mlle Stangerson and the assassin, with which the concierges had nothing to do.

'As far as the concierges were concerned, the poaching idea explained everything. Allowing it in principle, I searched for a proof in their lodge, which, as you know, I entered. I found there, under their bed, some springs and brass wire. "I have it!" I thought. "These things explain why the Berniers were out at night in the park." I was not astonished at their maintaining a dogged silence before the examining magistrate, even under so grave an accusation as that of being accomplices in the crime. They did not want to confess they had been poaching. Poaching would save them from the Assize Court, but it would lose them their situation; and as they were perfectly sure of their innocence in regard to the crime, they hoped this would soon be discovered, and that their poaching would continue to be unsuspected. There would always be time for them to speak before it was too late. I hastened their confession by the promise signed by M. Stangerson – a document which I handed to them myself. They gave all the necessary "proofs", were set at liberty, and conceived for me a deep gratitude. Why did I not have them released sooner? Because I was not sure that there was nothing more than poaching to be brought against them. I wanted to study the ground. As the days went by my convictions became more and more certain. The day after the events of the mysterious gallery, as I had need of some devoted persons, I decided to make the Berniers strongly attached to me by having them at once released from their captivity.'

I looked at Rouletabille, and once more I could not but be astonished at the simplicity of the reasoning which had led him to the truth in this matter of the suspected complicity of the concierges. Certainly it was a small matter, but I sincerely believed that very soon the young man would not fail to explain to us, with the same simplicity, the fantastic mystery of the Yellow Room, and that of the mysterious gallery.

We reached the Castle Inn, and walked in.

This time we did not see the landlord, but were received by the hostess with a pleasant smile. I have already described the room in which we found ourselves, and I have given an idea of the charming fair-haired woman with the gentle eyes who at once began to prepare our table.

'How's Mathieu?' asked Rouletabille.

'Not much better, Monsieur – not much better. He is still in bed.'

'Still his rheumatism?'

'Yes; last night I had again to give him an injection of morphine. It's the only thing that gives him any relief.'

She spoke in a soft voice. Everything about her expressed gentleness. She was truly a beautiful woman, a trifle indolent, with large, tender, caressing eyes. Mathieu must have been proud of such a wife. But what of her? Was she happy with her crabbed, rheumatic husband? The scene we had once witnessed did not lead us to believe that she could be; yet there was something in her general attitude that was not suggestive of despair. She vanished into the kitchen to prepare our luncheon, leaving on the table a bottle of excellent cider. Rouletabille poured it into earthenware mugs, filled his pipe, and quietly explained why he had sent for me, and asked for the revolvers.

'Yes,' he said, following with a dreamy eye the clouds of smoke he was puffing out – 'yes, my dear friend, I expect the assassin tonight.'

There was a brief silence, which I took care not to interrupt, and then Rouletabille went on: 'Last night, just as I was going to bed, M. Robert Darzac knocked at the door of my room. I opened it, and he confided to me that he was under the necessity of going the next morning – that is, today – to Paris. The reason which made this journey necessary was both peremptory – since it was impossible for him not to go – and mysterious, as he could not reveal to me the object of that journey. "I go," he said, "and yet I would give my life not to quit Mlle Stangerson at this moment." He did not hide from me that he believed her to be once more in danger. "If something happened in the course of the coming night," he added, "I should not be greatly surprised. Yet I go away – I must go away. I cannot be back at Glandier before the day after tomorrow, in the morning."

'I asked him to give me some kind of explanation, and this is all he said: this idea of a pressing danger threatening Mlle Stangerson had come to him wholly owing to the coincidence which existed between his absences and the attacks on her. On the night of the mysterious gallery incidents he had been obliged to be away from Glandier; on the night of the Yellow Room drama he was unable to be at the château – and, in fact, we knew he was not there. At least, we know it officially, from his own declaration. That M. Darzac should again absent himself today with such a thought in his mind must have been because he is obliged to obey a will stronger than his own. That is what I thought, and I said as much to him. He replied, "Perhaps!" I asked him whether the will stronger than his own was Mlle Stangerson's. He gave me his word it was not, and said his decision to go to Paris had been taken without any instructions from her.

'In short, he repeated that his belief in the possibility of a fresh attack being made on her was wholly based on the extraordinary coincidence which he had noticed, and which the examining magistrate himself had mentioned to him. "If anything happened to Mlle Stangerson," he said, "it would be terrible for her and terrible for me; for her, because she would be once more between life and death; for me, who could not defend her in case of attack, and unable to say where I had spent the night. Now I quite understand the suspicions that weigh upon me. The examining magistrate and Frédéric Larsan – the latter shadowed me the last time I went to Paris, and I had all the trouble in the world to get rid of him – are not far from believing me guilty."

' "Why do you not at once tell the name of the assassin, since you know it?" I cried.

'M. Darzac appeared extremely troubled by my question, and replied to me in a tone of hesitation: "I – I know the name of the assassin? Who could have told it to me?"

'I at once replied: "Mlle Stangerson."

'Then he became so pale that I thought he was going to faint, and I saw that I had struck home. *Both Mlle Stangerson and he knew the name of the assassin.* When he had recovered himself, he said to me: "I shall leave you now, Monsieur. While you have been here I have been able to appreciate your exceptional intelligence and your unequalled ingenuity. I have a service to ask of you. I am, perhaps, wrong to fear that an attack will be made during the coming night; but, as one must act with foresight, I rely on you to make such an attack impossible. Take all needful steps to isolate, to guard Mlle Stangerson. Watch about her room like a good watch-dog. Do not sleep. Do not allow yourself a single moment's rest. The man we dread is prodigiously cunning; his cunning has probably never been equalled in the world. That very cunning will save Mlle Stangerson if you watch, for it is impossible that he should not know that you are watching, because of his great cunning. And, knowing that, he will not venture to attempt anything."

' "Have you spoken of all this to M. Stangerson?"

' "No."

' "Why not?"

' "Because I do not wish M. Stangerson to say to me, as you did just now: 'You know the name of the assassin!' If you are surprised at my words, 'The assassin may come tonight', you can readily imagine what M. Stangerson's amazement would be if I spoke them to him. I have told you all this, M. Rouletabille, because I have a very great confidence in you. I know that you do not suspect me."

'The poor man was speaking as well as he could, by fits and starts. He was suffering. I pitied him, the more so because I felt sure that he would rather be killed than tell me who the assassin was, just as Mlle Stangerson would sooner allow herself to be assassinated than denounce the man of the Yellow Room and of the mysterious gallery. That man must have a terrible hold on her, or on them both, in a terrible manner, and they must dread nothing so much as that M. Stangerson should learn that his daughter is in the power of her assassin.

'I promised M. Darzac to watch through the whole of the night. He insisted that I should organise a really impassable barrier round

Mlle Stangerson's room, the boudoir where the nurses were sleeping, and the drawing-room where, ever since the affair of the mysterious gallery, M. Stangerson had slept – that is, round the whole of her apartments.

'By his insistence I understood that M. Darzac asked me, not only to make it impossible for the expected man to reach Mlle Stangerson's room, but to make that impossibility so clear that the man should at once realise the situation, and disappear without leaving any trace of his approach. That was how I explained to myself the final words with which he took leave of me: "When I am gone, you may speak to M. Stangerson of your suspicions for tonight; also to Old Jacques, to Frédéric Larsan, to everybody in the château, and so organise until my return a watch which, in the eyes of all, will be entirely your idea."

'The unfortunate man went off, not knowing quite what he was saying, for my silence and my eyes unmistakably told him that I had guessed three-quarters of his secret. Yes, yes; truly he must have been at his wits' end to have come to me at such a moment, and to abandon Mlle Stangerson, with that terrible idea of "coincidence" in his mind.

'When he had gone I thought the whole matter over. I realised that I must be more cunning than cunning itself, so that the man, if he should go during the night to Mlle Stangerson's room, would not for a second suspect that his coming had been expected. Yes, that was the idea – to prevent him from entering, even if he had to be shot, but to allow him to go far enough, so that, dead or alive, one should clearly see his face. For he must be got rid of; Mlle Stangerson must be freed from this constant danger of assassination!

'Yes, my friend,' said Rouletabille, after having placed his pipe on the table and emptied his mug of cider, 'I must distinctly see the fellow's face, so as to make sure that it is the one I have seen within the "circle of my judgment".'

At that moment the hostess reappeared, bringing the traditional bacon omelette. Rouletabille chaffed her a little, and she took it with the most delightful good-humour.

'She is much gayer when Mathieu is confined to his bed with rheumatism than when he is about the place and well,' Rouletabille remarked softly.

But I had no eyes, either for Rouletabille's little game, or for the smiles of the hostess. I was entirely absorbed in the last words of my young friend, and in the strange request Darzac had made to him.

When he had finished eating his omelette, and we were again alone, Rouletabille went on: 'When I sent you my telegram the first thing this morning, I had only the word of M. Darzac that "perhaps" the assassin would come tonight. Now I can tell you that he will *certainly* come. I expect him.'

'What gave you that certainty? Is it – '

Rouletabille interrupted me: 'Don't, dear boy; you're sure to make a silly remark. I know what you want to say.' Then he added: 'I have been sure that he would come since half-past ten o'clock this morning – that is to say, before your arrival – and, consequently, before we saw Arthur William Rance at the window in the court of honour.'

'Really!' I said. 'But tell me, why have you been sure since half-past ten?'

'Because at half-past ten I had the proof that Mlle Stangerson was making as many efforts to allow the assassin to enter her room tonight as Robert Darzac, in addressing me, had taken precautions against his entering it!'

'Is it possible?' I exclaimed. Then I whispered: 'But have you not told me that Mlle Stangerson adores M. Darzac?'

'I told you so, because it is the truth.'

'Then you don't think it strange – '

'Everything in this affair is strange, my friend; but take my word for it, the strangeness of which you know is nothing to the strangeness that awaits you!'

'One should have to admit, then,' I said, 'that Mlle Stangerson and her assassin have relations together – at least, they write to one another – '

'Admit it, my friend – admit it! You risk nothing. I have told you about the letter left on the table by the assassin on the night of the mysterious gallery affair – the letter which disappeared into the pocket of Mlle Stangerson. Who can deny, then, that in that letter the assassin commanded her to grant him a meeting, and also that as soon as he was sure of Darzac's departure, he made it known to her that the meeting must be for tonight?'

My friend laughed silently. There were moments when I wondered whether he was not laughing at me!

The door of the inn opened. Rouletabille was on his feet so quickly that one might have thought he had been lifted from his seat by an electric discharge.

'Mr Arthur Rance!' he exclaimed.

The American stood before us, phlegmatically bowing.

Chapter 20

An act of Mlle Stangerson

'You recognise me, Monsieur?' asked Rouletabille.

'Perfectly well,' replied Arthur Rance. 'I recognise in you the little boy at the buffet.' [The face of Rouletabille turned crimson with anger at being called a 'little boy'.] 'And I have come down from my room to shake hands with you. You're a jolly little boy!'

The American stretched out his hand. Rouletabille's brow relaxed. He shook hands, and introduced Mr Arthur Rance to me, and then invited him to share our luncheon.

'No, thanks! I am lunching with M. Stangerson.'

Arthur Rance spoke our language perfectly, almost without accent. Rouletabille said: 'I did not expect to have the pleasure of seeing you again, Monsieur. Were you not to have left our country the next day, or two days after the reception at the Élysée?'

My friend and I, apparently indifferent during this conversation, lent a very attentive ear to every word spoken by the American.

The purple-red face of the man, his heavy eyelids, certain nervous twitchings – all were proofs of his addiction to drink. How came it that this sorry specimen of humanity was the guest of M. Stangerson, and even a friend of his?

I was to learn a few days later from Frédéric Larsan, who, like ourselves, had been surprised at the presence of the American at the château, that Mr Arthur Rance had only been a drunkard for about the last fifteen years – that is to say, only since the departure of the professor and his daughter from Philadelphia. At the time when the Stangersons lived in the United States they had been on very intimate terms with Arthur Rance, who was one of the most distinguished phrenologists of the New World. Thanks to original experiments, he had been able to make the science of Gall and Lavater progress considerably. Then it has to be remembered, to explain the intimacy with which Mr Rance was received at Glandier, that he had one day rendered a great service to Mlle Stangerson by stopping, at the peril of his life, the runaway horses of her carriage. It was even probable that the outcome of that incident had led to considerable intimacy between him and the professor's daughter, but to nothing that could be termed love.

Where had Frédéric Larsan picked up this information? He did not tell me, but he appeared to be pretty sure of his statements.

If we had known these details at the moment when Arthur Rance joined us at the Castle Inn, it is probable that his presence at the château would not have puzzled us, but they could not have failed to increase the interest which we took in this new personage. The American must have been about forty-five years of age. He answered in a perfectly natural tone the question of Rouletabille.

'When I heard of the attempt on her life, I put off my return to the States. I wished to assure myself that Mlle Stangerson had not been mortally injured, and I shall not leave until she is quite well again.'

Arthur Rance then took the lead in the conversation, withholding answers to some of Rouletabille's questions, giving us, without our inviting him to do so, his personal ideas on the subject of the drama – ideas which, as well as I could make out, were not far from Frédéric Larsan's. He mentioned no name, but one did not need to be very clever to realise what his opinion really was. He told us that he knew of the efforts young Rouletabille was making to unravel the tangled skein of the Yellow Room mystery. He explained that M. Stangerson had told him all that had taken place in the mysterious gallery. While listening to Mr Rance one constantly had the impression that he had Robert Darzac in his mind. Several times he expressed regret that M. Darzac was absent from the château when all those dramatic events were occurring, and his meaning was perfectly clear. Finally, he expressed the opinion that M. Darzac had been well inspired, very clever, in installing himself on the spot, as M. Joseph Rouletabille was bound, sooner or later, to discover the assassin! The last words he said were obvious irony. Then he rose, bowed to us, and left the inn.

Rouletabille watched him through the window, and said: 'A singular person, that!'

I asked: 'Do you think he'll spend the night at Glandier?'

To my amazement, the young reporter replied that 'it was a matter of total indifference to him'!

I passed on to the question of our programme for the afternoon. All I need say is that Rouletabille took me to the grotto of Ste Geneviève, and all the time he affected to speak of anything but that which was on his mind. In this way evening came. I was astonished not to see him make any of the preparations I had expected. I spoke to him about it when night was come, and we were together in the room. He replied that all his arrangements were already made, and that the assassin this time could not escape him.

As I expressed some doubt, reminding him of the man's disappearance in the gallery, and that the same thing might occur again, he replied that he hoped it would – that, in fact, it was exactly what he wished to occur this time. I did not insist, knowing by experience how useless and tactless it would have been. He told me, however, that from early morning, by his care and that of the concierges, the château had been watched in such a manner that nobody could approach it without his being informed, and that so long as no one came from outside, he was perfectly easy with regard to the persons inside the château.

It was then half-past six by the watch he drew from his waistcoat-pocket. He rose, made me a sign to follow him, and, without taking any precaution, without trying to deaden the sound of his footsteps, without enjoining silence, he led me through the gallery. We reached the straight gallery, and went along it to the landing, which we crossed. We then continued our way along the same gallery, but in the left wing, and passed Professor Stangerson's apartment.

At the end of that gallery, before the keep was reached, there was a room which was then occupied by Arthur Rance. We knew that, because we had seen the American at the window which looked out on the court of honour. The door of that room stood across the gallery, and so terminated it in the left wing. It directly faced the east window at the end of the straight gallery (right wing), where Rouletabille had placed Old Jacques on the famous night, and commanded an uninterrupted view of the straight gallery from end to end of the château – left wing, landing, and right wing. Naturally, one could not see from there the turning gallery in the right wing.

'That turning gallery,' said Rouletabille, 'I reserve for myself. You, when I ask you to do so, will come here and do what I may beg you.'

And he made me enter a little dark triangular closet built in a bend of the wall to the left of the door of Arthur Rance's room. From this recess I could see all that took place in the gallery as well as if I had been in front of Arthur Rance's door, and I was able to watch that door as well. The door of the closet, which was to be my place of observation, was fitted with a glass window. It was quite light in the gallery, where all the lamps were burning. It was quite dark in the closet, which thus formed a capital place for a spy.

For what was I doing there, if not playing the part of a spy, or vulgar detective? It was repugnant to me, and, in addition to my natural instincts, was not the dignity of my profession opposed to such an occupation? If the President of the Corporation of Barristers had seen me! If they heard of my conduct at the Law Courts, what would the Bar Council say? Rouletabille did not even suspect that I should think of refusing the service he asked, and, in fact, I did not refuse him. In the first place, I should have feared to be taken by him for a coward; secondly, I reflected that I might always pretend that it was right to seek the truth, as a lover of it, in every place or direction; and, finally, because it was too late for me to draw back. Why had I not these scruples sooner? Because my curiosity was stronger than all else. Moreover, I could say that I was going to help save a woman's life, and there are no professional rules to forbid so noble a purpose.

We returned along the gallery. As we reached the door of Mlle Stangerson's apartment it was opened by the butler, who was serving at the dinner-table – M. Stangerson had for three days dined with his daughter in her drawing-room – and, as the door remained ajar, we distinctly saw Mlle Stangerson, taking advantage of the butler's absence, and of the fact that her father was stooping to pick up something he had dropped on the floor, pour the contents of a phial into his glass.

Chapter 21

On the watch

This act, which staggered me, did not appear greatly to affect Roule-tabille. We returned to his room, and, not even speaking of the scene we had just witnessed, he gave me his final instructions for the night. We were first going to dine. After dinner I was to go to the dark closet, and wait there as long as was necessary for the purpose of seeing anything.

'If *you see* before me,' he explained, 'you must let me know. You will see sooner than I shall if the man reaches the straight gallery by another way than by the turning gallery, since you will have a view along the whole length of the straight gallery, while I shall only command a view of the turning gallery. To warn me, you will merely undo the cord holding the curtain of the window which is nearest the dark closet. The curtain will fall of itself, and cause at once a square of shadow where there had been previously a square of light, since all the lamps in the gallery are lit. To do this, you need only stretch your hand out of the closet, for the curtain is within easy reach. I will be in the turning gallery. One sees through the windows there all the squares of light in the straight gallery. When *your* square disappears I shall understand.'

'And then?'

'Then you will see me appear at the corner of the turning gallery.'

'What am I to do then?'

'You will immediately come towards me, keeping behind the man, but I shall already be upon him, and shall have seen whether his face *comes within my circle*.'

'The circle which you have traced by the aid of your reason?' I added, with a smile.

'Why do you smile? It is quite unnecessary! However, take advantage of the few moments that remain to amuse yourself, for I swear to you that in a few moments you will see no occasion for laughter!'

'And if the man escapes?' I asked.

'So much the better!' said Rouletabille phlegmatically. 'I don't want to capture him. He may take himself off down the stairs and by the entrance-hall on the ground-floor, and that before you reach the landing, since you are at the far end of the gallery. I will let him go after I have seen his face. That's all I want. Afterwards I shall arrange matters in such a way that the man will cease to exist for Mlle Stangerson, even although he continues to live. If I took him alive Mlle Stangerson and M. Darzac would, perhaps, never forgive me, and I wish to preserve their esteem. They are noble souls.

'When I see Mlle Stangerson empty a sleeping-draught into her father's glass so that he may not be awakened tonight by the conversation which she is going to have with her assassin, you may imagine that her gratitude to me would be rather small if I took to her father the man of the Yellow Room and the mysterious gallery with his hands bound and his mouth open! It is, perhaps, a great piece of luck that on the night in the mysterious gallery the man vanished as by magic. I understood as much when I noticed the radiant look of relief which illuminated the features of Mlle Stangerson as soon as she learned that he had escaped. I have come to understand that, to save the unfortunate lady, it is less important to capture the man than to close his mouth, whatever the means used for the purpose. But to kill a man – to kill a man! That's no trifle! Besides, it's no business of mine, unless the man makes it impossible for me to deal with him otherwise. On the other hand, to compel him to silence without any help or information from the lady is a task that involves the guessing of everything, with nothing to go upon. Fortunately, my friend, I have guessed – or, rather, I have reasoned – and I only ask of the man who is coming tonight to show me his face, so that it may enter – '

'Into your mental circle?'

'Exactly! And his face will not surprise me.'

'But I thought you already saw his face on the night when you sprang into the room?'

'Imperfectly. The candle was on the floor, and, then, his long beard.'

'This evening he will not have it?'

'I think I can say for certain that he will. But the gallery is light, and now I know – or, at least, my brain knows – and my eyes will see.'

'If the whole matter consists in seeing him, and allowing him to escape, why are we armed?'

'Because, if the man of the Yellow Room and of the mysterious gallery knows that I know, he is capable of anything. Then we shall have to defend ourselves!'

'And are you sure he will come tonight?'

'I am positive! Mlle Stangerson, at half-past ten o'clock this morning, in the cleverest way in the world, arranged to be without her nurses tonight. She gave them leave of absence for twenty-four hours under some plausible pretext, and has expressed a wish to have only her father to watch over her while they are away. He is to sleep in the boudoir, and has accepted his new duty with grateful joy. The coincidence of M. Darzac's departure (after what he had said to me), and the exceptional precautions of Mlle Stangerson to ensure her being alone, do not leave room for doubt. The coming of the assassin, which Darzac dreads, Mlle Stangerson is herself preparing.'

'That is terrible!'

'Yes.'

'And what we saw her do was to send her father to sleep?'

'Yes.'

'In short, for tonight's business, we are but two?'

'Four. The Berniers will watch. It is better so, though I think their watch will be useless. But Bernier may be useful to me afterwards if there is any killing.'

'You think, then, there may be?'

'Yes, if *he* wishes it.'

'Why did you not warn Old Jacques? You make no use of him today?'

'No!' replied Rouletabille, in a sharp tone.

I remained silent for a while; then, desirous of getting at the bottom of Rouletabille's mind, I asked him point-blank: 'Why not tell Arthur Rance? He may be of great assistance to us.'

'Look here!' said Rouletabille, with irritation. 'Do you want to let everybody into Mlle Stangerson's secrets? Let us go to dinner; it is time. This evening we dine with Larsan in his room, unless he is still at the heels of M. Darzac! He sticks to him like a leech! But never mind! If he is not there now, I am quite sure he will be there tonight. That's a fellow I am going to beat at his own game.'

At that moment we heard a noise in the next room.

'It must be Frédéric Larsan,' said my friend.

'I forgot to ask you,' I said. 'When we are with the detective, we are not to make the slightest reference to tonight's expedition? Is that the idea?'

'It goes without saying. We are working alone tonight – entirely for ourselves.'

'And all the glory will be for us – '

Rouletabille laughed, and replied: 'Just so!'

We dined with Frédéric Larsan in his room. We found him there. He told us he had only just arrived, and invited us to sit at the table. The dinner passed in a very congenial way, and I had no difficulty in understanding that the cheerfulness of Rouletabille and Larsan was due to the feeling of certainty they each experienced of having the solution at last.

Rouletabille told the great Frédéric that I had come on my own account to see him, and that he had kept me to help him in the heavy task of writing he had to get through that night for the *Époque*. I was going back to Paris, he said, by the eleven o'clock train, taking his 'copy' with me, which was a sort of *feuilleton*, in which he recounted the principal events of the mystery of Glandier. Larsan smiled at this explanation, like a man who is not deceived, but refrains out of politeness from expressing the least opinion about things which do not concern him.

Using a thousand precautions in their language, and even in the intonation of their voices, Larsan and Rouletabille conversed at length on the subject of Mr Arthur Rance's presence at the château, of his past in America, about which they both wished they knew more – at least, so far as his relations with the Stangersons were concerned. At one moment Larsan, who seemed to me to be unwell, said with an effort: 'I think, M. Rouletabille, that we've not much left to do now at Glandier, and that we shall not sleep here many more nights.'

'That's what I think, M. Frédéric.'

'You think, then, my friend, that the whole affair is finished?'

'I do, indeed, think that the affair is now finished, and that we have nothing more to find out,' Rouletabille retorted.

'Do you realise who the assassin is?'

'And you?'

'I do.'

'So do I,' said Rouletabille.

'Can it be the same person we two – '

'I don't think so, unless you have changed your mind,' said the young reporter, interrupting Larsan; and he added with great emphasis: 'M. Darzac is an honest man!'

'Are you sure of that?' asked Larsan. 'Well, I am sure of the contrary! It's a fight between us, then?'

'Yes, a fight. *And I shall beat you*, M. Frédéric Larsan!'

'Youth never doubts anything,' said the great Frédéric in conclusion, laughing, and holding out to me his hand.

Rouletabille repeated like an echo: 'Never – anything.'

Suddenly Larsan, who had risen to bid us good night, pressed both his hands to his chest, and staggered. He had to lean on Rouletabille to save himself from falling. He had grown extremely pale.

'Good Heavens!' he cried. 'What is the matter with me? Can I have been poisoned?'

He looked at us with haggard eyes. Vainly we questioned him; he did not answer us. He had sunk into an armchair, and we could not get a word from him. We were extremely anxious, both on his account and on our own, for we ourselves had partaken of all the dishes of which Frédéric Larsan had eaten. At last he seemed to be out of pain, but his heavy head had fallen back, and his tightly closed eyelids concealed his eyes. Rouletabille stooped over him, and listened to the beating of his heart.

When he rose, my friend's face was as calm as a minute before it had been agitated. He said: 'He is asleep.'

He led me to his room, after having closed the door of Larsan's room.

'It was the sleeping-draught?' I asked. 'Does Mlle Stangerson wish to send everybody to sleep tonight?'

'Perhaps,' replied Rouletabille, who was thinking of someone else.

'But we – What about us?' I exclaimed. 'How do we know that we have not been dosed with the same sleeping-draught?'

'Do you feel indisposed?' Rouletabille asked, with perfect self-control.

'Not in the least.'

'Do you feel at all sleepy?'

'No.'

'Well, then, my friend, smoke this excellent cigar.'

And he handed me a choice Havana which M. Darzac had given him, while he lit his pipe – his eternal pipe!

We remained in his room until ten o'clock without a word being said by either of us. Buried in an armchair, Rouletabille smoked. He seemed thoughtful, and his eyes had a far-away look. At ten o'clock he took off his boots, and made a sign to me to do the same. When we were in our socks, he said, so low that I guessed rather than heard the word he uttered.

'Revolver!'

I drew my revolver from my coat-pocket.

'Cock it!' he whispered.

I did as he directed.

Then he moved towards the door of the room, opened it with infinite precaution, so that it made no sound. We were now in the turning gallery. Rouletabille made another sign to me. I understood that I was to take up my position in the dark closet.

When I was some distance from him he rejoined me and embraced me; then I saw him, with the same cautiousness, returning to his room. Astonished by his salute, and somewhat disquieted by it, I arrived at the straight gallery without difficulty, crossed the landing, and reached the dark closet.

Before entering it I examined the cord of the curtain. I found I had merely to touch the cord with one finger for the curtain to fall by its own weight, and thus hide the square of light from Rouletabille – the signal agreed upon. The sound of a footstep made me stop before the door of Arthur Rance's room. He was not yet in bed, then. But how was it that he was in the château at all, since he had not dined with M. Stangerson and his daughter? At least, I had not noticed him at the table with them when we saw the act of Mlle Stangerson.

I withdrew into the dark closet. I was perfectly comfortable in there. I saw the whole extent of the gallery. Clearly, nothing whatever could happen there without my seeing it. But what was going to happen there? Something, perhaps, of the gravest import. Again I thought of Rouletabille's disquieting embrace. People do not salute their friends in that way except on great occasions, or when they are about to incur danger. I was going to incur danger, then?

My hand closed on the butt of my revolver, and I waited. I am no hero, but I am not a coward.

I waited for about an hour. During that interval I noticed nothing unusual. Out of doors the rain, which had fallen violently towards nine o'clock, had now ceased.

My friend had told me that nothing, probably, would occur before midnight or one o'clock in the morning. It was hardly half-past eleven, however, when I heard the door of Arthur Rance's room open. I heard the slight creaking it made as it turned on its hinges. It was as if it had been pushed from inside with the greatest stealth. The door remained open for a minute, which seemed a long time to me. As this door opened into the gallery – that is to say, out-wards – I could not see what was happening in the room or behind the door.

Just then I heard a strange noise, repeated for the third time, and coming from the park. I had attached no more importance to it than one does to the howling of cats wandering in the gutters at night-time. But the third time the mewing was so sharp and odd that I recalled what I had heard about the cry of the Good Lord's beast. As, down to that day, the cry had accompanied every tragedy at Glandier, I could not help shuddering at it.

Directly afterwards I saw a man appear outside the door, and close it after him. I could not at first recognise him, for he turned his back to me, and was stooping over a rather large parcel. Having closed the door and picked up the parcel, he turned towards the dark closet, and then I saw who he was. The man who was coming out of Arthur Rance's room was the gamekeeper – the Green Man. He had on the same costume as he was wearing when I saw him on the road in front of the Castle Inn the first day I came to Glandier, and which he wore when Rouletabille and I met him coming out of the château. No doubt it was the gamekeeper. As the cry of the Good Lord's beast was sounding for the fourth time he put down his parcel in the gallery, and went to the second window from the dark closet. I did not move, fearing to betray my presence.

When he stood at the window he put his head against the glass panels and peered into the park. He remained in that position for half a minute. The night was lit at intervals by the moon, which would disappear suddenly behind heavy clouds. The Green Man raised his arms twice, making signs which I did not understand; then, leaving the window, he again took up the parcel and moved along the gallery to the landing.

Rouletabille had directed me: 'When you see anything, undo the cord that holds up the window-curtain.' I was certainly 'seeing something'! Was this what Rouletabille expected? That was not my business, and I had only to do what I had been told. I unfastened the cord. My heart was beating as if it would burst. The man reached the stair-landing, but, to my amazement, just as I expected him to continue his way along the gallery, I saw him descend the stairs leading to the entrance-hall.

What was I to do? I looked, bewildered, at the heavy curtains, which had now dropped before the window. The signal had been given, and yet I did not see Rouletabille appear at the corner of the turning gallery. Nothing happened. Nobody came. I was greatly perplexed. Half an hour passed, which seemed an age to me. What was I to do now, even if I saw anything else unusual? The signal had been given; I could not give it a second time. On the other hand, to venture into the gallery at that moment might upset all Rouletabille's plans. After all, I had nothing to reprove myself with, and if anything unexpected by my friend had happened, he could only blame himself for it. Being no longer able to be of any assistance by warning him, I took the risk. I left the dark closet, and, still in my socks, and picking my steps as I listened intently, made my way towards the turning gallery.

Nobody was in that gallery. I went to the door of Rouletabille's room and listened, but could hear nothing. I knocked gently. There was no answer. I turned the handle and entered the room.

Rouletabille lay at full length on the floor.

Chapter 22

The incredible body

With unspeakable anxiety I bent over the form of the reporter, and was rejoiced to find that he was only sleeping. And it was the same unnatural and profound sleep that had overcome Frédéric Larsan. My friend, too, had fallen a victim to the sleeping-draught which had been mixed with our food. How was it that I had not met with a similar fate? I reflected that the narcotic must have been put in our wine, for in that way all would be explained – I do not drink during meals. Endowed by Nature with a premature rotundity, I am restricted to the so-called 'dry diet'. I shook Rouletabille with great energy, but did not succeed in making him open his eyes. This sleep of his was, no doubt, the work of Mlle Stangerson.

She had certainly thought that she had even more to fear from the watchfulness of this young man, who foresaw everything, who knew everything, than from her father. I recalled that the butler, when serving us, had recommended an excellent Chablis, which most likely had come from the table of the Professor and his daughter.

More than a quarter of an hour passed. I resolved, in these extreme circumstances, when we had so much need to be wide awake, to resort to strong measures. I threw a pitcher of cold water over Rouletabille's head. At last he opened his eyes – his poor, dull eyes, lifeless and sightless. I smacked his cheeks smartly, and lifted him up. I felt him stiffen himself in my arms, and heard him murmur: 'Go on – but don't make a noise.' To smack his cheeks without making a noise seemed a rather difficult task to me. I pinched and shook him again, and at length he was able to stand up. We were saved!

'They have sent me to sleep,' he said. 'Ah, I spent an abominable time before giving way to sleep. I struggled. But it is over now. Don't leave me!'

He had no sooner uttered those words than our ears were thrilled by a frightful scream that rang through the château – a veritable death-shriek.

'Heavens!' Rouletabille roared. 'We shall be too late!'

He tried to rush to the door, but he was dazed still, and fell against the wall. I was already in the gallery, revolver in hand, dashing like a madman towards the room of Mlle Stangerson. At the moment when I arrived at the junction of the turning and the straight gallery I saw a man escaping from her apartment, who in a few strides reached the landing.

I was not master of my actions. I fired. The report of the shot made a deafening noise, but the man continued his flight down the stairs. I ran behind him shouting: 'Stop, stop, or I'll kill you!' As I rushed after him down the stairs I came face to face with Arthur Rance, coming from the gallery in the left wing of the château, shouting: 'What is it? What is it?' We reached the foot of the stairs almost at the same time. The window of the hall was open. We distinctly saw the flying form of a man. Instinctively we fired our revolvers in his direction. He was not more than ten paces in front of us. He staggered, and we thought he was going to fall. We sprang out of the window, but the man dashed suddenly away with renewed vigour. I was in my socks, and the American was barefooted. We could not hope to overtake the man if our revolvers failed to reach him. We fired our last cartridges at him, but he still sped on. However, he was flying along the right side of the court of honour towards the end of the right wing of the château. He would not be able to escape, for in that corner, surrounded by ditches and huge gates, there was no other exit than the door of the little room occupied by the gamekeeper.

The man, though evidently wounded by our bullets, was not twenty yards ahead of us. Suddenly a window above our heads in the gallery behind us opened, and we heard the voice of Rouletabille calling desperately: 'Shoot, Bernier – shoot!'

And the night, at that moment clear with moonlight, grew brighter with a sudden flash.

By its light we saw Bernier standing with his gun on the threshold of the keep.

He had taken good aim. The shadow dropped, but as it had reached the end of the right wing of the château it dropped behind the angle of the building – that is to say, we saw it fall, but it only sank to the ground on the other side of the wall, which we could not see.

Bernier, Arthur Rance, and myself reached that spot twenty seconds later. The shadow was lying dead at our feet.

Evidently awakened from his lethargic sleep by the cries and the shouting, Larsan opened the window of his room and called to us, as Arthur Rance had done: 'What is it? What is it?'

We were bending over the shadow – the mysterious dead form of the man. Rouletabille, now quite awake, joined us just then, and I cried to him: 'He is dead! he is dead!'

'So much the better,' he replied. 'Take him into the entrance-hall of the château.' But upon second thoughts he added: 'No, no! Let us take him into the gamekeeper's room.'

Rouletabille knocked at the door. Nobody answered from the interior, which, naturally, caused me no surprise.

'He is evidently not there, or he would have already come out,' said the reporter. 'Let us carry the man to the hall, then.'

Since we had reached the dead man, the night had become so dark, owing to the passing of a dense cloud, that we could only feel his form without distinguishing his features, and yet our eyes were anxious to know. Old Jacques, who joined us then, helped us to transport the body to the hall of the château. There we laid it on the lower step of the stairs. On the way I had felt upon my hands the warm blood which was dripping from the man's wounds.

Old Jacques flew to the kitchen, and returned with a lantern. He held it close to the face of the dead, and we recognised the game-keeper – he whom the landlord of the Castle Inn called the Green Man, and whom an hour earlier I had seen coming out of Arthur Rance's room carrying a parcel. But what I had seen I could only report to Rouletabille when we should be alone, and I did so a few minutes later.

* * *

I must mention the intense amazement, the cruel and overwhelming disappointment, shown by Rouletabille and Frédéric Larsan, who had joined us in the hall. They both felt the body, they looked at the dead face, at the green clothes, and repeated: 'Impossible! It is impossible!'

Rouletabille even exclaimed: 'It is enough to send one mad – to drive one to throw the whole thing up!'

Old Jacques exhibited an hysterical sorrow, broken by strange lamentations. He declared that there had been some mistake, and that the gamekeeper could not be the assassin of his mistress. We were compelled to order him to keep quiet. Had his own son been slain he could not have lamented more, and I explained his exaggeration of feeling by his fear lest it should be thought that he rejoiced in this dramatic death. For everybody knew Old Jacques had detested the gamekeeper. I noticed that, while all the rest of us were more or less undressed, barefooted, or in our socks, Old Jacques was completely attired.

Rouletabille, meanwhile, had not quitted the body. Kneeling on the flagstones of the hall, lighted by the lantern of Old Jacques, he was loosening the game-keeper's clothing. He laid bare the man's chest. It was still bleeding.

Suddenly snatching the lantern from the hand of Old Jacques, Rouletabille held it quite close to the gaping wound. Then he rose and said in a singular tone, with a touch of bitter irony: 'This man, whom you think you killed with the bullets of your revolvers and guns, died from a knife-stab in his heart!'

I thought once more that Rouletabille had gone mad, and in my turn bent over the corpse. I was then able to satisfy myself that the body bore, indeed, no trace of a bullet-wound, and that the only wound there was one inflicted by a sharp blade in the region of the heart.

Chapter 23
The double trail

I had not yet recovered from the bewilderment into which this discovery had plunged me when my young friend touched me on the shoulder and said: 'Follow me.'

'Where?'

'To my room.'

'What are you going to do there?'

'Reflect.'

I confess that I was in such a condition of mind as to make it impossible for me to think calmly, or even to think at all; and on this tragic night, after events the horror of which was only equalled by their incoherence and mystery, I found it difficult to realise how, between the gamekeeper dead, and Mlle Stangerson perhaps dying, Rouletabille could pretend to reflect. He did this, however, with all the coolness shown by great soldiers amid the din of battle. He closed the door, offered me a seat, sat down opposite me, and, of course, lit his pipe.

I watched him thinking, and then I fell asleep. When I woke it was daylight. My watch indicated eight o'clock. Rouletabille was no longer in the room; his armchair was empty. I rose, and was beginning to stretch my limbs, when the door opened, and my friend entered. I saw at a glance that while I slept he had not wasted his time.

'Mlle Stangerson?' I at once asked.

'Her condition, though extremely alarming, is not hopeless.'

'Is it long since you left this room?'

'I went out at dawn.'

'You have been working?'

'Hard.'

'And you have discovered?'

'A double set of footprints – most remarkable – which *might* have perplexed me.'

'They no longer do so?'

'No.'

'Do those footprints explain anything to you?'

'Yes.'

'Concerning the "incredible body" of the gamekeeper?'

'Yes, and it is quite credible now. I discovered this morning, whilst walking round the château, two distinct sets of footprints side by side, made at the same time last night. I say "at the same time", as if two persons had been walking together. This double set of footprints quitted all other footprints in the centre of the court of honour, and went in the direction of the oak-grove. I was leaving the court of honour, following the traces, when I was joined by Frédéric Larsan, who immediately became interested in my work, for this double track was really worth sticking to. I saw there the double footprints of the affair of the Yellow Room – those made by rough hobnailed boots, and those made by the elegant boots. But whilst in the Yellow Room affair the rough bootmarks only joined the elegant ones near the lake, and afterwards disappeared – which led Larsan and me to the conclusion that the two kinds belonged to one and the same person, who had simply changed boots – in the present case, however, both the rough and the elegant bootmarks were there together. This, of course, upset my former conclusions. Larsan seemed to share my trouble, and so we examined those footprints over and over again with the greatest care. I took from my pocket-book the paper measurements. The first was the one I had made from the impressions made by Old Jacques's rough boots, found by Frédéric in the lake. It fitted perfectly over one of the rough prints we saw. The second paper pattern was that of the elegant bootmarks. It also fitted over the corresponding traces, but there was a slight difference in the toe of the boot. We could not say from this comparison that the footprints were those of the same person, neither could we swear to the contrary, for the unknown man might not have worn the same boots.

'Still following the course of the two sets of footprints, Larsan and I were led by them out of the oak-grove, and found ourselves on the border of the lake which we had seen on our first search. But this time no footprints stopped there, for the two sets, still together, followed the little path leading to the high-road to Épinay. There we came upon a part of the road which had been recently macadamised, on which, in consequence, it was impossible to see anything; so we returned to the château without exchanging a word.

'On reaching the court of honour we separated, but our thoughts having travelled in the same direction, we met again at the door of

Old Jacques's room. We found the old servant in bed, and at once noticed that his clothes, which had been taken off and thrown upon a chair, were in a lamentable state, and that his boots, the soles of which were exactly like those we knew, were plastered with mud. It was certainly not in helping to carry the gamekeeper's body from the end of the court of honour to the hall, nor in going to the kitchen to fetch a lantern, that he had got his boots in that state, and his clothes drenched, since no rain was falling at the time.

'His face was not pleasant to look upon. He was obviously exhausted, and his blinking eyes met ours at first with terror.

'We questioned him. He began by telling us that he had gone to bed immediately after the arrival of the doctor, whom the butler had been sent for; but we so pressed him, so clearly proved that he was lying, that he finally confessed he had been away from the château. Naturally, we asked his reason. He said that he had had a headache, and needed to go into the open air, but that he had not gone farther than the oak-grove. We then described to him the road he had taken as well as if we had ourselves seen him traversing it. The old man sat up and began to tremble.

' "You were not alone!" cried Larsan.

' "You saw – then?" gasped Old Jacques.

' "Whom?" I asked.

' "The black phantom!"

'Old Jacques then told us that for several nights he saw the "black phantom". It appeared in the park at the stroke of midnight, and glided through the trees with incredible ease. It seemed to pass through the trunks of the trees! Twice Old Jacques had seen the phantom through his window by the light of the moon. He had risen and gone in search of the strange apparition. The night before last he had very nearly overtaken it, but it had vanished at the corner of the keep. Finally, he said that last night, having gone out of the château with his mind disturbed by the idea of a fresh crime, he had suddenly seen the black phantom issue from somewhere in the middle of the court of honour. He had followed it, at first cautiously. He had passed by the oak-grove, and reached the road to Épinay. There the phantom had suddenly disappeared.

' "You did not see its face?" Larsan enquired.

' "No; I saw nothing but the black veils."

' "And after what had passed in the gallery, you did not seize it by the throat?"

' "I couldn't; I was too terrified! I had hardly strength enough to follow it."

' "*You did not follow*, Old Jacques," I said, in a threatening tone; "you went *with* the phantom as far as the road to Épinay. You walked arm-in-arm with the phantom!"

' "No!" he cried. "It came on to pour with rain – I turned back! I don't know what became of the black phantom!"

'But his eyes were turned away from me as he spoke.

'We left him. When we were outside, "An accomplice?" I asked Larsan in a meaning tone, looking him full in the face to discover what was passing in his mind.

'Larsan raised his arm, saying: "How can I tell? Can one be sure of anything in such a case as this? Twenty-four hours ago I would have sworn that there was no accomplice!"

'And he left me, saying he was going to Épinay.'

When Rouletabille had finished this recital, I asked him: 'Well, what do you conclude from it all? As for me, I cannot see my way a bit; I cannot grasp anything. But you – what do you know?'

'Everything!' he exclaimed. 'Everything!'

I had never seen him look so happy. He rose and shook hands with me.

'Then explain to me – ' I began.

'Let us go and enquire about Mlle Stangerson,' he said abruptly.

Chapter 24

Rouletabille knows the two halves of the assassin

Mlle Stangerson had been nearly assassinated for the second time. Unfortunately, the injuries she received in this second attack were worse than those she had sustained in the first. The three wounds which the knife of the assassin had made in her bosom on the tragic night kept her a long time between life and death, and when at last life proved the stronger, and there was hope she would escape her terrible fate, it was found that while she gradually recovered the use of her senses, she did not recover her reason. The least reference to the horrible tragedy made her delirious, and I believe it is no exaggeration to say that the arrest of M. Darzac, which took place at the Château du Glandier the day after the discovery of the body of the game-keeper, deepened still more the mental abyss into which we saw that fine intellect sink.

M. Robert Darzac arrived at the château at about half-past nine. I saw him hurrying through the park, his hair and his clothes in disorder, entirely covered with mud, and altogether in a fearful state. His face was deadly pale. Rouletabille and I were looking out of the window in the gallery. M. Darzac saw us, and uttered a cry of despair.

'I am too late!'

Rouletabille cried: 'She lives!'

A minute later M. Darzac entered Mlle Stangerson's room, and through the door we heard him sobbing.

* * *

'Fatality!' groaned Rouletabille, by my side. 'What infernal gods are causing the misfortunes of this family? If I hadn't been sent to sleep, I should have saved Mlle Stangerson from the man; I should have silenced him for ever – and the gamekeeper would not have been killed.'

* * *

M. Darzac came to us bathed in tears. Rouletabille told him everything, and how he had provided for Mlle Stangerson's safety as well as his, Darzac's; how he would have succeeded in sending the man away for ever, having seen his face; and how his plan had been drowned in blood, owing to the sleeping-draught.

'Ah! if only you had had complete confidence in me!' said the young man, in a low voice. 'If you had told Mlle Stangerson to have confidence in me! But here everybody distrusts everybody else – the daughter distrusts her father, and even her own fiancé. While you were telling me to do all I could to prevent the assassin from reaching her, she was preparing everything to help him! And I arrived too late, half-asleep, almost dragging myself to the room where the sight of the unfortunate lady, however, covered with blood, awakened me thoroughly.'

At the request of M. Darzac, Rouletabille described the scene. Leaning against the wall to save himself from falling, while we in the hall and in the court of honour were pursuing the assassin, he had made his way towards the victim's room. The doors of the antechamber being open, he entered. Mlle Stangerson lay insensible, thrown half-across the desk, with eyes closed. Her dressing-gown was red with blood, which was flowing in streams from her bosom. It seemed to Rouletabille, still under the influence of the sleeping-draught, that he was the victim of a hideous nightmare.

Automatically he returned to the gallery, opened the window, shouted to us, ordered us to stay, and then went back to the room. Presently he crossed the deserted boudoir, entered the drawing-room, the door of which was ajar, shook M. Stangerson, who was lying on the sofa, and waked him, as I had previously waked himself. The professor sat up, with haggard eyes, and let himself be led by Rouletabille into the room, where, seeing his daughter, he uttered a heart-rending cry. Ah, Rouletabille is awake now, and both now, uniting their tottering strength, carried the victim to bed.

Then Rouletabille rejoined us, desperate for information. Before leaving the room, he stopped near the desk. On the floor there was a parcel, an enormous parcel. How came that parcel there, near the desk? The serge covering was loose. Rouletabille knelt down. Papers, documents, photographs were heaped together in it. He scanned them: 'New Differential Condensing Electroscope', 'Fundamental Properties of the Intermediary Substance between Ponderable Matter and Imponderable Ether'. Truly, what is this mystery, and this astounding irony of fate which makes somebody restore to M. Stangerson all these useless papers – which he will hurl into the fire the next day – at the very moment when his child is being slain?

* * *

On the morning following that horrible night we saw M. de Marquet reappear, with his registrar and his gendarmes. We were all inter-rogated, except, naturally, Mlle Stangerson, who was in a condition bordering on coma. Rouletabille and I, having conferred together, said what we had mutually agreed to say. I took good care not to mention the sleeping-draught and my presence in the dark recess. In fact, we kept to ourselves everything that could lead to the suspicion that we had anticipated the deed; also anything that might suggest that Mlle Stangerson had expected the assassin. The unfortunate woman was, perhaps, about to pay with her life for the mystery with which she surrounded her murderers. It was not our business to render such a sacrifice useless.

Arthur William Rance told everybody, quite naturally – so natur-ally that I was amazed at it – that he had seen the gamekeeper for the last time about eleven o'clock. He had come, he said, to fetch his bag, which the gamekeeper was to carry for him at an early hour next morning to the Saint-Michel Station, and had been kept to a late hour by him while they talked together about poachers, game, and shooting. Arthur Rance was, in fact, to have left the château in the morning, and intended to walk, according to his habit, to Saint-Michel Station. He had, therefore, taken advantage of an intended early errand of the gamekeeper to the village to get rid of his luggage.

M. Stangerson confirmed all this, and added that he had not had the pleasure of Arthur Rance at his table, as his friend had said good-bye to himself and daughter at about five o'clock. Mr Arthur Rance had merely had tea served in his own room, pleading that he was slightly indisposed.

Bernier, the concierge, in accordance with Rouletabille's instruc-tions, reported that he had been required by the gamekeeper himself that night to watch poachers (the gamekeeper could not contradict him); that the meeting-place was the oak-grove, and that, finding the gamekeeper did not appear, he had gone in search of him. He had nearly reached the château, and had passed the little door of the court of honour, when he saw a man running with all his might on the opposite side towards the right wing of the château. He heard revolver-shots at the same moment behind the man. Rouletabille, who had appeared at one of the windows of the gallery, saw him, Bernier, and called upon him to fire the gun he was carrying. He had fired, and believed that he had not only injured, but killed the man, until Rouletabille, on opening the man's clothing, found that he had been killed, not by a bullet, but by the stab of a knife. Bernier added that he could make nothing of this fantastic affair, since, if the body that had been found was not of the man at whom we had all fired, the fugitive must needs be somewhere still. Now, in the little yard where we had all met round the corpse there was no room for anyone, dead or living, without our seeing it.

Thus spoke Bernier, but the examining magistrate reminded him that, where we stood, in the corner of the court, it was very dark, for we had been unable to recognise the gamekeeper until we had removed his body to the entrance-hall of the château, and a lantern had been brought.

To this Bernier retorted that 'if they had not been able to see the other body, dead or living, they must anyway have trodden on it, considering the very small size of the courtyard. Also, there were five of us in that restricted space – not including the dead man – and it would have been strange if the other body had escaped notice! The only door that opened into the court was that of the gamekeeper's room, and it was closed. The key of it had been found in the Green Man's pocket.'

However, as this argument of Bernier's – which, at first sight, appeared logical – led to the conclusion that we had shot dead a man who had died from a stab in his heart, the examining magistrate did not waste much time over it. It was evident to all of us that he was persuaded we had missed the man we were pursuing, and that we had come upon a body that had nothing to do with our affair. For him, the corpse of the gamekeeper was a different affair altogether. He wished to prove it at once, for it was likely that this new affair tallied with ideas he had recently formed concerning the life of the game-keeper, his acquaintances, and his recent intrigue with the wife of the landlord of the Castle Inn, and also agreed with the reports made to him of the threats uttered against the Green Man by Mathieu. For at one o'clock in the afternoon Mathieu, in spite of his rheumatic pains and the protests of his wife, was arrested and taken under escort to Corbeil. Nothing compromising, however, had been discovered at his home. But his threats, made even on the previous day in the presence of some waggoners, who repeated them, compromised him more than if the knife used to kill the Green Man had been found under his bed.

We were thus flurried by many events, as terrible as they were inexplicable, when, to crown our amazement, we saw Frédéric Larsan return to the château, which he had left after seeing the examining magistrate. He was accompanied by a railway clerk.

Rouletabille and I were in the hall with Arthur Rance, arguing about the guilt or innocence of Mathieu – at least, Mr Rance and I were conversing, for Rouletabille seemed to have gone off in some distant dream, paying scarcely any attention to what we were saying.

The examining magistrate and the registrar were in the small green drawing-room, into which Robert Darzac had taken us when we arrived for the first time at Glandier. Old Jacques had been sent for by the magistrate, and had just entered the room. M. Darzac was upstairs in Mlle Stangerson's room with M. Stangerson and the doctors. Frédéric Larsan entered the hall with the railway clerk. Rouletabille and I at once recognised this clerk by his tiny blonde beard.

'It is the clerk of the Épinay-sur-Orge Station!' I exclaimed.

And I looked at Larsan, who replied, smiling: 'You are right. He's the booking-clerk at Épinay-sur-Orge.'

Larsan caused himself to be announced to the magistrate by the gendarme on duty at the drawing-room door. Old Jacques came out, and Frédéric Larsan and the clerk were at once introduced. Some minutes passed – perhaps ten minutes. Rouletabille was very impatient. The door of the drawing-room was again opened. The magistrate called to the gendarme, who entered the room, and presently came out, went upstairs, and at the end of a minute or two came down again. He then opened the drawing-room door, and, without closing it behind him, said to the magistrate: 'M. Robert Darzac will not come.'

'What? He'll not come?' cried M. de Marquet.

'He says he cannot leave Mlle Stangerson in her present state.'

'Very well,' said M. de Marquet, 'since he will not come to us, we will go to him.'

M. de Marquet and the gendarme mounted the stairs. He made a sign to Larsan and the booking-clerk to follow him. Rouletabille and I completed the procession.

On reaching the door of Mlle Stangerson's room, the magistrate knocked. A chambermaid appeared. It was Sylvia, a little damsel with sorrowful features and hair in disorder.

'Is M. Stangerson here?' asked M. de Marquet.

'Yes, Monsieur.'

'Tell him that I wish to speak with him.'

The professor came to us. He was weeping. It was, indeed, painful to watch him.

'What do you want now?' he asked the magistrate. 'May I not, at such a moment, be left in peace, Monsieur?'

'Monsieur,' said the magistrate, 'it is absolutely necessary that I should at once have an interview with M. Robert Darzac. Can you not induce him to quit Mlle Stangerson's room? Otherwise, I shall be compelled to enter it in the name of the law.'

The professor made no reply. He looked at the magistrate, at the gendarme, at all who were present, as a condemned man might look at his executioners, and went back into the room.

M. Robert Darzac immediately came out. He was already very pale and wan, but when he saw the booking-clerk behind Larsan his features became yet more distorted by anguish. His eyes were haggard, and he could not repress a deep and hollow groan.

We all noticed the tragic expression of that distressed face, and were unable to refrain from exclamations of pity. We felt that something definitive was happening to decide the fate of Robert Darzac. Frédéric Larsan alone had a radiant face, exhibiting the triumphant joy of a dog who has at last seized his prey. The magistrate said to M. Darzac, pointing to the young booking-clerk: 'Do you recognise this gentleman?'

'I do,' said M. Darzac, in a tone which he vainly tried to make firm. 'He is a clerk on the railway at the station of Épinay-sur-Orge.'

'This young man,' continued M. de Marquet, 'declares that you stepped out of a train at Épinay-sur-Orge – '

'Last night,' said M. Darzac, completing the sentence, 'at half-past ten. It is true.'

There was an interval of silence.

'M. Darzac,' the magistrate went on, in a tone of deep emotion – 'M. Darzac, what were you doing last night at Épinay-sur-Orge, at a very short distance from the place where an attempt to assassinate Mlle Stangerson was made?'

M. Darzac remained silent. He did not lower his head, but he closed his eyes – either to hide his sorrow, or for fear that something of his secret should be read in them.

'M. Darzac,' the magistrate insisted, 'can you tell me how you employed your time last night?'

M. Darzac reopened his eyes. He seemed to have recovered all his self-control.

'No, Monsieur.'

'Reflect, Monsieur; for if you persist in your strange refusal, I shall be under the necessity of keeping you at my disposal. *M. Robert Darzac, in the name of the law, I arrest you*!'

The magistrate had no sooner pronounced these words than I saw Rouletabille move quickly towards M. Darzac. He was certainly going to speak, but M. Darzac stopped him with a gesture. Besides, the gendarme had already approached his prisoner.

At that moment a despairing cry rang through the room.

'Robert! Robert!'

We recognised the voice of Mlle Stangerson, and at her tone of sorrow we all shuddered. Larsan himself turned pale this time, and M. Darzac, responding to the pathetic appeal, flew back to the room.

The magistrate, the gendarme, and Larsan followed closely behind him; Rouletabille and I remained on the threshold. The scene was heart-breaking! Mlle Stangerson, whose face had the pallor of death, had risen on her bed, in spite of the two doctors and her father. She held out her trembling arms towards Robert Darzac, on whom Larsan and the gendarme had laid hands. Her eyes were wide open; she saw, she understood. Her mouth seemed to utter a word – a word that expired on her bloodless lips, which nobody heard – and suddenly she fell back in a swoon.

The gendarme hastily drew M. Darzac out of the room. Larsan went to fetch a carriage, and we stopped in the hall. Everyone was greatly affected. M. de Marquet had tears in his eyes. Rouletabille took advantage of this general emotion to say to M. Darzac: 'Shall you defend yourself?'

'No,' replied the prisoner.

'Then I will defend you, Monsieur.'

'You cannot do it,' said the unfortunate man, with a faint smile. 'What we have not been able to do – Mlle Stangerson and I – *you* cannot do.'

'I *will* do it!' And the voice of Rouletabille was strangely calm and confident. He went on: 'I will do it, M. Robert Darzac, because I know more than you!'

'Nonsense!' murmured Darzac, almost angrily.

'Do not be uneasy! I will not know anything beyond what may be necessary to save you!'

'You must know nothing at all, young man, if you would have a claim to my gratitude!'

Rouletabille shook his head, and approached very close to M. Darzac.

'Listen to what I am going to say,' he whispered, 'and let me give you confidence. You know only the name of the assassin, and Mlle Stangerson only knows one half of him; *but I know his two halves – I know him entirely!*'

Robert Darzac had in his wide-open eyes an expression which clearly showed that he had not understood a word of what Rouletabille had said.

The carriage then arrived, driven by Frédéric Larsan himself. Darzac and the gendarme entered it; Larsan remained on the box. The prisoner was taken to Corbeil.

Chapter 25
Rouletabille goes on a journey

That same evening Rouletabille and I left Glandier. We were very glad to do so, as there was nothing to detain us there. I declared that I threw up the attempt to solve so much mystery, and Rouletabille, giving me a friendly tap on the shoulder, told me he had nothing more to learn at Glandier, because Glandier had told him everything.

We reached Paris about eight o'clock, dined rapidly, and then, as we were fatigued, separated, agreeing to meet next morning at my lodging.

At the time agreed on, Rouletabille entered my room. He was dressed in an English check suit, had an ulster on his arm, a cap on his head, and a bag in his hand. He told me he was going on a journey.

'How long shall you be away?' I asked.

'A month or two,' he answered. 'It depends.'

I did not venture to question him further.

'Do you know,' he said, 'what was the word Mlle Stangerson uttered before she fainted, when her eyes were fixed on M. Darzac?'

'No. Nobody heard it.'

'I beg your pardon,' replied Rouletabille; 'I heard it. She said, "Speak."'

'And will M. Robert Darzac speak?'

'Never!'

I would have liked to prolong our interview, but he warmly shook hands with me, wished me good-bye, and I had only time to ask him: 'You don't fear that, during your absence, fresh attempts will be made on Mlle Stangerson's life?'

'I fear nothing of the sort, now that M. Darzac is in prison,' he replied.

Having spoken these strange words, Rouletabille left me.

I was destined to see him no more until the trial of M. Robert Darzac in the Assize Court, when my young friend appeared *to explain the inexplicable.*

Chapter 26

In which Joseph Rouletabille is impatiently expected

On January 15, two months and a half after the tragic events I have related, the *Époque* published in its leading column on the front page the following sensational article.

The jury of Seine-et-Oise are today called upon to decide one of the most mysterious affairs in the judicial annals. No case ever presented so many obscure, incomprehensible, inexplicable points; and yet the prosecution has not hesitated to place in the dock a man respected, esteemed, beloved by all who knew him – a young savant, the hope of French science, a man whose whole existence has been devoted to study, and who has ever been a model of probity.

When Paris heard of the arrest of M. Robert Darzac, a universal protest was made. The entire Sorbonne, dishonoured by this act of the examining magistrate, proclaiming their faith in the innocence of the fiancé of Mlle Stangerson. M. Stangerson himself protested that the law had been led into error. Nobody doubts that, if the victim could speak, she would claim from the twelve jurors of Seine-et-Oise the man whom she desires to make her husband, and whom the prosecution would send to the scaffold. It is, therefore, to be hoped that at an early date Mlle Stangerson will recover her reason, which has been momentarily overthrown in the horrible mystery of Glandier. Must she, then, be doomed to lose her reason for ever by hearing that the man she loves has perished – died at the hands of the executioner? We ask this question of the members of the jury, and we propose to deal with them without delay.

We have decided not to allow twelve worthy men to commit an abominable judicial error. We know that terrible coincidences, accusing traces, the enigmatical employment of M. Darzac's time, the total absence of an *alibi*, must have led the magistrates to their conviction; but, having vainly searched elsewhere for the truth, they are resolved to find it in M. Darzac's guilt. The charges are, in appearance, so overwhelming that a detective so well informed, so intelligent, and so generally successful as M. Frédéric Larsan, may well be excused for having been blinded by them. Hitherto everything has gone against M. Robert Darzac during the examining magistrate's inquiry. Today we are going to defend him before the jury, and will solve the entire mystery of Glandier, *for we are in possession of the truth*!

If we have not spoken sooner, it was because the interests of the cause we seek to defend compelled us to wait.

Our readers have probably not forgotten the private enquiries, of which we published an account, relating to the left foot of the 'Rue Oberkampf', the famous robbery of the Universal Credit Bank, and the 'Gold Ingots of the Mint' case. In all those cases we were enabled to discover the truth, even before the wonderful ingenuity of Frédéric Larsan could reveal it. Those enquiries were made by our youngest reporter, Joseph Rouletabille, a youth of eighteen years of age, who tomorrow will be famous. When the affair of Glandier took place, our young reporter went to the spot, compelled all doors to open to him, and settled down in the château, from which all other representatives of the Press had been excluded. Side by side with Frédéric Larsan he sought the truth. Horrified, he realised the complete and dangerous error into which that celebrated detective, with all his genius, was sinking. In vain he tried to draw Larsan away from the false trail he was following. The great Frédéric would not be taught a lesson by this 'boy-journalist'. We know now where Larsan's error has led M. Robert Darzac.

Now, France must know, the entire world must know, that on the same evening that M. Darzac was arrested young Rouletabille entered the office of our Editor, and said to him: 'I am going on a journey. I cannot tell how long I shall be away – perhaps one, two, three months – perhaps I shall never return! Here is a letter. If I am not back by the day on which M. Robert Darzac appears before the Assizes, open this letter in court, after all the witnesses have been heard. Arrange the matter with M. Darzac's counsel, for M. Robert Darzac is innocent. This letter contains the name of the assassin. I won't add the proofs, for I am now going in search of those proofs; but the envelope contains, at least, the irrefutable explanation of the man's guilt.'

Our reporter departed. We were a long time without news of him, but a week ago a stranger called upon our Editor and said: 'Act in accordance with the instructions of Joseph Rouletabille, if it becomes necessary to do so. The truth is in the letter.' This gentleman would not give us his name.

Today, January 15, is the great day of the Assizes. Joseph Rouletabille has not returned, and perhaps we shall never see him again. The Press has its heroes, its martyrs to duty, the obligations of their profession being to them the first of all duties. It is quite possible that Joseph Rouletabille has given his life for the sake of his professional duty! We shall know how to avenge him.

Our Editor will go this afternoon to the Court of Assize at Versailles with the letter – the letter which contains the name of the assassin.

At the head of the article was a portrait of Rouletabille.

*   *   *

Parisians who flocked that day to the Assize Court at Versailles in the trail of what was known as the 'Mystery of the Yellow Room' will certainly not have forgotten the extraordinary and tumultuous crowd at the Saint-Lazare Station. No more seats were to be had in the ordinary trains, and several additional trains had to be run. The article in the *Époque* had roused everybody, excited universal curiosity, and whetted the passion for discussion. Blows were exchanged between the partisans of Joseph Rouletabille and the fanatical supporters of Frédéric Larsan, for – strange fact – the excitement of the people arose less from the thought that perhaps an innocent man might be sentenced to death than from the interest they took in their individual theories of the Mystery of the Yellow Room. Each had his own explanation, to which he held fast. Those who explained the crime in the same way as Frédéric Larsan would not admit any doubt as to the perspicacity of that popular detective, and others who had solutions differing from that of Larsan naturally claimed that they must be identical with that of Joseph Rouletabille, with which they were not yet acquainted. With copies of the *Époque* in their hands, the 'Larsans' and the 'Rouletabilles' argued, and hustled one another on the steps of the Law Courts at Versailles, and even in the court itself! An unusually strong force of gendarmes were present to cope with the enormous crowd.

Such of the innumerable crowd as could not gain admission remained until the evening around the building, hungry for news, welcoming even the most fantastic rumours. They were kept clear of the entrance of the Law Courts with the greatest difficulty by the gendarmes and soldiery. At one moment a rumour was current that M. Stangerson himself had been arrested in court, and had confessed to being the assassin of his own daughter! It was pure madness. Nervous excitement had reached the highest pitch. Rouletabille had not yet arrived. People pretended to know him and to recognise him, and when a young man with a 'pass' crossed the open space which separated the crowd from the building, scuffles took place. People trampled on one another. There were cries of 'Rouletabille! There's Rouletabille!' Witnesses who more or less vaguely resembled the portrait published in the *Époque* were cheered as they went by. The arrival of the Editor of the great newspaper was also the signal for manifestations. Some applauded, others hissed. There were many women in the crowd.

* * *

In the court the trial proceeded under the direction of M. de Rocoux, a magistrate imbued with all the prejudices of lawyers, but thoroughly honest. The names of the witnesses had been called over. I was one of them, naturally; others were those who, from far or near, had been connected with the mystery of Glandier – M. Stangerson, who looked ten years older, and was unrecognisable; Larsan; Mr Arthur William Rance, with face as red as ever; Old Jacques; Mathieu, the innkeeper, who was brought into court handcuffed between two gendarmes; Mme Mathieu, all tears; the two Berniers, the two nurses, the butler, all the domestics of the château, the clerk of Post Office No. 40, the booking-clerk from Épinay, several friends of M. and Mlle Stangerson, and all the witnesses for M. Darzac, the prisoner. I had the good fortune to be heard amongst the earliest witnesses called. This allowed me to be present at nearly the whole of the subsequent proceedings.

I need scarcely say that the place was crowded to excess. Barristers were sitting on the very steps of the bench, and behind the magistrates, in their red robes, representatives of other tribunals were present. M. Robert Darzac appeared in the dock between the gendarmes, so calm, tall, and handsome that a murmur of admiration rather than of compassion greeted him. He immediately bent forward towards his counsel, Maître Henri Robert, who, assisted by his chief secretary, Maître André Hesse, then at the beginning of his career, was already engaged in examining the documents and notes before him.

Many expected that Professor Stangerson would have gone to the accused and shaken hands with him, but the names of the witnesses were called over, and they had left the court without the occurrence of that sensational incident.

At the moment when the jurors took their seats it was remarked that they appeared to be deeply interested in a rapid conversation which the Editor of the *Époque* was carrying on with Maître Henri Robert. The former then took his place on one of the front seats reserved for the public. Some were surprised that he did not follow the other witnesses to the room allotted to them.

The reading of the indictment was got through, as usual, without incident. I shall not here report the lengthy cross-examination to which M. Darzac was subjected. He answered the questions promptly in a most natural manner, but at the same time very reservedly. All that he was able to say seemed reasonable; all that he withheld appeared to tell terribly against him, even in the estimation of those who felt that he was innocent. His silence on certain points – of which the reader is aware – told against him, and it seemed that his reticence must utterly destroy him. He resisted all the entreaties of the President of the Assizes and of the representatives of the Public Prosecutor. He was told that to remain silent in such circumstances meant being condemned to death.

'Very well, then,' he said, 'I must die! But I am innocent!'

With the tremendous ability which has made his reputation, Maître Henri Robert – M. Darzac's counsel – taking advantage of the incident, tried to show, by the very fact of his silence, the greatness of his client's character, and made allusion to those moral duties of which none but heroic characters are capable. The eminent barrister only succeeded, however, in strengthening the confidence of those who knew M. Darzac, but others remained prejudiced. The hearing was suspended, and a little later the witnesses were called in turn.

Rouletabille had not yet arrived. Every time a door opened all eyes turned first towards it, and then to the Editor of the *Époque*, who remained impassive. At last he was seen to feel in his pocket and draw from it the letter. A loud murmur followed this movement.

I do not intend to report here all the incidents of the trial. I have sufficiently retraced all the steps of the affair to render unnecessary for the reader any fresh description of the events that occurred at Glandier, and of the obscurity surrounding them. I am anxious to come to the really dramatic moment of that memorable day.

It occurred on the resumption of the trial, when Maître Henri Robert was questioning Mathieu, who, in the witness-box between gendarmes, defended himself against the charge of having murdered the Green Man.

His wife was called, and confronted with him. Bursting into tears, she confessed that she had been infatuated with the gamekeeper, and that her husband had suspected it; but she again affirmed that he had nothing to do with the murder of her lover. Maître Henri Robert thereupon asked the court to hear Frédéric Larsan on the matter.

'In a short conversation which I had with Frédéric Larsan during the suspension of the hearing,' the famous counsel declared, 'he has given me to understand that the death of the gamekeeper may be explained otherwise than by the intervention of Mathieu. It will be interesting to know the views of Frédéric Larsan.'

Frédéric Larsan was introduced. He explained himself very clearly.

'I see no necessity,' he said, 'for the introduction of Mathieu into all this. I have told M. de Marquet so. But the murderous threats of this man evidently compromised him in the eyes of the examining magistrate. To me it appears that the assassinations of Mlle Stangerson and of the gamekeeper are one and the same affair. The assassin of Mlle Stangerson, flying through the court of honour, was fired upon; it was thought that he had been struck, that he was killed; but, as a matter of fact, he only stumbled just as he disappeared behind the angle of the right wing of the château. There the criminal encountered the gamekeeper, who, no doubt, tried to oppose his flight. The assassin had still in his hand the knife with which he had stabbed Mlle Stangerson; he stabbed the gamekeeper in the heart, and the gamekeeper fell dead on the spot.'

This very simple explanation appeared very plausible, more so than many of those who were interested in the mysteries of Glandier had thought.

The President then asked: 'What became of the assassin?'

'He evidently hid himself in an obscure corner at the end of the yard, and, after the departure of the people carrying away the body to the château, he was able to disappear quietly.'

At that moment, from the back of the public gallery, a youthful voice was raised. In the midst of the general amazement it was heard to say: '*I agree with Frédéric Larson as to the stabbing of the gamekeeper, but I disagree as to the manner in which the assassin escaped from the end of the court.*'

Everybody turned round. The ushers sprang toward the speaker, and commanded silence. The President of the Tribunal angrily asked who had dared to speak, and ordered the immediate expulsion of the intruder. But the same clear voice was heard again: '*It is I, M. le Président – I – Joseph Rouletabille!*'

Chapter 27

In which Joseph Rouletabille appears in all his glory

There was a terrible commotion. The cries of fainting women were heard. No attention was paid to the majesty of the Law. All was wild confusion. Everybody wanted to see Joseph Rouletabille. The President announced that he would have the court cleared, but nobody listened. Meanwhile, Rouletabille jumped over the balustrade which separated him from the seated public, used his elbows unsparingly, and reached his Editor, who embraced him warmly, and took his letter from the Editor's hands, put it into his pocket, and made his way, hustled and hustling, to the witness-box. His face was beaming with keen joy; his head was truly a red ball, made brighter still by the fiery gleam of his two large, round eyes. Rouletabille was wearing the same English suit that I had seen him wear on the day of his departure, but in what a state! The same cap was on his head, and the same ulster on his arm. He said: 'I beg your pardon, M. le Président! The steamer was late. I have only just arrived from America! I am Joseph Rouletabille!'

There was a general outburst of laughter. Everybody was glad of the lad's arrival. It seemed as if a great weight had been lifted from the consciences of all. Everybody breathed more freely, for everybody felt certain that he really brought the truth with him – that he was now going to make it known.

But the President of the Assize Court was furious.

'Oh, you are Joseph Rouletabille, are you?' he replied. 'Well, young man, I must teach you what comes of contempt of court. For the present, while the Court will consider your case, I keep you in detention in virtue of my discretionary power.'

'But, M. le Président, I *wish* to be at the Court's disposal. That's the very thing I'm asking. That's what I have come here for – to place myself at the disposal of the Law. If my entrance has been a trifle noisy, I humbly apologise to the Court. I beg you to believe, M. le

Président, that nobody has a greater respect for the Law than I have. But I entered in the only way I could.'

And he began to laugh. Everybody laughed, too.

'Take him away!' the President ordered.

But Maître Henri Robert intervened. He began by excusing the young man, who, he said, was actuated by the best intentions in the world. He made the President understand that it would be difficult to pass over the evidence of a witness who had lived at Glandier during the whole of the mysterious week; above all, of a witness who claimed he could prove the innocence of the accused, and make known the name of the assassin.

'You are going to tell us the name of the assassin?' the President asked, wavering but sceptical.

'That's what I have come for, M. le Président,' said Rouletabille.

People were about to applaud, but the energetic 'Hush!' of the Court attendants restored silence.

'Joseph Rouletabille,' said Maître Henri Robert, 'has not been regularly subpoenaed as a witness, but I hope that M. le Président, in virtue of his discretionary power, will be kind enough to examine him.'

'Very well,' the President replied, 'we will question him. But first let us proceed by order.'

The Advocate-General rose.

'It would perhaps be better,' the representative of the Public Prosecutor remarked, 'that this young man should at once tell us the name of the person he denounces as the assassin.'

The President acquiesced with an ironical remark.

'If M. l'Avocat-Général attaches some importance to the evidence of M. Joseph Rouletabille, I see no reason why this witness should not tell us at once the name of "his" assassin.'

The silence was complete. One might have heard a pin drop.

Rouletabille remained silent, and looked with sympathy at M. Robert Darzac, who, for the first time since the beginning of the trial, seemed perturbed and deeply anxious.

'Well,' cried the President, 'we are ready to hear you. We were waiting for the name of the assassin.'

Rouletabille very quietly felt in his waistcoat-pocket, drew a huge, thick watch from it, and, having looked at the time, replied: 'M. le Président, I cannot tell you the name of the assassin before half-past six o'clock. We have four solid hours before us.'

The President seemed delighted. Maître Henri Robert and Maître André Hesse were much annoyed.

The President said: 'This little joke has gone on long enough. You may retire, Monsieur, into the witnesses' room. I keep you under arrest.'

Rouletabille protested.

'I assure you, M. le Président,' he cried, in his sharp, clear voice, 'that when I have told you the name of the assassin, you will understand why I could not tell it to you before half-past six. Take my word for it – the word of Joseph Rouletabille. But, meanwhile, I can give you some explanation in regard to the assassination of the gamekeeper. M. Frédéric Larsan, who has seen me at work at Glandier, can tell you with what care I have studied this whole affair. Although I disagree with him, and declare that, by having M. Robert Darzac arrested, he charges an innocent man, M. Larsan does not doubt my good faith, and realises the importance of my discoveries, which have often corroborated his own.'

Frédéric Larsan then said: 'M. le Président, it will be interesting to hear M. Joseph Rouletabille – the more so as we do not agree.'

A murmur of approval greeted the words of the detective. Like a good sportsman, he accepted the duel. The struggle between these two intellects, both eager to solve the same tragic problem, both arriving at different conclusions, promised to be most fascinating.

As the President remained silent, Frédéric Larsan continued: 'We agree, M. Rouletabille and I, as to the stabbing of the gamekeeper by the assassin of Mlle Stangerson, but, since we do *not* agree on the question of the flight of the assassin from the end of the court of honour, it would be interesting to know how M. Rouletabille explains that flight.'

'Certainly it would be interesting,' said my friend.

There was a general outburst of laughter. The President instantly declared that, if it were repeated, he would not hesitate to have his threat carried out, and the Court cleared.

'Really,' added the President, in conclusion, 'in such an affair as this I do not see anything to provoke laughter.'

'Nor do I,' said Rouletabille.

People before me stuffed their handkerchiefs into their mouths to repress further merriment.

'Now, young man,' said the President, 'you have heard what M. Frédéric Larsan has just said. How, according to your view, did the assassin escape from the end of the little courtyard?'

*   *   *

Rouletabille looked at Mme Mathieu, who smiled sadly at him.

'Since Mme Mathieu,' he said, 'has frankly admitted her weakness, and has not concealed the fact of her admiration for the gamekeeper, I am free to tell you that she often met him at the keep. These meetings became more frequent when the innkeeper, her husband, was confined to bed by his rheumatism. Mme Mathieu would come to the château at night, wrapped in a large black shawl, which disguised her, and made her look like a sombre phantom, which sometimes gave Old Jacques some uneasy nights. She had learned to imitate the cry, the sinister cry, of the cat of Mother Agenoux, an old sorceress of Ste Geneviève des Bois. The gamekeeper, when he heard this cry, would at once leave the keep to open the little postern for Mme Mathieu. When the repairs to the keep were recently being made, their meetings took place in the new room at the extremity of the right wing of the château, which was separated from the butler's apartment by only a thin partition.

'Mme Mathieu had left the gamekeeper in perfect health before the dramatic events in the little court. She and her admirer came from the keep together. I learnt these details, M. le Président, by the examination which I made of the footmarks in the court of honour the next morning. Bernier, the concierge, whom I had placed with his gun on the watch behind the keep, as I will allow him to explain for himself, could not see what passed in the court of honour. He did not arrive there until a little later, attracted by the revolver-shots. He fired in his turn.

'In the darkness and the silence of the court of honour Mme Mathieu was bidding the gamekeeper good-night. She then walked to the open gate of the court, and he returned to his room at the end of the right wing of the château. He had nearly reached his door when the reports of revolvers rang out. He turned back anxiously. He had nearly reached the corner when a shadow rushed at him and stabbed him in the heart. He died, and his body was immediately picked up by persons who believed they had secured the murderer, but were in reality carrying away the murdered.

'Meanwhile, what is Mme Mathieu doing? Surprised by the revolver-shots and by the invasion of the court of honour, she makes herself as small as she can in the darkness. The court of honour is very large, and, finding herself near the gate, she might easily have passed out unseen. But she did not pass out. She remained, and saw the body carried away. In an agony of mind that may readily be imagined, urged by a tragic foreboding, she walked to the hall of the château, and cast her eyes on the stair, lit by Old Jacques's lantern, the stair on which the body of the gamekeeper was stretched. She saw, and fled.

'Did Old Jacques notice her? Anyhow, he joined the black phantom that had caused him to have so many sleepless nights. That very night, before the crime, he had been wakened by the cries of the Good Lord's beast, and had, through his window, seen the black phantom. He had hastily dressed himself, which explains why he arrived fully clothed in the hall when we brought the body there. Doubtless he tried that night to get a nearer view of the phantom. He recognised her. Old Jacques is an old friend of Mme Mathieu. She probably confessed to him her infatuation for the gamekeeper, and besought him to screen her at that difficult time. Her condition after seeing the dead body of her admirer must have been pitiable. Old Jacques did pity Mme Mathieu, and accompanied her through the oak-grove out of the park, and beyond the lake to the road to Épinay. From there she had but a little way to go to reach home.

'Old Jacques returned to the château, and, seeing how legally important it was for Mme Mathieu that her presence at the château should remain unknown, did his utmost to hide from us this dramatic episode of a night already burdened with terrible incidents.

'I need not ask Mme Mathieu or Old Jacques to confirm these explanations. I know things occurred as I have just related them. I will simply appeal to the memory of M. Larsan, who, no doubt, understands how I learned all this, for he saw me the next morning bent over the double trail – the footprints of Old Jacques and of Mme Mathieu.'

Rouletabille turned to the innkeeper's wife, and bowed to her, saying: 'Madame's footprints bear a strange resemblance to the elegant footprints of the assassin.'

Mme Mathieu trembled, and gazed at the young reporter with a look of eager curiosity. What was he saying? What did he mean?

'Madame,' Rouletabille went on, 'has an elegant foot, long, and rather large for a woman. Its imprint, but for the pointed toe, is similar to that of the assassin.'

There was a movement in the audience. With a gesture Rouletabille repressed it. One might have thought that it was he who was now keeping the audience in order.

'I hasten to say,' he continued, 'that all this is of little importance, and that a detective who would build up a case on such superficial indications as these, without supporting them by a general idea, would make straight for judicial error. M. Robert Darzac also, has feet like the culprit, yet he is not the assassin.'

These words created a great sensation.

The President asked Mme Mathieu: 'Was it so that things happened with you that night, Madame?'

'Yes, M. le Président,' she replied. 'One might believe M. Rouletabille had been behind us.'

'You saw the assassin flying to the end of the right wing, Madame?'

'Yes, as I saw, a minute afterwards, people carrying the body of the gamekeeper.'

'But what became of the assassin? You remained alone in the court of honour. It would be quite natural for you to have seen him there. He was ignorant of your presence and the time had come for him to make his escape.'

'I saw nothing, M. le Président,' said Mme Mathieu. 'At that moment the night became very dark.'

'M. Rouletabille, then,' said the President, 'will explain to us how the assassin made his escape?'

'Certainly!' the young man replied, with so much assurance that even the President could not refrain from smiling. Rouletabille continued: 'It was impossible that the assassin could escape by ordinary means from the end of the court where he had entered unseen by us. If we had not *seen* him, we should have *touched* him. The place is a little bit of a courtyard – a tiny square surrounded by ditches and high iron railings. The assassin would have had to tread on us – or we on him. This square was as securely enclosed by its ditches and iron railings, and by ourselves, as the Yellow Room.'

'Then, since the man was confined in that narrow square, tell us how it was that you did not find him there. I have been asking you this question for the last half-hour!'

Rouletabille once more took his huge watch from his waistcoat-pocket, observed the time, and said in a quiet tone: 'M. le Président, you may ask me that for another three hours and thirty minutes, but I shall not be able to answer you before half-past six!'

This time the murmurs were neither hostile nor those of disappointment. The audience were beginning to have faith in Rouletabille. They were amused by his assurance, and by his daring to fix a time for the President, just as he might make an appointment with a comrade.

As for the President, after wondering whether he ought to be angry, he decided to be amused by this youth, as was everyone else.

Rouletabille was sympathetic, and the President already began to like the young man. Besides, Rouletabille had so clearly defined the part played by Mme Mathieu in the affair, and explained so clearly every one of her acts that night that M. de Rocoux felt compelled to take him almost seriously.

'Well, M. Rouletabille,' he said at last, 'it shall be as you please; but don't let me see any more of you till half-past six o'clock!'

Rouletabille bowed to the President, and, wagging his big round head, made his way to the witnesses' room.

* * *

He looked for me, but did not see me. I gently made my way through the crowd, and left the court almost at the same time as Rouletabille. He greeted me with effusion. He was happy and loquacious, and shook both my hands with jubilation. I said to him: 'I will not ask you, my friend, what you have been doing in America. No doubt you would answer me as you have answered the President – that you cannot tell me anything before half-past six.'

'No, no, my dear Sainclair – no! I am going to tell you at once why I went to America, because you are a friend. I went to America in search of the name of the second half of the assassin!'

'Really! The name of the second half – '

'Exactly. When we left Glandier for the last time I knew the two halves of the assassin, and the name of one of his halves. It was the name of the other half which I went to America to discover.'

We were then entering the witnesses' room. They crowded about Rouletabille with warm greetings. The reporter was very amiable, except towards Arthur Rance, to whom he showed marked coolness.

Frédéric Larsan came in. Rouletabille went up to him and shook his hand in that particularly powerful manner of which he had the painful secret, which left one's fingers nearly broken. In showing him so much sympathy, Rouletabille must have felt perfectly sure of having got the better of the great detective. Larsan, equally sure of himself, smiled, and, in his turn, asked what he had been doing in America. Then my friend, in a charming way, took him by the arm and told him several anecdotes about his voyage. After a while they moved away in conversation about more serious matters, and I discreetly left them. Moreover, I was anxious to return to the court, where the examination of witnesses was being continued. I resumed my seat, and realised at once that the public felt very little interest in what was going on, but were impatiently awaiting the hour of half-past six.

* * *

Half-past six at last!

Joseph Rouletabille was again called. To describe the excitement with which the crowd watched him as he walked to the witness-box would be impossible. Everyone present held his breath. Robert Darzac rose to his feet; he was as pale as death.

The President said gravely: 'I do not compel you to take the oath, Monsieur. You have not been regularly summoned, but I hope there is no need to explain to you the great importance of what you are about to say in this court.' And he added warningly: 'The great importance of your words – *to you*, if not to others!'

Rouletabille, who was not in the least degree disturbed, looked him steadily in the face, and replied: 'Yes, Monsieur.'

'Now then,' said the President, 'we were speaking a little time ago of that little corner of the courtyard where the assassin sought refuge, and you promised to tell us at half-past six o'clock how he got away from it, also, what is his name. It is twenty-five minutes to seven, M. Rouletabille, and we know nothing from you yet.'

'Quite so, Monsieur,' began my friend, in the midst of a silence so solemn that I cannot remember ever to have experienced the like of it. 'I have told you that the end of the court was closed, and that it was impossible for the assassin to escape from the square without being seen by the persons who were in search of him. That is the exact truth. When we were there, in the little square end of the court, the assassin was with us!'

'And you did not see him! That's exactly what the prosecution declares!'

'But we all saw him, M. le Président!' cried Rouletabille.

'And you did not arrest him!'

'I was the only one who knew he was the assassin. It was important to me that he should not be immediately arrested. Moreover, at the time I had no other proof than my personal conviction. Yes, my reason alone proved to me that the assassin was there, and that we were looking at him. I have taken my own time to bring today to this Assize Court an irrefutable proof, a proof which, I may declare, will satisfy everybody!'

'Speak out, Monsieur – speak out, then! Tell us the name of the assassin!'

'You will find it amongst the names of those who were in that corner of the courtyard,' replied Rouletabille, who did not appear to be in the least hurry.

The public began to be impatient.

'The name? The name?' several voices murmured.

'I delay this declaration of mine a little, M. le Président, because I have certain reasons for doing so.'

'The name? The name?' the crowd repeated.

'Silence!' interjected the usher.

The President said: 'You must tell us the name at once, Monsieur. Those who were at the end of the court were, first of all, the dead gamekeeper. Was *he* the assassin?'

'No, Monsieur.'

'Old Jacques?'

'No, Monsieur.'

'The concierge, Bernier?'

'No, Monsieur.'

'Mr Arthur William Rance, then? There only remain Mr Arthur William Rance and yourself. You are not the assassin, are you?'

'No, Monsieur.'

'Then you accuse Mr Arthur William Rance?'

'No, Monsieur.'

'I no longer understand you! What are you leading up to? There was nobody else at the end of the court.'

'I beg your pardon, Monsieur. There was no other person at the end of the court, nor under it; but there was someone *above* it – someone who was leaning out of his window at the end of the court.'

'Frédéric Larsan!' cried the President.

'*Frédéric Larsan!*' replied Rouletabille in a thundering voice. And, turning towards the public, who were already making protestations, he shouted to them with a strength of which I had not thought him capable: '*Frédéric Larsan, the assassin!*'

There was a general outcry. It was expressive of amazement, indignation, scepticism, and, in some cases, of enthusiasm for the youth who was bold enough to make such a tremendous accusation. The President did not attempt to quell the uproar. When it had subsided under the energetic 'Hush!' of those who were impatient to know more, Robert Darzac was distinctly heard to murmur: 'It is impossible! He is mad!'

The President spoke. 'You dare to accuse Frédéric Larsan, Monsieur! See what an impression your accusation has made! M. Robert

Darzac himself calls you a madman! If you are not mad, you must have proofs.'

'Proofs, Monsieur? You want proofs? Well, I am going to give you one to begin with!' cried the piercing voice of Rouletabille. 'Let Frédéric Larsan be called into court!'

'Usher,' cried the President, 'call Frédéric Larsan!'

The usher hurried to the door of the witnesses' room, opened it, and disappeared. The little door remained open; the eyes of all were turned towards it. The man returned, and advanced to the centre of the court.

'M. le Président,' he said, 'Frédéric Larsan is not there. He went away about four o'clock, and has not been seen since.'

'My proof – there you have it!' Rouletabille shouted triumphantly.

'Explain yourself. What proof?' asked the President.

'My irrefutable proof,' said the young reporter. 'Don't you see it in the very flight of Larsan? I can swear to you that he will not return! You will see no more of Frédéric Larsan!'

People were murmuring at the back of the court.

'If you are not mocking the Law, Monsieur, why did you not take advantage of his presence with you in this court to accuse him face to face? At least, he would have been able to answer you!'

'What answer *could* be more complete than this one, M. le Président? He does not answer me! He will never answer me! I accuse Frédéric Larsan of being the assassin, and he runs away! You consider that to be no answer, Monsieur?'

'We refuse to believe – we cannot believe that Larsan, as you say, has fled! Why should he have fled? He did not know that you were going to accuse him!'

'Oh yes, Monsieur, he did know, since I told him so myself, not very long ago!'

'You did that! You believe Larsan to be the assassin, and you gave him the means of escaping?'

'Yes, M. le Président, I did that,' replied Rouletabille proudly. 'I have nothing to do with the Law, neither do I belong to the police. I am merely a journalist, and it is not my business to get people arrested. I serve truth in my own way – that is *my* business. You, the magistrates, are here to protect Society as best you can, and that is *your* business. But you will never get me to provide heads for the executioner to cut off! If you are just, M. le Président – and you are – you will find that I am right. Did I not tell you a short time ago that you would understand why I could not pronounce the name of the assassin before half-past six? I had calculated the time necessary to warn Frédéric Larsan, and allow him to take the 4.17 train to Paris, where he would place himself in safety. One hour to reach Paris, one hour and a quarter to enable him to destroy all traces of his flight – that brought us to half-past six o'clock! You will not find Frédéric Larsan' – Rouletabille here fixed his eyes on M. Darzac – 'Larsan is too cunning. He is a man who has always escaped you, and whom you have long pursued in vain. If he is not quite as clever as I am' – Rouletabille laughed heartily as he spoke, and laughed alone, for nobody felt inclined to laugh with him – 'he is cleverer than all the police on earth. The man who four years ago managed to join the detective staff, and in that capacity become famous under the name of Frédéric Larsan, is notorious for other reasons, and considerably more so under another name which is also well known to you. Frédéric Larsan, M. le Président, is *Ballmeyer*!'

'Ballmeyer!' cried the President.

'Ballmeyer!' Robert Darzac exclaimed, springing to his feet. 'Ballmeyer! It was true, then!'

'Aha, M. Darzac! you do not think I am mad now?' said Rouletabille.

'Ballmeyer! Ballmeyer! Ballmeyer!' Nothing else was heard in the court.

The President suspended the hearing.

One can readily imagine the excitement and uproar that reigned during this interval of the proceedings. The public had enough to think and talk about. Ballmeyer! Everybody thought that 'decidedly the youngster was a marvel!' Ballmeyer! The report of his death had been spread a few weeks before. Ballmeyer, then, had escaped death, as all his life he had escaped the police. Is it necessary that I should recount here the doings of Ballmeyer? For twenty years they have filled the law reports and the newspapers, and though some of my readers may have forgotten the affair of the Yellow Room, the name of Ballmeyer has certainly not faded from their memory.

Ballmeyer was the true type of the Society swindler. He was a 'perfect gentleman'. There was no abler sleight-of-hand man than he. There was no Apache more terrible and audacious. Received in the best society, admitted to membership of the most exclusive clubs, he had robbed families of honour and punters of their money with a skill never surpassed. On certain difficult occasions he had not hesitated to make use of the knife and the sheep's-bone. As a matter of fact, he never hesitated, and no enterprise was too great for him.

Having fallen into the hands of the Law, he escaped on the morning of his trial by throwing pepper into the eyes of the guards who were taking him to the Assize Court. It became known later that on the day of his flight, while the keenest detectives were after him, he was quietly, without even having 'made up' his face, seated in the stalls of the Theatre Français watching the first performance of a new play!

He afterwards left France to 'work' America, and the police of the State of Ohio one day laid hands on this extraordinary bandit. But the next day he escaped again. It would require a volume to tell the complete story of Ballmeyer. This was the man who had become Frédéric Larsan! It was this boy, this Rouletabille, who had discovered that! It was this youngster who, although he knew the past of Ballmeyer, permitted him once more to laugh at the world by giving him the means of escape!

In respect of this I could not but admire Rouletabille, for I knew that his purpose was to serve both M. Robert Darzac and Mlle Stangerson by freeing them from the blackmailer without allowing him to speak.

The crowd had not yet recovered from the amazement caused by the young reporter's revelations, and I had already heard some of the most excited amongst them saying, 'Admitting that the assassin was Frédéric Larsan, that doesn't explain how he got out of the Yellow Room,' when the hearing was resumed.

* * *

Rouletabille was immediately called to the witness-box, and his examination – for he had to submit to an interrogatory rather than make a deposition – was resumed.

'You have told us,' said the President, 'that it was impossible to escape from the end of the court. I admit that. I will even admit that since Frédéric Larsan was leaning out of the window above you, he was still in the little court. But to leave that court, to reach that window, how did he proceed?'

'I have said that he did not escape by ordinary means,' Rouletabille replied. 'He had, consequently, fled in an extraordinary way, for the end of the court was only closed in the ordinary sense, whilst the Yellow Room was *absolutely* closed. It was possible to climb up the wall of the court – a thing impossible in the Yellow Room. He could then spring on to the veranda, and from there, while we were bending over the body of the gamekeeper, gain access to the gallery by the window just above it. Larsan, after that, had nothing more to do than to open the window and speak to us. It was all mere child's play to an athlete of Ballmeyer's ability. And here, M. le Président, you have the proof of my statements.'

Rouletabille then drew from his pocket a small packet, which he opened, producing from it a strong peg.

'Here, M. le Président,' he said, 'is a peg which fits perfectly into a small hole still to be seen in the cornice supporting the terrace. Larsan, who foresaw everything, and thought of all possible means of flight to or from his room – a necessary precaution when one is playing the game he played – had previously fixed this peg into a stone. One foot on the stone post which stands at the angle of the château, the other foot on this peg, one hand on the cornice of the gamekeeper's door, the other on the veranda, and Frédéric Larsan disappears in the air, the more easily because he is extremely nimble and quick, and, furthermore, because that evening he was not in the least under the influence of a sleeping-draught, as he wished us to believe.

'We dined with him, M. le Président, and at dessert he played off on us the trick of the gentleman who suddenly feels terribly sleepy, for he wanted to appear to have been drugged, so that the day after no surprise should be expressed that I, too, had been the victim of an opiate whilst dining with him. From the fact that we both shared a similar fate he would be unsuspected; for I, M. le Président, had been thoroughly sent to sleep, and by Larsan himself! If I had not been in that condition Larsan would not have been able to enter Mlle Stangerson's room, and the crime would not have been committed.'

A groan was heard. It came from M. Darzac, who could not control his great sorrow.

'You can understand,' added Rouletabille, 'the fact of my room being next to his was particularly annoying to Larsan that night, for he knew – or, at least, he might have suspected – that I should be on the watch. Naturally, he could not believe that I suspected him, but I might see him just as he was leaving his own room to go to Mlle Stangerson's. Before entering Mlle Stangerson's room he waited till I was asleep, and my friend Sainclair was busy trying to arouse me.

'Ten minutes later Mlle Stangerson was being murdered, and was screaming.'

The President then asked: 'How did you come to suspect Larsan?'

'My good sense pointed him out to me, M. le Président, and so I had my eye on him. But he is a terribly smart fellow, and I had not foreseen the sleeping-draught trick. Yes, my good sense pointed him out to me. But I required a tangible proof – I wanted, as it were, to see him with my eyes after seeing him at the "right end of my judgment".'

'What do you mean by the "right end of your judgment"?'

'Well, M. le Président, judgment has two ends – the right and the wrong. There is but one on which you can lean with safety, and that is the right end. You know it because nothing can make it give way or break, whatever you do or whatever you say. The day after the affair of the mysterious gallery, when I was in a worse state than the most stupid of those dull fools who don't know how to use their judgment because they cannot exercise it, whilst I was broken in spirit and in despair through those deceptive superficial clues, I raised my head, and, leaning on the "right end of my judgment", became at once buoyed up with hope.

'There I satisfied myself that the assassin whom we were all pursuing could not on that occasion have left the gallery either by ordinary or extraordinary means. Then with the "right end of my judgment" I drew a circle, within which I enclosed the problem. Around this circle I mentally wrote these blazing words: "Since the assassin cannot be outside the circle, he is within it!" Who did I see within my circle? The "right end of my judgment" showed me that, besides the assassin, who must necessarily be within it, there were Old Jacques, M. Stangerson, Frédéric Larsan, and myself. These made, including the assassin, five persons. Now, when I searched within the circle – or, if you prefer it, in the gallery, to speak materially – I found only four persons in all. It was demonstrated that the fifth could not have fled – could not have got out of the circle. So that I had within my circle one person who was really two – that is to say, a being who, in addition to his own personality, was the person of the assassin. Why had I not already perceived that fact? Simply because the question of a "double" had not occurred to me.

'With which of the four persons enclosed within my circle had the assassin been able to double himself without my having perceived it? Obviously not the persons whom I saw, at any moment, independently of the assassin. Thus, I had seen *at one and the same time* in the gallery M. Stangerson and the assassin, Old Jacques and the assassin, myself and the assassin. The assassin, therefore, could not be M. Stangerson, or Old Jacques, or myself. Had I seen Frédéric Larsan and the assassin at the same time? No! Two seconds passed, during which I lost sight of the assassin; for, as I have noted in my papers,

he arrived two seconds before M. Stangerson, Old Jacques, and myself at the junction of the two galleries. Those two seconds were
sufficient to Larsan to run into the turning gallery, snatch off his
false beard, turn round, and rush towards us as if, like us, he were in
pursuit of the assassin. Ballmeyer had done things more difficult than
this. And you will easily understand that to him it was child's play to
"make up" in such ways that he appeared at one time with a red beard
to Mlle Stangerson, and at another to a post-office clerk wearing a
brown beard that made him look like M. Robert Darzac, whom he
wished to ruin.

'Yes, the "right end of my judgment" brought together those two
persons, or, rather, *the two halves* of this one person – which I had
never seen at the same time – Frédéric Larsan and the unknown man
I wanted – and made of them the mysterious and formidable being of
whom I was in search – the assassin.

'That revelation completely upset me. I tried to recover by occupy-
ing myself with those external clues which had, till then, led me
astray, which I must naturally bring within the circle traced by the
"right end of my judgment".

'What, in the first place, were the principal external clues which
that night had led me away from the idea of Larsan as the assassin?

'1st. I had seen the unknown person in the room of Mlle Stangerson, and, running to the room of Frédéric Larsan, I had found him
there, dull with sleep.

'2nd. The ladder.

'3rd. I had placed Frédéric Larsan at the end of the turning gallery,
and told him I was going to spring into the room of Mlle Stangerson
to try and capture the assassin. Then I returned to Mlle Stangerson's
room, where I found my unknown!

'The first external clue did not embarrass me much. It is probable
that when I came down the ladder, after having seen the unknown
person in Mlle Stangerson's room, he had already finished what he
was doing there. Then, while I was re-entering the château, he went
back to Larsan's room, changed his clothes rapidly, and when I
knocked at the door, showed the face of Frédéric Larsan, as sleepy as
could be.

'The second clue – the ladder – did not embarrass me more. It was
evident that if the assassin was Larsan he did not need a ladder to enter
the château, since his room was next to mine; but the ladder was
there to make people believe the assassin had come from outside –
a thing quite necessary to Larsan's scheme, since M. Darzac was

not at the château that night. Finally, the ladder was there in case of emergency, to facilitate Larsan's flight.

'But the third clue altogether misled me. Having placed Larsan at the end of the turning gallery, I could not see why he had taken advantage of the moment when I had gone to the left wing of the château to M. Stangerson and Old Jacques to return to Mlle Stangerson's room. It was a most dangerous thing to do. He risked being caught, and he knew it. And he was very nearly caught, not having had time to return to his post, as he certainly had hoped to do. He must have had a very urgent reason for going to Mlle Stangerson's room. As for myself, when I sent Old Jacques to the end of the straight gallery, I naturally thought that Larsan was still at his post at the end of the turning gallery; and Old Jacques himself, to whom I had given no details, in going to his post did not look to see whether Larsan was at his or not.

'Old Jacques only thought of carrying out my instructions quickly. What, then, was the unforeseen reason which induced Larsan to go to the room the second time? What was it? I thought it could only be some obvious sign of his presence there – a sign which would betray him. He had forgotten something of great importance while in the room. What was it? Had he found it again? I recollected the candle on the parquet-floor, and the stooping man. I asked Mme Bernier, who used to clean the room, to search it thoroughly, and Mme Bernier found in a crevice of the parquet a pince-nez – *this pince-nez*, M. le Président!'

Rouletabille drew from his pocket the pince-nez with which we already are acquainted.

'When I saw this pince-nez,' he continued, 'I was dismayed. I had never seen Larsan wearing eye-glasses. If he did not wear them, it was because he had no need of them. He had still less need of them at a moment when complete liberty of action was so necessary to him. What did this pince-nez mean? It did not enter into my "circle". Unless it belonged to a long-sighted person! This thought flashed across my mind. As a matter of fact, I had never seen Larsan reading. He might, then, be long-sighted. They would certainly know at the Detective Department whether he was. They would, perhaps, know this pince-nez – the pince-nez of *long-sighted Larsan*, found in the room of Mlle Stangerson after the affair of the mysterious gallery. That would indeed be terrible for Larsan! In this way the return of Larsan to the room was explained. And, as a matter of fact, Larsan-Ballmeyer is long-sighted, and this pince-nez, which they will probably recognise at the Detective Department, is his property.

'You see now, Monsieur, what my system is,' Rouletabille continued. 'I do not rely upon external clues to tell me the truth; I simply ask them not to conflict with the truth which the "right end of my judgment" has pointed out to me.

'To make quite sure of the truth in regard to Larsan – for Larsan, as an assassin, was an exception, necessitating that I should protect myself by proof positive – I made the mistake of wishing to see his face. I have been well punished for it. I really think the "right end of my judgment" avenged itself by punishing me for not having – since the affair of the mysterious gallery – relied solely and in complete confidence upon it. I ought, indeed, to have entirely neglected to search for proofs of Larsan's guilt anywhere but in my judgment. Then Mlle Stangerson was struck down.'

Rouletabille stopped, coughed. He was deeply moved.

* * *

'But,' asked the President, 'what had Larsan intended to do in that room? Why did he twice attempt to assassinate Mlle Stangerson?'

'Because he adored her, M. le Président.'

'That is evidently a reason.'

'Yes, Monsieur. An absolute reason. He was madly in love, and because of that and many other things, was capable of committing any crime.'

'Did Mlle Stangerson know it?'

'Yes, Monsieur; but she was ignorant of the fact that the man who was pursuing her was Frédéric Larsan, otherwise he could not have installed himself at the château, and could not, on that night in the mysterious gallery, have gone with us into Mlle Stangerson's room after the affair. I noticed, moreover, that he remained in the darkest corner of the room, and that he continually bent his head down. He must have been searching for the lost pince-nez. Mlle Stangerson was compelled to bear the attacks of Larsan under a name and disguise unknown to us, but which *she* may already have known.'

'And you, Monsieur Darzac,' asked the President, 'you may perhaps have heard something on this point from Mlle Stangerson. How is it that she has never spoken about it to anyone? It might have put the law on the track of the assassin, and, if you are innocent, would have spared you the pain of being accused.'

'Mlle Stangerson has told me nothing,' replied M. Darzac.

'Does what this young man has said appear possible to you?' the President asked.

M. Robert Darzac replied imperturbably: 'Mlle Stangerson has told me nothing.'

The President turned again to Rouletabille: 'How do you explain that, on the night of the murder of the gamekeeper, the assassin brought back the papers stolen from M. Stangerson? How do you explain the means by which the assassin gained admission to the locked room of Mlle Stangerson?'

'Oh, as to the last question, I think it is easily answered. A man like Larsan-Ballmeyer could have obtained, or had made, the keys he required. As for the theft of the documents, I believe that Larsan had not at first thought of it. Closely watching Mlle Stangerson, and having made up his mind to prevent her marriage with M. Robert Darzac, he followed her and M. Darzac into the *Magasins du Louvre* one day, and got possession of the reticule which she lost, or was robbed of. In that reticule there was a key with a brass head. He did not know the importance of it till it was revealed to him by the advertisements which appeared in the newspaper. He wrote to Mlle Stangerson, "Poste Restante", as the advertisement requested. No doubt he asked for a rendezvous, informing her at the same time that he, who had the reticule and the key, was the person who had for some time pursued her with his love. He received no answer.

'He went to Post Office No. 40, and ascertained that his letter was no longer there. He had already adopted the ways and the bearing of M. Darzac, and, as far as possible, had dressed like him, for, having determined to win Mlle Stangerson at any cost, he had prepared everything, so that, whatever might happen, M. Darzac, the beloved of Mlle Stangerson, M. Darzac whom he detested, and whom he was resolved to ruin, should be taken for the guilty one.

'I say, whatever might happen; but I believe that Larsan had not then thought he would go as far as to murder. In any case, his precautions were taken to compromise Mlle Stangerson under the disguise of M. Darzac. He was very nearly the same size as M. Darzac, and had almost the same sized feet. It was not difficult for him, after taking an impression of M. Darzac's footprints, to have similar boots made for himself. Such tricks were mere child's play to Larsan-Ballmeyer.

'Well, he received no answer to his letter; no appointment was made, and he still had the precious key in his pocket. Since Mlle Stangerson would not come to him, he would go to her. His plan had long been formed. He had procured all necessary information about the château and the pavilion. One afternoon, while M. and Mlle Stangerson were out for a walk, and while Old Jacques was away too, he introduced himself by the vestibule window. He was alone for the moment, and was in no hurry. He examined the furniture, and noticed a small cabinet of curious form, resembling a safe, with a small keyhole. Ah, that was interesting! As he had with him the little key with the brass head, he thought of it – a natural association of ideas.

'He tried the key in the lock; the door opened. The cabinet was full of papers and documents. They must be very precious to have been put away in so peculiar a receptacle, and the key of it to be of so much importance. Oh! That might prove useful – a little blackmailing – it might assist him in his amorous designs. He quickly made a parcel of the papers, and took it to the lavatory in the vestibule.

'Between the expedition to the pavilion and the night of the murder of the gamekeeper, Larsan had had time to see what those papers were. What was he to do with them? They were rather compromising. That night he took them back to the château. Perhaps he hoped that by returning those precious documents, which represented the labours of twenty years, he might win some sort of gratitude from Mlle Stangerson. Everything is possible with a man like Larsan-Ballmeyer. In short, whatever may have been his reason, he took the papers, and was happy to get rid of them.'

Rouletabille coughed, and I understood what his cough meant. It was evident that he was embarrassed at this point of his explanation by his wish not to give the true motive for the frightful attitude of Larsan towards Mlle Stangerson. His argument was too incomplete to satisfy everybody, and the President would no doubt have made some remark about it, had my ready-witted friend not cried suddenly: '*Now we arrive at the explanation of the Yellow Room!*'

*　　*　　*

There was, in the court, a general movement of chairs, slight rustlings, and energetic 'Hushes!' Curiosity was roused to the highest pitch.

'But,' said the President, 'it seems to me, according to your hypothesis, Monsieur Rouletabille, that the mystery of the Yellow Room is wholly explained. It was Frédéric Larsan himself who explained it to us, merely deceiving us as to the identity of the assassin by putting M. Robert Darzac in place of himself. It is evident that the door of the Yellow Room was opened when M. Stangerson was alone, and that he allowed the man who was coming out of his daughter's room to pass without stopping him – perhaps even on her own entreaty – to avoid scandal!'

'No, M. le Président,' protested the young man. 'You forget that Mlle Stangerson was stunned, and consequently unable to make such an appeal; neither could she have locked and bolted herself into her room. You also forget that M. Stangerson has sworn the door had not been opened.'

'That, however, is the only way in which things can be explained, Monsieur. The Yellow Room was shut up as close as an iron safe. To use your own expression, it was impossible for the assassin to make his escape by ordinary, or even extraordinary, means. When the room was entered he was not found there. Therefore he must have escaped.'

'It is quite unnecessary, M. le Président.'

'How can that be?'

'There was no need to escape, *if he was not there.*'

'What! He was not there?'

'Obviously not! Since he *could not* be there, he was *not* there! One must always lean upon the "right end of one's judgment", M. le Président.'

'But what of all the traces of his movements?' the President objected.

'That, M. le Président, is the wrong end of reason. The right end indicates this to us: from the time when Mlle Stangerson shut herself in her room to the moment when her door was burst open, it was impossible that the assassin could have escaped from that room; and as he was not found in it, it was because, from the moment when the door was closed to the moment when it was forced open, the assassin was not in the room!'

'But the traces!'

'Ah, M. le Président, once again this is only apparent evidence, by which so many judicial errors are committed, because it "leads you to believe what it likes". It must not, I repeat, be used to reason by. One must think first, and afterwards find out whether the external clues can be included within the circle of one's argument. I have formed a very small circle of incontrovertible truth; the assassin was not in the Yellow Room. Why was he thought to be there? Because of the traces of his movements. But he may have been there before. Nay, reason tells me that he *must* have been there before. Let us examine these traces, and whatever else we know of the affair, see whether they do not agree with the idea of his being there *before* Mlle Stangerson shut herself into her room in the presence of her father and Old Jacques.

'After the publication of the article in the *Matin*, and a conversation which I had with the examining magistrate during the journey from Paris to Épinay-sur-Orge, the proof that the Yellow Room was mathematically closed appeared to me complete, and consequently that the assassin had left it before Mlle Stangerson went to her room at midnight.

'The external signs then seemed to go terribly against my reasoning. Mlle Stangerson had not been her own assassin, and they proved that it was not a case of suicide. The assassin, then, had come *before*. But how was it that Mlle Stangerson had not been attacked till *afterwards*? Or, rather, that she appeared not to have been attacked until afterwards? Naturally I had to reconstruct the affair into two phases – two phases separated from one another by several hours. The first phase, during which an attempt had really been made to assassinate Mlle Stangerson – an attempt which she had kept secret; the second phase, as the effect of a nightmare she had. Those who were in the laboratory had thought that she was being assassinated!

'At the time I had not yet been in the Yellow Room. What were the injuries to Mlle Stangerson? Marks of strangulation, and a formidable blow on the temple. The marks of strangulation did not trouble me much; they might have been made before, and Mlle Stangerson hidden them under a collarette, a boa – anything. For, since I was obliged to divide the affair into two phases, I was compelled to think that Mlle Stangerson had concealed all the events of the first phase; she, no doubt, had reasons sufficiently strong for doing this, since she had said nothing to her father, and was compelled to tell the story of the attempt made on her life by the assassin – whose passage she could not deny – to the examining magistrate, as if it had taken place in the night, during the second phase. She was compelled to speak then as otherwise her father would have asked: "What have you hidden from us? What does your silence mean after such an attack?"

'She had concealed, then, the marks made by the man on her throat. But there was the formidable blow on the temple! That I could not make out. The less so when I learned that a sheep's-bone, the weapon of the crime, had been found in her room. She could not hide the fact that she had been struck on the head, and yet evidently that wound must have been inflicted during the first phase, since it necessitates the presence of the assassin. I imagined that this wound was much less severe than it was said to be – in which I was wrong – and I thought that Mlle Stangerson had concealed the wound by arranging her hair over her temples in "bandeaux".

'As to the mark on the wall, made by the hand of the assassin, who was wounded by Mlle Stangerson's revolver, it had evidently been made *before*, and so the assassin must have been wounded during the first phase; that is to say, when he was there. All the traces of the assassin's passage had naturally been left during the first phase – the sheep's-bone, the black footprints, the old cap, the handkerchief, the blood on the wall, on the door, and on the floor. It is absolutely clear that if those traces were still all there Mlle Stangerson – who wished to keep the whole matter secret – had not yet had time to remove them. This led me to suppose that the first phase of the affair had taken place not very long before the second.

'If, after the first phase – that is to say, after the assassin's escape – after she herself had hastily returned to the laboratory, where her father found her working, she could have gone back again to her room for a minute, she would at least have hidden the sheep's-bone, the cap, and the handkerchief lying upon the floor. But she did not attempt it, her father not having quitted her. After the first phase, then, she did not return to her room till midnight. Someone had entered it at ten o'clock – Old Jacques, who, as was his practice every night, closed the shutters, and put a match to the night-light. Owing to the disturbed state of her mind – while at the desk in the laboratory, where she pretended to be at work – she had doubtless forgotten that Old Jacques would be going into her room! She was startled; she begged Old Jacques not to trouble himself, not to go into her room. All this was mentioned in the article in the *Matin*. Old Jacques entered all the same, but perceived nothing, so dark was the Yellow Room.

'Mlle Stangerson must have lived through two awful minutes! However, I imagine that she did not know there were so many traces of the assassin left in her room. She had probably – after the first phase – only just time to conceal the marks of the man's fingers on her throat, and to hurry away. Had she known that the bone, the cap, and the handkerchief were on the floor, she would have gathered them up when she retired at midnight. She did not see them, however, as she undressed by the faint glimmer of the night-light. She went to bed exhausted by so many events and by fear – fear that had made her retire as late as possible to her room.

'I was thus forced to come to the second phase of the drama, in which it appeared that Mlle Stangerson was really *alone* in the room, since the assassin had not been found in it, and I had, naturally, to make the external signs come within "the circle of my judgment", as I have explained.

'But there were other external signs! And they required explanation. Revolver-shots had been fired during the second phase. Cries of "Help! Murder!" had been raised. What conclusion could the "right end of my judgment" draw from such circumstances? First, with regard to the cries. Since there was no assassin in the room, they could only be due to *nightmare*! A great noise had been heard. There seemed to have been a struggle; furniture had been overthrown. After reflection I was forced to this conclusion: Mlle Stangerson was sleeping, haunted still by the terrible scene of the afternoon. She dreamed. Nightmare filled her feverish brain with pictures of crime, of murder. She saw once more the assassin hurling himself upon her; she screamed, "Help! Murder!" and wildly felt for the revolver she had placed within her reach on the table by her bedside. But her hand dashed against the table with sufficient force to overturn it. The revolver fell to the floor, and, in falling, was discharged, lodging a bullet in the ceiling. From the outset this bullet in the ceiling appeared to me to have been the result of accident. It showed at least the possibility of an accident, and so fitted in with my theory of the nightmare that it was one of the reasons why I no longer doubted that the crime had been committed much earlier, and that Mlle Stangerson, being endowed with great firmness of character, had kept it secret.

'Mlle Stangerson, in a frightful state of agitation, had awakened. She tried to get up, but fell on the floor exhausted, overturning some of the furniture, and even crying "Help! Murder!" and finally fainted.

'However, *two* revolver-shots were said to have been fired that night at the time of the second phase. My theory of the tragedy demanded that two shots should have been fired, one in each of the two phases, and not two in the last – one *before*, to wound the assassin, and one *after*, at the time of the nightmare. Now, was it quite certain that during the night two shots had been fired? The report of the revolver was heard in the midst of the noise of the falling furniture. When questioned by the examining magistrate, M. Stangerson spoke of a *dull* sound which he had heard first, followed by a *ringing* sound. What if the dull sound had been caused by the fall of the marble-topped table on the floor? It was *necessary* that that explanation should be the right one. I became certain it was the right one when I learned that the concierges, Bernier and his wife, had not heard – although quite close to the pavilion – more than *one* revolver-shot. They said so to the examining magistrate.

'Thus I had almost reconstructed the two phases of the drama when, for the first time, I entered the Yellow Room. The gravity of the wound on the victim's temple, however, did not enter "the circle of my judgment". This wound, then, had *not* been made by the assassin with the sheep's-bone at the time of the first phase, for it was too serious a wound: Mlle Stangerson could not possibly have concealed it by dressing her hair in the Madonna style with "bandeaux" over the temples, as I had supposed. Had that wound, then, been made at the time of the second phase during the nightmare scene? I asked this of the Yellow Room, and the Yellow Room answered me.'

Rouletabille drew from the same little package a piece of white paper, neatly folded in four, and took from it an invisible object, which he held between his thumb and forefinger, and carried to the President.

'This, M. le Président, is a hair, a blonde hair, from the head of Mlle Stangerson. I found it sticking to one of the corners of the overthrown table, the marble top of which was certainly stained with blood. Certainly a very tiny stain, but most important, for it told me that, on rising bewildered from her bed, Mlle Stangerson had fallen heavily on the corner of the marble top, and had been wounded on the temple. The marble retained this hair, which must have been on Mlle Stangerson's forehead, although she did not have her hair dressed in "bandeaux".'

Once more the crowd applauded; but as Rouletabille immediately continued his deposition silence was instantly restored.

'I had still to learn – besides the name of the assassin, which I only discovered a few days later – at what moment the first phase of the drama had taken place. The interrogation of Mlle Stangerson, though calculated to deceive the examining magistrate, with that of M. Stangerson, disclosed it to me. Mlle Stangerson described very exactly how she had employed her time that day. We had established the fact that the assassin introduced himself into the pavilion between five and six o'clock; let us say that it was a quarter-past six when the professor and his daughter resumed their work. The drama could only have been enacted while the professor was away. What I had to do, then, was to find within that short space of time *the moment when the professor and his daughter were not together.*

And that moment I found in the interrogatory which took place in Mlle Stangerson's room, in the presence of M. Stangerson.

'It was said that the professor and his daughter returned to the laboratory about six o'clock. M. Stangerson made the following statement: "At that moment I was accosted by my gamekeeper, who detained me for a while." The professor then had a conversation with the gamekeeper. The man spoke to him about thinning out the woods and about poachers. Mlle Stangerson was no longer there. She had already gone to the laboratory, since the professor said further: "I left the gamekeeper and rejoined my daughter, who was already at work."

'The drama must needs have been enacted during those short moments. I can clearly see Mlle Stangerson re-enter the pavilion, and go to her room to take off her hat, and then find herself suddenly face to face with the scoundrel who was pursuing her. The man had been in the pavilion for some time. He had arranged his plan so that everything would occur during the night. He had taken off the boots of Old Jacques; he had removed the papers from the cabinet, and had afterwards slipped under the bed. The time had appeared very long to him. He had got up, had gone again into the laboratory, into the vestibule, had looked out into the garden, and had seen coming towards the pavilion Mlle Stangerson – *alone*! He would never have dared to attack her then if he had not thought she was absolutely alone. For him to suppose she was quite alone, the conversation between M. Stangerson and the gamekeeper must needs have taken place at a bend in the path where there was a cluster of trees which hid the two men from the assassin's sight. His plan was decided upon. He would be more at his ease alone with Mlle Stangerson in the pavilion, then, than he would be in the middle of the night with Old Jacques above, sleeping in the attic. And so he shut the vestibule window, which explains why neither M. Stangerson nor the gamekeeper, who were at some distance from the pavilion, heard the revolver-shot.

'The criminal went back to the Yellow Room. Mlle Stangerson arrived. What passed must have been as quick as lightning! Mlle Stangerson probably screamed out, or tried to do so. The man seized her by the throat. He was perhaps going to stifle her – to strangle her; but her hand had sought and grasped the revolver which she had been keeping in the drawer of her bedside table since she began to fear the man's threats. The assassin was already brandishing over her head that weapon so terrible in the hands of Larsan-Ballmeyer – a sheep's-bone. She fired. The shot wounded the assassin in the hand; the sheep's-bone dropped on the floor, covered with the blood of the man's wound. He staggered, clutched at the wall for support – imprinting upon it the marks of his red fingers – and, fearing another bullet, fled.

'She saw him pass through the laboratory. She listened. What was he doing in the vestibule? He was a long time at the window. At last he jumped from it. She flew to the window and shut it. And now, had her father seen? Had he heard? Now that the danger was over all her thoughts were of her father. Gifted with superhuman energy, she would hide all from him if it were not too late. So, when M. Stangerson returned, he found the door of the Yellow Room closed, and his daughter in the laboratory, bent over her desk, already at work!'

Rouletabille turned towards M. Darzac.

'You know the truth,' he cried. 'Tell us, if that is not what happened.'

'I know nothing about it,' replied M. Darzac.

Rouletabille folded his arms, and said: 'You are a hero, Monsieur Darzac, but if Mlle Stangerson were in a condition to realise that you are accused she would release you from your oath – she would beg of you to tell all she confided to you; moreover, she would herself come here to defend you!'

The prisoner did not stir, nor did he pronounce a word. He only looked sadly at Rouletabille.

'Well, then,' said the young reporter, 'since Mlle Stangerson is not here, I must do it myself; but believe me, M. Darzac, the best way – the only way – to save Mlle Stangerson and to restore her reason is for you to get yourself acquitted.'

A thunder of applause greeted this last phrase. The President did not even attempt to repress the enthusiasm of the crowd. Robert Darzac was saved. It only needed a glance at the jurors to be certain of it. Their attitude emphatically bespoke their conviction.

The President then said: 'But what is the mystery which makes Mlle Stangerson, when somebody has twice tried to assassinate her, conceal such a crime from her father?'

'That, M. le Président, I don't know,' said Rouletabille. 'It's no business of mine.'

The President once more endeavoured to induce M. Darzac to speak out.

'You still refuse, Monsieur, to tell us how you were spending your time while attempts were being made on the life of Mlle Stangerson?'

'I cannot tell you anything, Monsieur.'

The President turned an appealing look at Rouletabille.

'One may well suppose, M. le Président, that the absences of M. Robert Darzac were closely connected with Mlle Stangerson's secret. That is why M. Darzac feels bound to remain silent. Suppose that Larsan, who in his three attempts took every possible means to turn suspicion on to M. Darzac, had fixed, exactly on those three occasions, certain rendezvous for M. Darzac at some compromising places – rendezvous where the mysterious affair was to be discussed. M. Darzac would rather be found guilty than explain anything connected with Mlle Stangerson's secret. Larsan was clever enough to have planned even that.'

The President, half-convinced, but still curious, asked again: 'But what can that mystery be?'

'Ah, Monsieur, I cannot tell you!' said Rouletabille, bowing to the President. 'Only I think you know enough now to acquit M. Robert Darzac – unless Larsan should return; but I don't think he will,' he added, with a happy, hearty laugh.

Everybody laughed with him.

'One more question, Monsieur,' said the President. 'Admitting your theory, we know that Larsan wished to divert suspicion to M. Robert Darzac; but what interest had he in turning it also on Old Jacques?'

'The interest of the detective, Monsieur, in showing himself to be a marvellous unraveller of intricacies, by destroying the proofs he had himself accumulated. That was very clever indeed. It is a trick that had often enabled him to divert suspicion from himself. He proved the innocence of one person before accusing another. You must understand, M. le Président, that such a scheme as this had evidently been thought out and prepared a long time in advance by Larsan. I can assure you that he had seen to every detail, and knew thoroughly everybody and everything at Glandier. If it interests you to know how Larsan became acquainted with the place, I may tell you that he had at one time made himself the official messenger between the laboratory of the Detective Department and M. Stangerson, who had been asked to make certain experiments for it.

'By that means he had been able, before the crime, to enter the pavilion twice. He had "made up" in such a way that Old Jacques afterwards did not recognise him; he had taken advantage of his visit to the pavilion to rob Jacques of a pair of old boots and a cap, which the servant had tied up in a handkerchief, probably with the intention of taking them to one of his friends – a charcoal-burner on the road to Épinay. When the crime was discovered, Old Jacques, who naturally recognised those things as belonging to him, pretended not to know them – at least, not at once. They were too compromising, and this explains his confusion when we spoke to him about them. It is all perfectly obvious. I drove Larsan into a corner, and made him confess the whole thing. He did so, indeed, with gusto. For if he is a ruffian – which, I hope, nobody doubts any longer – he is also an artist. He has his own way of doing things. He acted in a similar way in the "Universal Credit Bank" case, and in that of the "Gold Ingots of the Mint". Those cases will have to be revised, M. le Président; for a good many innocent persons have been sent to prison since Larsan-Ballmeyer has belonged to the Detective Department!'

Chapter 28

In which it is proved that one does not always think of everything

Great excitement; murmurs, applause! Maître Henri Robert asked
for an adjournment of the trial to another session, to make further investigations. The Advocate-General concurred. The trial
was postponed. M. Robert Darzac was provisionally liberated,
and Mathieu was unconditionally released, his innocence having
been established. Larsan was searched for in vain. M. Darzac escaped
the frightful calamity which had for a while threatened him,
and, having called on Mlle Stangerson, was enabled to hope that,
with constant and devoted care, she would some day recover her
reason.

As for Rouletabille, he was naturally the lion of the hour. When he
left the Law Court of Versailles, the crowd carried him shoulder-
high. Newspapers all over the world published accounts of his great
achievements and reproduced his photograph; and he, who had interviewed so many celebrated personages, became celebrated himself,
and was interviewed in his turn. I may add that the modest youngster
did not appear to lose his head over it.

We returned from Versailles together, after having dined at the
Smoking Dog. In the train I asked Rouletabille all sorts of questions
which, during our meal, I had refrained from putting, knowing he
did not like to 'work' while eating.

'My friend,' I said, 'this affair of Larsan is quite sublime, and
worthy of your wonderful brain!'

He stopped me, and begged me to talk more simply, pretending
that nothing would ever console him for seeing so fine an intellect as
mine ready to fall into the hideous abyss of imbecility, precipitated
thither by admiration for himself.

'I will come to the point then,' I said, a little nettled. 'All that has
passed does not in the least enlighten me as to your motive in going
to America. If I rightly understood you, when you last left Glandier
you had already found out all about Frédéric Larsan. You knew that

he was the assassin, and you had nothing more to learn as to the way he had attempted to carry out the assassination?'

'Exactly! And you,' he said, trying to turn the conversation – 'you suspected nothing?'

'Nothing!'

'It is incredible!'

'But, my dear friend, you took very great pains to hide your thoughts from me, and I don't see how I could have surmised them. When I arrived at Glandier with the revolvers, did you already suspect Larsan?'

'I did. I had just been thinking out the "mysterious gallery" affair in the way I have explained to the judges this afternoon; but the return of Larsan to Mlle Stangerson's room had not then been made clear to me by the discovery of the long-sighted pince-nez. Moreover, my deduction was only mathematical, and the idea of Larsan being the assassin appeared to me so formidable that I resolved to wait for some external proofs before venturing to admit it any further. Nevertheless, the idea worried me, and I sometimes spoke to you of the detective in a manner that ought to have roused your suspicions about him. I no longer mentioned, as I had done before, his good faith; I no longer said to you that he was mistaken; I spoke of his system as a miserable system, and my contempt – which you thought was meant for the detective – was really meant, in my mind, less for the detective than for the *criminal* I already suspected him to be!

'Remember in what tone I once asked you, "Now, does this idea really mislead Larsan? That is the question – that is the question – that is the question!" Those words, three times repeated, ought to have given you some inkling of my suspicions. But I watched you – you did not seem to guess my hidden meaning, and I was pleased; for I was not absolutely certain of Larsan's guilt until the discovery of the pince-nez. But after that discovery, which explained the return of Larson to Mlle Stangerson's room, I was really happy – perfectly happy! I remember it all! I rushed into my room like a madman, and cried to you "I'll beat Larsan – I'll beat the great Frédéric!"'

'Those words referred to the bandit, not the detective. And that same evening, when I was requested by M. Darzac to watch over Mlle Stangerson, I restrained myself until ten o'clock, dining with Larsan – taking no special precautions whatever. I kept quiet, and did nothing, because he was there opposite me. At that moment, again, you might have suspected that it was he alone I feared. And, again, when I said to you, in reference to the approaching arrival of the assassin, "I am quite sure that Frédéric Larsan will be here tonight."

'But there was one important object which ought at once to have proved to us the identity of the criminal – a thing which convicted Frédéric Larsan, and which we both allowed to escape us – you and I. Have you forgotten the story of the bamboo cane? Yes, in addition to the reasoning, which, to all logical minds, convicted Larsan, there was the story of the cane, and this alone should have denounced him to all observant minds.

'I was altogether astonished to note that, during the legal inquiry, Larsan made no use of the cane against M. Darzac. Had not that cane been purchased by a man whose description corresponded with that of M. Darzac? Well, a little while ago, before he stepped into the train that took him away, I asked Larsan why he had not made any use of the cane. He answered that he never had any intention of using it in the way I suggested; that he had never imagined anything against M. Darzac in connection with it; and that we had greatly embarrassed him that evening at the inn near the station at Épinay, by proving that he was lying to us.

'You know he said to me that he had obtained the stick in London, whilst the mark on it showed that it had come from Paris. Why, instead of thinking, "Frédéric is lying. He was in London; he could not have had this Paris cane in London!" why did we not say, "Frédéric *certainly* lies! He was not in London, since he bought that stick in Paris"? Frédéric a liar! Frédéric really in Paris at the time of the crime! A starting-point for suspicion that! And when, after your enquiry at Cassette's, you told me that the stick had been bought by a person dressed like M. Robert Darzac, when we were positive, having M. Darzac's word for it, that it was not he who had purchased the stick; and further, when we were sure, thanks to the poste-restante affair, that there was a man in Paris assuming the identity of M. Darzac, and we wondered who this man could be, who, disguised as Darzac, entered Cassette's on the evening of the crime, and bought a stick which we found in Larsan's hands, why – why – why did we not instantly think, "What if this unknown person, disguised as Darzac, who buys the stick which Larsan has in his hands, were – were Larsan himself?"?

'Of course, his position as an official detective did not lend colour to this supposition, but when we saw the eagerness with which Larsan accumulated evidence against Darzac – the rage with which he pursued the unfortunate man – we might have been struck by Frédéric's huge lie. Now, how was it he never used the cane as one found near M. Darzac? It is very simple – it is really so simple that we never thought of it!

'Larsan bought it after he was slightly wounded in the hand by Mlle Stangerson's shot, solely for the look of the thing – to keep his hand continually closed – not to be tempted to open it, and let the wound be seen. Do you understand now? Larsan told me all this himself, and I remember having more than once remarked to you how strange it seemed that Larsan's hand *never quitted that cane*! At table, when I dined with him, having let go of his cane, he took up a knife with his right hand, and never put it down during the meal.

'I recollected all these details when my mind was fixed on Larsan, but too late for me to use them. For instance, on the evening when Larsan pretended to be asleep, I bent over him and looked in his hand without his suspecting it. There was only a small piece of court-plaster hiding what remained of a very slight wound – so slight, indeed, that Larsan might have said it had been made by anything but the bullet of a revolver. Nevertheless, so far as I was concerned, a new outward proof entered straightway within "the circle of my judgment". The bullet, as Larsan told me this afternoon before he disappeared, only grazed the palm of his hand, but caused an abundant flow of blood.

'If we had been more perspicacious at the moment when Larsan lied – and more dangerous – it is certain that he would have used, to ward off suspicion, the very story we had imagined – the story of the discovery of Darzac's stick. But events occurred in such rapid succession that we forgot all about the cane. All the same, we considerably worried Larsan-Ballmeyer without suspecting it.'

'But, my friend,' I interrupted, 'if Larsan had no intention of using the cane against Darzac when he bought it, why did he so closely "make up" to resemble him when he went to buy it?'

'Because he had only just reached Paris, after committing the crime at Glandier, and had, immediately afterwards, disguised himself as Darzac – a disguise which he has repeatedly used in his criminal task, with what intention you know. But his wounded hand was even then worrying him, and, as he was passing the Avenue de l'Opéra, he thought he would buy a stick, and did so at once. It was eight o'clock. Think of it! A man looking like Darzac bought a cane which I found in the hand of Larsan, and I – I – I, who had guessed that the drama had already taken place – that, in fact, it had just taken place at that time – I, who was almost persuaded of Darzac's innocence – never suspected Larsan! Really, there are moments when – '

'There are moments,' I said, 'when the greatest intelligence – '

Rouletabille stopped me there, and although I still asked him questions, I found he was no longer listening to me – he was sound asleep, and I had all the trouble in the world to wake him when we reached Paris!

Chapter 29
The mystery of Mlle Stangerson

During the following days I found an opportunity to ask Rouletabille what he had been to America for. He did not answer me much more precisely than he had done in the train from Versailles, and he turned the conversation to other points of the affair.

At last, one day, he told me.

'Can't you see that I needed to find out the true personality of Larsan?'

'No doubt,' I replied; 'but why did you go to America to find it?'

He smoked his pipe and turned his back to me. Evidently I was encroaching upon the mystery of Mlle Stangerson. Rouletabille thought that this mystery, which bound her and Larsan together in a manner so terrible – a mystery of which he, Rouletabille, could find no explanation in her life in France – must have its origin in her life in America. And so he had crossed the Atlantic in search of a solution. There he would discover who this Larsan really was, and would acquire the materials necessary for compelling him to remain silent.

Rouletabille went to Philadelphia –

And now, what was this mystery which had compelled the silence of Mlle Stangerson and M. Robert Darzac? After so many years, after all the stories invented by scandalmongering newspapers, now that M. Stangerson knows and has forgiven everything, everything may be told.

There is but little to say, but it will serve to put matters straight, for there have been people who have dared to accuse Mlle Stangerson!

Mlle Stangerson, from the very beginning of this sad affair, has always been a victim.

The beginning goes back to a distant date when, as a young girl, she lived with her father in Philadelphia. There at a party, at the house of one of her father's friends, she met a compatriot, a

Frenchman, who succeeded in fascinating her by his attractive manners, his wit, and his love. He was said to be rich. He asked the famous professor for the hand of his daughter. M. Stangerson made enquiries about this M. Jean Roussel, and very soon found he had to deal with an adventurer. 'M. Jean Roussel' was only one of the many transformations of the celebrated Ballmeyer, who, being 'wanted' in France, had fled to America.

M. Stangerson did not know this, nor did his daughter. She only discovered it for herself in the following circumstances. Not only did M. Stangerson refuse the hand of his daughter to M. Jean Roussel, but he forbade him his house. Mathilde, whose heart had opened to love, and who saw nothing in the whole world more beautiful and better than her Jean, was outraged at that. She did not conceal her discontent from her father, who, to quiet her, sent her to the banks of the Ohio, to the house of an old aunt at Cincinnati. Jean joined the young girl there, and, in spite of her great veneration for her father, she resolved to betray the watchfulness of her aunt, and run away with Jean, taking advantage of the facilities afforded by American laws to get married at once.

This was done. But they did not go farther than Louisville. There one morning someone knocked at the door of the newly-wedded couple. It was the police, come to arrest M. Jean Roussel, which they did, in spite of the protestations and tears of Professor Stangerson's daughter. At the same time they informed Mathilde that her husband was no other than the famous Ballmeyer.

Desperate, and after a fruitless attempt at self-destruction, Mathilde returned to her aunt at Cincinnati. The old lady nearly died of joy at seeing her again. For a week she had not ceased searching for her niece, and had not dared to tell M. Stangerson. Mathilde made her swear that her father should know nothing. This was exactly the elder lady's desire, for she felt somewhat responsible for what had occurred. A month later Mlle Stangerson returned to her father, repentant, and with a heart dead to love. She only asked one thing: never again to see her husband, the terrible Ballmeyer – of whose death a report was spread a few weeks later – but to be able to pardon herself for her fault, and to restore her self-respect by a life devoted to study and boundless devotion to her father.

She kept her word.

At the moment, however, when, having confessed everything to Robert Darzac, and believing Ballmeyer to be dead, after having so completely expiated her fault, she had promised herself the supreme joy of marriage to a true friend – destiny had resuscitated Jean Roussel, the Ballmeyer of her youth. He told her he would never allow her to marry M. Robert Darzac – that he still loved her, which, alas, was true!

Mlle Stangerson did not hesitate to confide in M. Darzac; she showed him the letter in which Jean Roussel – Larsan – Ballmeyer recalled the first hours of their union in the charming little vicarage which they had rented at Louisville – 'The vicarage has lost nothing of its charm, nor the garden of its brightness.' The wretch pretended to be rich, and claimed the right of taking her back there. She had declared to M. Darzac that if such a dishonour came to the knowledge of her father, she would kill herself. M. Darzac had sworn that he would reduce the American to silence, either by terror or by force, even although he had to commit a crime to effect this. But M. Darzac was no match for a man like Larsan-Ballmeyer, and would have been defeated but for the daring youngster, Rouletabille.

As for Mlle Stangerson, what could she do in the presence of such a monster? The first time when, after threats which had put her on her guard, he suddenly stood before her in the Yellow Room, she tried to kill him. Unfortunately she did not succeed. From that time she was the marked victim of this invisible being, who could blackmail her to the end of her days, who lived by her side without her knowing it, who demanded meetings in the name of their mutual love. On the first occasion she had refused the meeting demanded in the letter addressed to her at Post Office No. 40; and the result was the tragedy of the Yellow Room. The second time, warned by another letter from him which reached her by post – which found her in her sick-room – she had avoided meeting him by taking refuge in the boudoir with her nurses. In that letter the wretch had informed her that, since, owing to her condition, she could not come to him, he would go to her, and would be in her room on such a night at such a time. Knowing she had everything to fear from Ballmeyer's audacity, she abandoned her room to him. This was the episode of the mysterious gallery.

On the third occasion she arranged a meeting because her persecutor, before leaving her empty room on the night of the mysterious gallery, had written an ultimatum, which he had left on her desk. In his note he insisted on an effective meeting, for which he fixed the date and hour, promising to return to her then her father's papers, but threatening to burn them if she still tried to avoid him. She did not doubt that he had those precious documents in his possession – she had, in fact, for years suspected him of being the thief who had stolen her father's papers in Philadelphia, and she knew him well enough to understand that if she did not obey him the records of so much labour, so many experiments, and scientific aspirations would soon be reduced to ashes.

She decided to see the man who had been her husband face to face, and attempt to soften him, since she could not avoid him. She arranged the meeting. What passed between them may be imagined. The supplications of Mathilde, the brutality of Larsan-Ballmeyer. He insisted upon her renunciation of Darzac. She proclaimed her love for him. He struck her down, with the thought of sending the other man to the scaffold. For he was clever, and the Larsan-disguise which he would assume when he left her, would, he thought, save him, whilst the other once again would not be able to account for the employment of his time. In this respect Ballmeyer's plot was well thought out, and the idea was very simple, as young Rouletabille had guessed.

Larsan blackmailed Darzac, as he blackmailed Mathilde, with the same weapons and the same mystery. In written offers, as imperative as orders, he declared himself ready to transact business, to deliver up all the love letters of the past, and, above all, to disappear, if they would pay him his price. Darzac had to go to the meeting-place which Ballmeyer appointed under the threat of disclosure the very next day, just as Mathilde had been compelled to consent to the rendezvous which the man had given her. M. Robert Darzac went to Épinay, where an accomplice of Larsan – a strange being whom we will meet again some day – kept him by force, and delayed him; and later on that same 'coincidence' which Darzac when charged with the crime refused to explain, was to be the means of making him *lose his head on the scaffold*.

Ballmeyer, however, had reckoned without Joseph Rouletabille.

*   *   *

It is not here, now that the Mystery of the Yellow Room has been explained, that we intend to follow Rouletabille, step by step, in America. We know the young reporter; we know the powerful means of getting information seated in the two bumps on his forehead, which enabled him to trace back the whole of the past lives of Mlle Stangerson and Jean Roussel. In Philadelphia he learned everything about Arthur William Rance; he learned of his act of devotion, and of the rewards he thought himself entitled to claim for it. The rumour of his marriage with Mlle Stangerson had previously found its way to the drawing-rooms of Philadelphia, the indiscretion of the young savant, the fact of his unwearied pursuit of Mlle Stangerson, even in Europe, the disorderly life he led under the pretence of drowning his sorrows. These things did not commend him greatly to Rouletabille, but they serve to explain the coldness with which the young man had met him in the witnesses' room. Moreover, Rouletabille had soon seen that the Rance affair had nothing whatever to do with the Larsan-Stangerson affair.

He discovered the alarming Roussel-Stangerson adventure. Who was this Jean Roussel? Rouletabille went from Philadelphia to Cincinnati. There he found the old aunt and made her speak. The story of Ballmeyer's arrest threw a light on everything. He went to see the vicarage, a pretty little dwelling in the old colonial style, which had, indeed, 'lost nothing of its charm'. Then, abandoning the track of Mlle Stangerson, he followed that of Ballmeyer, from prison to prison, from crime to crime. Finally, on the quays of New York, when he was returning to Europe, he learned that Ballmeyer had sailed five years previously, having in his pocket the papers of a certain honourable French merchant of New Orleans, called Larsan, whom he had murdered.

Does the reader now know the whole of the mystery of Mlle Stangerson? Not yet. Mathilde Stangerson had borne her husband, Jean Roussel, a child – a son. That child was born in the house of the old aunt, who arranged things so well that nobody in America ever knew anything about it.

What became of that son? That is another story, which I have not yet the right to relate.

* * *

About two months after these events I met Rouletabille, seated on a bench in the Law Courts, looking very melancholy.

'Well,' I said, 'what are you thinking of, my dear friend? You are looking rather sad. How are your friends getting on?'

'Have I really any friends besides yourself?'

'I hope that M. Darzac – '

'Certainly – '

'And Mlle Stangerson – how is she, by the way?'

'Better – much better.'

'You should not be sad then.'

'I am sad,' he said, 'because I am thinking of the perfume of the lady in black.'

'The perfume of the lady in black! I hear you constantly speaking of it. Won't you tell me at last why the thought of it haunts you so persistently?'

'Perhaps – some day; some day – perhaps,' said Rouletabille.

And he heaved a deep sigh.

THE END